ExposedI

Signs of Impurity

JAMES GAMBLE, PH.D.

ISBN: **0615532411**
ISBN-13: 978-0615532417

DEDICATION

This book is dedicated to my beautiful wife, Lucinda, and our two wonderful 'kids': JJ & Marcy.

CONTENTS

ACKNOWLEDGMENTS

I would like to acknowledge Jesus Christ as Lord.

I would also like to acknowledge all those leaders who stand firm on their Christian faith and hold true to its principles.

Finally, I would like to acknowledge all who have had the courage to endure impure religious leadership while continually increasing and sharing their faith.

Not your average acknowledgement page, is it?

INTRODUCTION

This book is a factitious story (a parable) that takes what may appear to be unrelated events in the gospels and illustrates their connection to God's overall plan for moving from the old phase of His relationship with us (a proctored relationship) to a new phase (a personal relationship). Missing pieces of history have been parabolically filled in. The intent here was not to account for untold portions of biblical history; that would be a violation of biblical principle. No – the desire, rather, is to offer a fresh interpretation of biblical principle; not violate it. The purpose for the fill–ins is to create a story that will flow to a point where the principles it teaches are fully achieved by the reader. That is the sole purpose of parables: to make the listener or reader wholly aware of principles being taught in the Scriptures while inspiring them to trust and live by the same. That was why Jesus used parables and if we use them it should be for the same reason and to the same effect. Parables should relay biblical principles in a way that is fully comprehensible. One should often make use of parables to share biblical principles.

This story illustrates how God's grace was enacted as a permanent fulfillment of the temporal corrective measures of law and liturgy. It also demonstrates how the role that others should play in our personal relationship with God was altered upon entering the period of grace. It shows that a great portion of the movement of God to draw His believers into this period of grace involved exposure of impure religious leadership who deceitfully professed their main focus was to proctor their followers into a proper relationship with God. The story teaches that taking personal accountability for one's growth into a proper relationship with God decreases the probability of being misled into an improper relationship with Him. Pay close attention to the facts in the story (if you are familiar with biblical facts) as well as the parabolic inferences and notice how they greatly relate to what commonly occurs in today's Christian province. It may strengthen your ability to stay focused on building and maintaining a personal relationship with God; which is what He wants with humanity. It may prevent you from being misled into an improper relationship with Him.

As I stated at the onset, this is a parable. I don't mean to insult your intelligence; but – in case you don't know – a parable is a factitious story that illustrates (in this case) a religious principle. It could also be used to illustrate a moral point of view. In that case, it would be no more than a fable.

The difference in parables and fables is that the former points out truths about one's religious views while the latter just points out ideologies accepted as generally good. I trust that the following story will prove to be a very informative and eye–opening parable for those of you who read this and are familiar with biblical facts and Christian principles. Perhaps it will make you reevaluate your perspective on religious leadership, both how you lead (if you are a leader) and how you allow others to lead you. It may not necessarily change that perspective – perhaps there's no need to, but prayerfully it will cause you to evaluate whether or not it warrants a change.

For those of you who are not familiar with biblical facts and Christian principles; well, this may prove to be just another fable. If that is the case, I hope then that it's a most interesting and comprehensible fable. I trust that it will stay true in accomplishing the goal of a fable. I hope that it provides you a refreshing story and offers you a few very good morals to live by or at least live with. I also pray that it leaves you more enlightened on biblical facts and Christian principles. Finally, I pray that it will consequently become more than just a fable for you by the time you complete the reading.

This story contains the elements that make up an expressive and attractive literary work. I have often read that there are two essentials to such a creation. There is courage displayed by the main character and, as one might expect, there is an overarching love story. This story purposely contains both, but it inherently encompasses a story of betrayal, vengeance and ultimately forgiveness–simply because of the nature of the parable. So, if you read the story for the literary entertainment it is designed to offer, I hope it proves adequate in that respect.

The story takes place during the time of the inception of Christianity–during its induction to the world. A lot of "what if" and "what really happened" questions have been asked and subsequent "perhaps then" and "maybe it was this" answers have been offered in this parable. As stated before, the intent here was not to try and fill in untold portions of biblical history. I hope Bible scholars will not read this and insist on suggesting that my intent is to provide new revelation on Bible history. If one or some should allege that as my intent, then they will be dreadfully wrong in their allegations. I understand that to present any information as if it were new revelation would be totally against biblical principle. Those who read the Bible and believe its truths and follow its principles know we are not to add to or take away anything from its history or its principles as we share it with others.

The names here have been modified slightly. This is not an attempt to protect the innocent, but rather an effort to assist the reader in relating to the story. Common names for people and places have replaced proper ones to hopefully make you, the reader, realize that the plots and activities in this story are so common, either of the characters in the events could have easily been you or me. In some cases, it may make you recognize that at some point(s) in your life it has been you. I've certainly found myself in the midst of some of the stories–both in good and bad scenarios. The summation of its purpose is that perhaps it will cause you to evaluate your perspective of how you should lead people (or allow them to lead you). It may even convince you to change your perspective. That is, if your perspective requires alteration. Again, I dare not assume that it requires a change.

The story is about a young man whose religious laws and practices required that he forgive others of any wrongdoings against him. Although the requirements were present in the written law, there were sub–requirements within the practice of law that contradicted those requirements. The law surrounding forgiveness contained a policy for acceptable vengeance. The system of laws and practices also contained elements in its composition that made no provision for forgiveness in certain situations. Did I state that clearly enough? Let me try again: One was required to forgive in some cases, but not required to forgive in other cases and there were even cases where there was no room for forgiveness. It was a clear contradiction of principles. Some of the contradictions were inherent to the system of laws and practices. Some were a result of misunderstandings within the religious population. Some, however, were intentionally introduced by impure motives of some of the religious leaders.

At one point in his life, the young man felt strongly that he was at a place in the religious maturation process where he could forgive any offense against him without invoking the law's acceptable vengeance clause. He felt certain he could forgive anything despite the elements of their system that made forgiveness impossible in certain situations. He felt that way until he was faced with a tragic transgression enacted against him. It was a wrongdoing that he ultimately deemed unforgivable. A spectrum of ensuing events caused him to reevaluate his entire philosophy on forgiveness.

Often we as Christians are faced with the same situation. Sometimes, life events force us to reevaluate our perspective on forgiveness as it relates to our belief system. Sometimes those events are a result of apparent contradictions or honest misunderstandings in our religious beliefs or practices. Sometimes the events are the result of impure leadership's intentionally introduced contradictions or misunderstandings. When we can unmistakably determine that the latter has occurred, we are left struggling against the desire to invoke an acceptable vengeance or 'no room for forgiveness' clause in our contract to follow that leadership.

With that said, let me introduce you to Bari. Bari had become a hard man—or I should say a *hardened* man. He hadn't intended on becoming that man. He certainly never expected to be at the place he found himself on that terrible day of judgment. Bari was on death row. The day had come when he was scheduled to die in merciless fashion, at the hands of an unsympathetic executioner, and in plain sight of all who cared to observe his physical termination. There were many who had come to observe the carrying out of Bari's death sentence. Government–imposed killings of that type often drew a crowd. For some reason people were attracted to such atrocities. It was normal to have a crowd of people on hand to witness the violent events, but on that day, for some unexplainable reason, the crowd was much larger than normal.

Bari never expected his life to end at the hands of the executioners; but the government–appointed slaughterers were just moments away from extinguishing him. A certain series of events acted out by impure leadership had changed Bari's religious perspective tremendously. In the midst of the change, he lost all respect for his religious and civic leaders. His perspective on the matter of clemency toggled from one of unconditional forgiveness to conditional forgiveness, to unconditional un–forgiveness. The un–forgiveness caused him to make statements and take actions without weighing the consequences of the same. It propelled him into a moment of rage, which ultimately flung him into the merciless court of justice that handed him the sentence of death. Although anyone with an ounce of compassion who'd followed Bari's path to that day would scream for leniency, those in the judgment seat would reason that justice must be blind; therefore, it must be merciless.

It's hard to determine the exact moment Bari decided to follow the path that brought him to that end. It's difficult to establish if his spiritual deterioration was the result of a single act or if it was a combination of acts that drove him to this point. Psychiatrists today would probably speculate and reference their Diagnostic and Statistical Manual to deduce a suggestive rationale for Bari's personal demise; but it might only be speculation. I suppose their answers would make sense and appear to be as accurate as humanly possible, but maybe sometimes assessment of such matters is beyond human comprehension. Perhaps sometimes they are Spiritually enacted and we just can't determine when, why, or how such uncharacteristic behaviors will announce themselves.

Okay. That's much deeper than we need to delve to understand the significance of Bari's transformation. We don't need to assess Bari's condition, the cause of it, or the effect of it on those close to him. We're more concerned about how and why his religious viewpoints changed so drastically. There is always a barrage of questions that follow the exposure of impure intentions of religious leadership. Those questions will always challenge our Christian perspective. If we want to maintain the correct Christian perspective, of course we know the answer is in the Scriptures. Sometimes those answers are as clear as unblemished crystal. Other times, however, we need the aid of a *parable* to recognize them.

1 CONTENT

Before you begin with Chapter 1, let me make sure you didn't just skip over the Introduction and jump right into the story. Some of us have a tendency to be impatient with introductions and just want to jump right on into the conversation. As boring as introductions can sometimes be, they help us establish the context of the conversation, the purpose of the meeting, etc. If you are guilty of intro-jumping, I need you to go back and read the introduction. You might miss a lot of this book's context and purpose if you have not done so. So if you skipped over it, just skip yourself on back, and then catch up. I'll wait...

Bari was a genuinely good man regardless of whose standards one cares to use in assessing his character. He treated everyone he encountered with the utmost respect. He absolutely refused to exhibit prejudice against a person's gender, color, nationality or creed. He made certain to greet a pauper as courteously as he would a king. He was as manner–able to orphaned children as he was to distinguished dignitaries. He neither showed favoritism towards his friends nor impartiality towards those who considered themselves his foes. He could look eye–to–eye with anyone and not regard himself as superior or inferior.

Bari wasn't a man of the cloth, but he took his religion as equally serious as any cleric did and perhaps more so than many. Routine visits to the temple were commonplace with him. He had the utmost respect for his religious leaders and their ideologies. He studied the books of his religion often and diligently so that he might live by them as best he could. He contributed to their religious cause as he knew to do–based on how their books taught them. He prayed often and with great expectation. He recognized the order of things both from a spiritual and natural perspective. He wasn't judgmental of those who followed the principles of his religion less vigorously than he; nor did he overly praise those who appeared to do so to a greater degree. He wasn't the least bit critical of those who chose not to follow his religious principles at all.

Bari didn't simply follow along behind the meaningless antics of a crowd of religious fanatics as he noticed to be the practice of some. There was purpose in all he did when conducting his religious activities. Every deed he performed from a religious standpoint was genuine. He understood the discipline factor of his religious duties and how they would improve his attempts at regulating himself in other areas of his life outside of his place of worship and even beyond his religious conviction. He understood the bonding effect of their gatherings and how it improved communal relations among his fellow citizens. He understood the eternal value in keeping with those practices.

Bari made every attempt to live peaceably among his fellow citizens and in harmony with his environment. When he conducted business for personal gain, he made certain to manage all transactions fairly. Because of that, he profited substantially from his business operations. To show gratefulness, he gave a generous portion of his earnings to those in need – the ones who could not sustain themselves. He never demanded anything from anyone he hadn't earned and never bickered about what he owed someone. He paid his debts on time and with all accrued interest.

He ensured that he made his personal contributions toward the conservation of natural resources. He never took more than he needed from the land or from the waters. He restored whatever he damaged when possible and made every attempt not to cause unnecessary impairment. When he planted his fields, he often tossed seed beyond the area of planting that they might be consumed by needy persons and non–domesticated animals that made their way onto his property. As a good gesture, he also released any fish that he did not expect to consume.

If there were ever a need he could meet for someone, he was more than eager to offer assistance. If he found himself in need, he felt no ignominy in being on the receiving end of a contribution. There was congruent balance in Bari's actions. No fault could be observed in Bari's life or his lifestyle. He was what most would deem a model citizen. He was a good man.

Bari's name was well–known and well–respected among the Weshuan communities. The people bequeathed him with celebrity status. They were all very familiar with the accomplishments of his kinsmen, both current and past. All in the vicinity absolutely adored his family. His relatives were esteemed in the high places as well as low. In the political arena, they had excelled to the highest level of local government. They had also left an impressive mark on those in the religious ranks over the years. The business community revered their name to no end. They had faired extremely well in the academic circles, also. There were few, if any, local citizens who did not appreciatively pay homage to his family's name.

Bari was the grandson of Mathes, a priest and a valiant warrior whose name came to prominence during the days of the revolt against the Kreges. You might wonder how Mathes could have been a priest *and* a warrior. Let me help you with that. He was a priest when the Kreges came in and forcibly colonized Bari's people. At the beginning of the incursion, Mathes did not display any desire whatsoever to resist the arresting overthrow. He simply continued his duties at the temple and subjected himself to the civil laws of the Kreges once they were in place.

Mathes' whole life, up to that point, had been devoted to temple duties. He was very meticulous in how he performed his religious operations. This dedication to the temple and its worship services allowed him very little interaction with the outside world. His rationale for lack of communication beyond temple services was that his duties came first. So, he spent his time perfecting his knowledge of their religious laws and improving his performance of their religious rites as well as enhancing his ability to teach and communicate the writings of their sacred books to his people. He had no political or social agenda outside of the temple environment; yet, he was an admired religious leader to his people – admired far greater than any politician or commercial mogul of his time. All were humbled by his knowledge of their religious law and with the mild manner in which he taught and judged them by it. (The Weshuan priests not only acted as educators of their law, but also judges.)

When the Kreges attacked and overthrew Weshua, Mathes hardly noticed the change in command. He never paid attention to the political realm, so he never knew what their leaders where involved with anyway. He refused to include himself in any resistance to socialization or events associated with protesting the takeover. As a priest, he was completely removed from the matter. When the upheaval concluded, he simply continued his duties at the temple and subjected himself to the new rules of the Kreges whenever he ventured outside of the temple.

For years the Kreges imposed their culture, their laws, and their beliefs onto Bari's countrymen. The Kreges decorated Weshuan government buildings with artifacts of their culture and paintings of their leaders (past and present). They propagated literature that introduced their ideologies and regulatory requirements. They introduced their foods, spices, and recipes to the Weshuan marketplaces and area restaurants (which consisted mostly of taverns or inns). They brought in their music, their contemporary style of clothing, and their revolutionary arts to the local Weshuan libraries and gathering places.

There was a two–fold purpose to the influential introduction of the Kreges' cultural elements. The paramount intention was to socialize Bari's people into acceptance of Kregian governance. The Kreges assumed that there would be less threat of rebellion if the people were accustomed to and interested in their culture. The second reason for the abrupt institution of Kregian principles and products was that it generated a handsome amount of revenue for both the Kreges' homeland and for Weshua. The exportation of their products meant boosted sales for Kregian farmers and merchants who sold those goods to the Weshuans at a higher price and greater profit than they could have attained in their native land. The products that were imported were heavily levied by the local Weshuan government. The taxes generated instant and continuous revenue for their government, making the arrangement attractive to the Weshuan politicians. They could raise the amount of taxes collected from the citizens without protest, simply because the people were willing to pay the extra tariff for the new and exotic products.

There were no arguments raised (at least overtly) regarding the changes imposed or influenced by the Kreges at the onset of their rule. Bari's people mumbled on occasion in closed chambers and concealed corridors when among their own, but hardly ever in public where Kregian authorities might overhear them. Some of Bari's people actually welcomed the many new foods, spices, and other articles of interest. They favored most of the music and a major portion of the art. The clothing quickly became fashion statements among the young and young at heart. They didn't bicker about the elevated costs of the imports. Cost was not an issue to the majority of the trend producers and fad architects and the many subjects who latched on to their vogues. They became so engrossed in the new styles they paid little or no attention to the elevated prices and exorbitant taxes. It was just the effect the Kreges intended with their introduction of the Kregian goods and culture.

All was well until the Kreges took matters to the extreme. One of the locally appointed Kregian rulers decided to introduce their worshipping practices in the temple dedicated to the God of Bari's people. The Kregian religion was in total contrast to that of the Weshuans. Their god was not the same. Their practices were not the same. What the separate parties considered permissible and non-permissible behavior was not the same. Nothing harmonized between the two religions. Yet, the Kreges decided they would perform their acts of worship on the holy grounds and in the hallowed halls and quarters of the Weshuan temple. The Kreges decimated the temple with practices that were totally against the ideologies Bari's ancestors had practiced and believed for countless generations.

Mathes and his peer religious leaders ferociously objected to the new practices. So did the Weshuan citizens who held fast to their religious beliefs and understood the procedures of temple worship. This constituted the vast majority of Bari's people. Not only were there the Weshuans religious leaders up in arms over the inappropriate activities in the temple, but there were also those outside of the temple who detested other aspects of the Kreges' cultural socialization. There were some Weshuans who believed that everything about their culture was sacred. Since many of the products, foods, and activities associated with the Kreges' culture were prohibited by Weshuan law and religious beliefs, many of Weshua's older citizens would take no part in the new culture at all. They had been tolerant of the taxes and new decrees (without choice), but they would not participate in the new regime's cultural renaissance. To ask them to do so would have created reason for complaint; perhaps even peaceful protest. The fact that the Kreges would perform degenerative acts in the temple was more than reason for protest, however. It was absolutely unacceptable. That was grounds for war.

It seemed the Weshuan people were much less tolerant of derision of their religious belongings and beliefs than they were of their personal effects. Well, that declaration may need slight modification. It seemed Weshuans were intolerant of *outsiders'* mockery of their religious belongings and beliefs. In some cases, sad to note, they seemed to disregard the recurring internal disrespect of their religious beliefs. In fact, after Mathes' term of service to the temple ended; disregard for its sanctity seemed to reach an all–time high. It grew to such a horrible state that their prophet Lamak brought a message to them with a grave warning from their God declaring they should stop the degradation and return to their proper respectful practice of Weshuan religious law. Otherwise, they would face a terrible fate.

Despite the degree of internal perversion of their principles and practices, however, members of their religious party totally refuse to allow outsiders to ridicule their rituals. Most governments are aware of such and do all they can to protect the rights of their citizens to worship in solitude. Their legislative systems struggle to maintain a "separation of church and state" in an all–out effort to allow religion to have its free course. That is, provided it doesn't attempt to invalidate personal rights or infringe criminal or civil law. For some reason, however, the Kreges acted out of the governmental norm. In retrospect, they found their actions were detrimental to their dictatorial dominance over the Weshuan people.

When the Kreges moved too far from the standard, it threw Bari's countrymen into a tumultuous state. With the riotous posture of the nation at its peak, Mathes had no problem assembling a militia and opposing the conduct of the superimposed government. Mathes and his comrades were able to rather easily force the Kreges not only out of their temple, but also out of their country – freeing their people of Kregian oppression. Afterwards, they restored the dignity and sanctity of their temple. They removed the idol gods. They sanitized the sacred ornaments. The burned the Kregian flags, paintings, wooden ornaments, and religious regalia. They restored the temple to its original state, rededicated it, and began worshiping as they had before the Kreges invaded their homeland.

The self–reigning freedom would be short–lived, however; because the Rhomine government (another dominant nation in the region) was waiting in the wings to move into the position of authority the Kreges had vacated at the forceful request of the Weshuans. This time the Weshuans were allowed to maintain their own governance at the local level; but overall Bari and his countrymen still were subject to the laws and customs of the Rhomines. So, it was out of one dictate and into the next. The Rhomines were smart enough, though (contrary to the Kreges), to maintain separation of church and state competently enough to allow Bari's people their rightfully desired and deserved religious freedom.

Mathes' heroic acts resonated in the minds of the citizenry. They venerated Mathe's love for his country, his concern for his people, and his knowledge of and adherence to their religious creed. His name riddled their history books and spoken memorials. A sculpture of his figure adorned many Weshuan businesses, government buildings, and private libraries. Several Weshuan sons bore Mathes' name in honor of such a great religious and civic leader. Ballads were written in his honor and sang at almost every outing, on nearly every excursion, and all around the marketplace. An almost weeklong annual celebration was held in admiration of the cleansing and rededication of the temple brought about by Mathe's hand. Even the prayer Weshuans prayed before meals in the blessing of their food incorporated his name. They thought very highly of Mathes from that day forward.

Although Mathes was revered as a hero outside of the temple, he was unanimously denied such veneration within the hallowed place of worship. The priests and workers who refused to take part in the military procedures were extremely grateful of his heroics—as much as anyone else. They were careful to make that known with every opportunity afforded them. They commended him whenever they made public appearances. His praises were imbedded in their routine discourses and addresses to the people. They endorsed his efforts whenever they attended a communal gathering. They made it known in every way possible that they truly appreciated Mathe's sacrifices in obtaining Weshua's independence from the Kreges – particularly their religious liberty.

Within the temple walls, however, they would not hold Mathes in such high esteem. In fact, they relieved him of his duties as priest. He was relegated to meeting his religious obligations and performing his worship activities as a common parishioner. Their rationale for Mathes' demotion was rather simple. At least, it was in their minds. It fell in line with what they knew and understood about their religious history. A person with blood on their hands could counsel and lead the people civically, but they could not do so in a religious capacity. The requirement was not a written rule, but it was certainly implied and adherence to those implications was mandatory.

Their religious books recorded that a great king once wanted to build a temple in honor of their God. The king was extremely well–known for his observance of their religious principles. He was also very well–known for his former war heroics. The people were so impressed by his accomplishments in war that they attributed a ballad to him. The ballad sang of his achievements being ten times greater than those of the king that served before him and his predecessor was quite successful in his own right. Beyond the military accomplishments of the great king, the people were truly impressed with the level of spirituality he had attained after ending his military career.

Once the decorated battle star had finally laid down his war tools and spiritually matured to a point where he was more in tune with his religious principles, his intentions were fixated on building a temple to their God. His convictions brought him to believe that since he had such a magnificent structure of a palace in which to be honored, his God should be reverenced with an even more elaborate edifice. He secured the finest materials and the most skillful craftsmen available to complete the task. According to their religious books, he prayed to his God as to how he should proceed in building the temple. The soul-saddening response was that he could not pursue his desires. Because the blood of war was on his hands, he was not allowed to erect a temple to their God. It seemed that forgiveness at that level was not available for such acts – not during his time. Subsequent to his death, however, his son was allowed to build the temple and adhered to the detailed plans his father had previously drafted for the proposed temple.

Since the celebrated king was prohibited from building the temple, the current leaders felt Mathes, now with bloodstains of war on his hands, should no longer serve in the temple. Consequently, they felt the same of the other priests and workers who took part in the eradication of the tyrants. Each of the clergymen who'd joined in the battles was asked to relinquish their rights and privileges as officers or servants in the temple. They all left the temple to serve or work in other capacities within their communities.

The rationale was sound to the group of religious leaders. Mathes concurred with their decision as well. Although he was the highest ranking and most respected among the leaders, he relinquished his post without opposition. He ended his life of religious servitude and joined the private sector working class.

Their sentence proved to be extremely beneficial for Mathes from an economic standpoint. He moved on to serve as a political leader in the community and was celebrated by all. Civil service awarded him the opportunity to accumulate wealth that he never would have accrued as a priest in the temple. The priests were not allowed to own property (land) or engage in professions that would produce income for them or for their families. Those needs were to be met by the people. The people would pay tribute to the temple for, among other things, provisioning for the priests. The priests were allowed to keep a small, set amount of the tributes the people brought into the temple. Their needs were always met by this small portion of the tribute, but it did not afford an opportunity for amassing any measure of wealth whatsoever. At least, that's how the temple functioned in the days of Mathes. Some changes had occurred in Bari's lifetime. It seemed by then priests and religious leaders lived better than the greater percentage of their parishioners. In fact, the number of constituents who lived better than them was probably in the meager tenth percentile.

Mathes, after having been released of his duties at the temple, became a very successful businessman as well. He was just and honest in his dealings, so people were more than eager to conduct business with him. Of course, the fact that he was their greatest modern–day hero worked very well in his favor. Few competed against him for the people's business. He lived well from his earnings, but he did not become conceited or complacent with his success. His work and business ethics remained impeccable.

When he decided to run for public office, no one dared compete against him. Once in office, he used his political and fiscal influence to serve the people outside of the temple just as he had used his religious clout to serve them inside the temple. He realized he was a very influential figure and made certain to use that influence for the betterment of the people and not for personal gain.

Outside of business and politics, he was still as devoted to their religion as ever. He made frequent trips back to the temple as a parishioner to pay his tribute and honor his God. He offered provisions to those in need. He continued to perform each deed and activity his religion and their traditions required of him.

Mathes had since passed on, but those Weshuans who knew him or knew of him (the aging members of their communities) often expressed how they observed the same qualities in Bari as once seen in Mathes. Bari illustrated the same dedication to their religion. He demonstrated the same goodwill toward his countrymen (anyone for that matter). He conducted business in an equally just and honest manner as did Mathes. The people often referred to Bari as "Mathes the Second" and insisted that he was the reincarnation of his grandfather (not literally, but as a matter of comparative honor).

Bari would revel in the attention and strived to not disappoint, but he dared not try and live up to the townspeople's valuation. He knew that his grandfather was an exceptional human being. Mathe's life story was that of history book caliber and those types didn't come along very often. Bari took delight in being heir to his grandfather's legend, but held no interest in being the link that continued Mathe's legacy for future generations.

Still, many in Bari's community felt because of his Mathes–like characteristics he should have been serving in the temple or in a very high political office. He was extremely knowledgeable of their religious laws and customs. He abided by their principles without waver. Since he was born in the lineage of the priests and temple workers, he had every right and qualification to do such work. (Birthright was a prerequisite for priesthood and temple service for Weshuans.) He owned the lawful privilege to be a temple worker and by the people's opinion should have been a leader in the temple.

Bari did not see temple service as a privilege, though. He regarded it as a responsibility. He viewed it as a seriously grave responsibility. He looked beyond the perks of having the people provide everything he needed and most of what he desired beyond his needs. He saw past having the authority to govern over people's personal affairs. He wasn't moved by the opportunity to make decisions that would affect citizen's lives for generations to come. He felt it was a very burdensome responsibility and Bari did not desire to have it. He did not even feel qualified to serve in the temple.

There were certain qualities described in the stories of Mathes that Bari felt he just did not possess in his character. He denied having the valiancy his grandfather exhibited in his lifetime. Bari was not the soldier–type. He did not have a warrior–like mentality. He never got loud or boisterous. He'd much rather walk away from confrontations than face them head on. He would also rather sit down and reason with opponents over differences instead of battling over those variances. He was neither a drinker nor a reveler. His language was never vulgar.

Of course, not all soldiers acted in that manner (certainly Mathes would not have), but those qualities often manifested themselves in the mightiest of warriors. Perhaps it was excessive male testosterone that generated such behavioral patterns. Perhaps it was the environmental influence that encouraged it. Perhaps it was just a show of dominance as displayed by animals when protecting their territory or attempting to impress and woo the female species. Whatever the source of such valiancy, Bari did not feel that he possessed them – at least not to the degree of the average warrior. He simply was not the combatant type. He was a gentleman. He was a husband. He was a businessman. He was a farmer. He worked hard and endlessly; so, he had a build resembling that of a warrior, but his demeanor was far from such.

Although the people felt he had just as much potential for politics as for priesthood, Bari didn't feel he possessed the political savvy once displayed by his grandfather, either. The fact of the matter is he did not care much for the politicians and their lavish, unregulated lifestyles. He didn't assign that classification to all politicians, but from his experiences, it matched the majority. There was very little moderation and/or accountability with most of the politicians he encountered in his social happenstances. Hence, he did not care to be associated with the type. He didn't publicly disrespect them or debase them in private conversation. He didn't campaign against their ways. He just simply chose not to espouse their characteristics or garner their friendship.

Bari knew that most Weshuans respected his family name, his ideologies, and his opinions; but he never used that knowledge to take advantage of folks. He never used his clout to sway a group or an individual into supporting a personal agenda that might go against what was best for the majority. He could not overlook the needs of the general public while catering to the desires of a select few influential people as he often witnessed of the politicians and wealthy class. He would never be able to overlook the bad effects of a political decision made in favor of a selfish agenda. He could not ignore the real issues that plagued his community while claiming to have conquered other issues that were mostly just fabricated to gain support from the voters. He never sought to side with one party or the other, but rather agreed with whoever proposed the best solutions to the worst problems.

Bari had no desire for recognition among the people as a great leader or a great thinker or a great "fill in the blank." He possessed a healthy amount of self–confidence, as a person should, but not to the point that it was injurious to his relationships. He never belittled someone else's worthiness to ostensibly increase his own. Bari could not grandstand in front of a group of total strangers as he often noticed of the condescending types. His ego wasn't hungry for attention that entailed: being acknowledged by name and title when walking into a room; being motioned to the front; being provided the best seat; or being waited upon for everything. He did not make much use of words that left common folk searching for an interpretation or that left them lost in the conversation or awed by his mastery of language arts. He contained such words in his vocabulary, but avoided using them at inopportune times. He communicated at the level of his audience: common language to common folk and impressive or expressive language to the elites.

Bari didn't feel he deserved the status once bestowed upon his grandfather, Mathes. He certainly did not feel he belonged among the ranks of the religious leaders and political powers. Besides all that, Bari was not fully convinced that being confined to the temple was the most effective way to lead people in spirituality.

He also didn't feel that having someone pay homage to his political prowess was the best way to proctor their municipality. He felt he could have a more positive impact on his community as a lay person intermingled among the populace. He believed that if he were living a life representative of their religious beliefs and civic duties while among the people, then it would generate a positive constant reminder of those principles. He did not disagree with the liturgical temple routines and honor shown to the leaders there and he wasn't altogether against political protocol. He just did not feel either of those positions of authority were his calling in life. Still, many believed contrary to Bari in that regard.

It took very little effort to recognize why Bari was admired so much by the Weshuan community, even beyond his accumulated wealth and the family reputation. He was relatively young, not yet thirty; he was well-educated. He was handsome and very fit. Not only that, he was married to a very beautiful young lady by the name of Yrma. Everything seemed to be working in his favor as well as hers. There was nothing undesirable about either of them.

Their marriage wasn't just one of convenience or arrangement as was the case for many marriages among the upper class in their culture. Theirs resembled one of fairytales. There were no quarrels. There were no opposing directional dreams competing with one another. They fully complimented each other. They shared the agony of their defeats as well as the glory of their successes. The temperament of their relationship did not fluctuate with situational circumstances. They both loved the same things and wanted what was best for each other. They had a youthful desire for each other that did not dissipate once the realities of married life had set in. The blissful longing lasted far beyond the honeymoon stage.

Bari wasn't an overbearing husband. As a cultural rule of thumb, the male was solely responsible for making decisions regarding their affairs. As such, many never consulted their spouses on any decisions regardless of how those choices affected the family. Bari, however, would not make any decisions without discussing risks, probable effects, pros, and cons with Yrma. Although such a thing was considered non–masculine within his culture, he did not feel any less of a man in doing so. He knew she had great insight and could offer valuable input in the decision–making process. He honored her opinion and made good use of it as often as possible. It made for an indispensable asset in their home and in his business.

Bari dedicated almost each day to the same uneventful tasks of days past. Each day began with prayer, then breakfast with his wife. As Yrma prepared their breakfast, Bari went to the well to draw enough water to supply the household and to last him and his workers for a day in the sun. The well was a short distance from the house in an open area of their land. All of his workers drew from the well for their household needs. Many of his neighbors drew from the well also despite its placement on Bari's property. They all had Bari's and Yrma's uninhibited consent to do so. He was very cordial to friends and workers on his way to and from the well, but spent very little time socializing during that time. In fact, those who knew him expected a hearty "Good morning," and not much else. They knew he was mission–oriented when making trips to and from the well. During leisure time he would talk as much as they wished, but not during periods of labor.

Upon his return from the well, he and Yrma would sit and have breakfast together. They had a breakfast nook attached to their kitchen that overlooked the valley encompassing the greater portion of their gorgeous homestead. What they considered their humble abode was a magnificent sight to behold:

> It was a docile place, not yet soiled with urban traits;
> still enveloped within the beauty of its natural state.
> Positioned all around it where rolling hills;
> circling perfectly plotted wide–open fields.
> The air around the place was so fresh and clean, one could feel it.
> (If societal soot had sickened the soul, then this place could heal it).
> The rivers and lakes and creeks and streams
> were so bountiful they nearly burst at the seams.
> Velvety green grass grew tall along the winding roads.
> Snow glistened on the distant mountains' steepest nodes.

There were fruit trees and olive trees and berries of all kind. To a nature lover, this place would have been the perfect find.

There was an indeed awe–inspiring view from their breakfast window. It served as a constant reminder that they should begin each day in gratitude – with the realization of how truly blessed they were. And that's exactly what they did during breakfast time while taking in the splendid view and reflecting on the good in life.

Bari and Yrma's property was less than fifty miles from the ocean and even closer than that to a nearby river. There were a couple of very large lakes (the locals actually referred to them as seas) and several streams, so fish were plentiful in the region. In fact, fish was a staple food for them and was a part of at least one meal on almost a daily basis. It was very uncommon to not see at least one fisherman along the banks of the bodies of water on any given day. Perhaps one out of every three men in the coastal region was a professional fisherman. Many of the others fished as a means of supplementing their families' food supply or just for game and recreation.

Bari was certainly affiliated with the latter. He was an excellent amateur angler. He made his own nets and formed his own hooks and lead weights. He had even mastered the art of spear fishing. He maintained a ten foot, four–pronged spear that he used to harvest the larger fish. There was a long rope attached to the end of the pole of the spear, which he also tied to his wrist. He walked along the banks and surveyed for sizeable fish making their way up and down the river. Once he identified a suitable target, he would set his sights on it and release his spear into flight. He was extremely accurate with the spear and rarely missed on an opportunity. Often a group of spectators formed around him whenever he handled the spear and vocally admired his gamesmanship in harvesting fish with a lance.

Bari could have easily made a living as a fisherman. He had the equipment and the skill sets to catch fish any time he desired to do so. There was certainly enough demand for the product. He could have marketed fish and done well, but he chose to farm instead. His rationale for deciding against fishing as a vocation was he was aware of the time away from family that the profession would require of him. He'd much rather remain home and work the fields alongside his family and friends than spend days at sea or traveling to and from the diverse fishing areas.

After breakfast, Bari made his way to the meadows for a full day's work. There was a seemingly unending amount of fieldwork to be done; but he was up to the challenge. He was a very skilled farmhand and craftsman. There was very little he could not accomplish with his hands. He constructed his own buildings. He birthed and tended to his own animals. He repaired his own equipment. He was an excellent woodcutter and carver. He built his own kiln and could prepare and finish showpiece quality pottery and bricks. Although he did have hired help, there were very few things, if any, that Bari had to rely on outside assistance for. So, he rarely left his daily routine because of inability to complete a task himself.

As Bari made his daily jaunts to the fields, Yrma remained and finished the day-to-day house chores. She had a few handmaids who assisted her just as Bari had field hands. The ladies would grind meal, prepare provisions for storage (to sustain them during winter or drought months), milk the cows and goats, gather the eggs, clean equipment, and prepare the daily meals. They delivered lunch to Bari and the workers at the same hour of each day. It was often the same menu: bread, fruit, pasta, vegetables, and fish prepared in olive oil. Occasionally, however, Yrma would surprise with fish prepared a different way or lamb and on rare occasion – beef.

Yrma and the maids prepared enough food for themselves as well as the male workers. They would take their lunchtime while away from the house delivering the meals to the men folk. They would all have prayer together and then eat lunch in a shaded area of whatever section of the farmstead the men were working at the time. Most of the workers and maidens were husband and wife teams, but there were unmarried personnel among them also.

The workers always ended lunch and returned to their chores at a specific time of day. Bari and Yrma would often linger a little while after lunch. A few of the maidens would wait around at a distance to escort Yrma back to the house while the others returned to their chores. It was a courtesy they showed their superior so she would not have to make the trek alone. Sometimes the men's work areas were quite a distance from the house.

The extra minutes afforded Bari and Yrma a little more opportunity for quality time together. They held discussions centered on chores that were to be completed by day's end. They determined ways to improve various processes such that less time or less effort was required to complete a recurring task. They talked about items to procure for the house during their next trip to the marketplace. They discussed having children and what their names would be.

They also talked current events. Lunchtime was a good time for each to share what they had heard from the workers since their last conversation on such things. News spread by word of mouth in those regions and times. Amazingly, it was accurately shared over broad areas in a short amount of time. It certainly wasn't as fast as modern microwave/cellular/satellite medium, but their communication system was adequately effective.

The two of them had a lot to talk about in respect to business and current events; but sometimes they simply carried on meaningless conversation sprinkled with jokes and laughter. They took great pleasure in sharing a cackle. The two savored their early afternoon time together. Sometimes, their after–lunch moments were briefer than others and occasionally they would leave when everyone else did. In either case, they would always bid one another farewell with a kiss and a smile and the impression that they longed for their next personal encounter.

Once lunchtime was ended, Yrma made her way back to the house to complete the remainder of her chores for the day and to begin dinner preparations. The maids continued with their duties around the house. They'd leave to go tend to their own homes long before the men were done in the fields. If there were any personal chores to be done, Yrma would complete those after the maids departed to their dwelling places. After they left, she performed her sewing tasks. She balanced their financial books. She created decorative articles for their home or just carried on with busy work. Occasionally, when she had the notion, she would just relax and do nothing at all. Her afternoons were basically her time to do with as she pleased and she did exactly that.

Bari went back to his farming activities after lunch, taking water breaks throughout the course of the day. Deviation in daily events would only occur when there was malfunctioning equipment or animals that needed special attention. He took good care of his animals, so they hardly ever were the cause of his break from the ordinary. Most often the case was defective equipment. He did not use metal to work his fields, so there was a more frequent case of broken hoe or plow or other instrument than if he'd used iron tools.

Metal tools would have certainly proven more efficient, but he chose not to use them. That was partly due to customary reasons and partly because of personal preference. Customarily, their people chose not to employ metal in working their fields. Personally, he felt that since metal was used so often for destruction of life (war), it should not be used for sustenance of life (cultivation). Some might see that as peculiar, but it made sense to the populace in Bari's region and time. It sort of went along with their conviction that blessings and curses should not proceed from the same mouth. Surely that's logical thinking for any region or time.

Bari wasn't totally sure if his reason for avoiding the use of metal in this case was more their custom or his own personal preference. Either way, he opted not to use the metal. He used a good grade of wood (olive or cedar), but still; wood is obviously not as durable as iron or even copper. So, it made for a more recurrent cause to stop the normal daily events and repair or replace equipment. Bari wasn't the least bit perturbed by it though. The stops were infrequent enough and besides that, he was not willing to trade principle for convenience. Stopping to fix or replace a broken tool every now and again wasn't going to hamper progress. Besides that, it was extremely rare that he would have to stop and replace a tool. It differed very little from other events that interrupted his workday, which were also rare. Perhaps a bad storm passed through; or a family member, friend or neighbor needed assistance. Brief pauses from his work in the fields were bound to occur. He felt he could tolerate tool repair as the infrequent cause of stoppage as well as he could anything else.

Bari had a huge parcel of land and almost an infinite number of livestock, so his work was never fully accomplished, even though he had hired help. If he wasn't planting crop, he was tending to crop. If he wasn't tending to crop he was harvesting crop. If he wasn't birthing livestock, he was feeding livestock. If he wasn't feeding livestock, he was porting them to and from the market. If he wasn't erecting buildings, he was performing maintenance on them. If he wasn't fishing, he was preparing his catch for storage. He also assisted Yrma with housework and cooking on occasion as her work also seemed to be without end. At times, she would help with dressing the fish he caught as well as other outside labor. Neither felt their responsibilities were too masculine or to feminine that they could not share in the work. Hence, there was never a time when they were without a task. On many occasions they had to leave work undone and force themselves to take leisure.

The farm land Bari owned was not the easiest to maintain, but it was manageable. It was extremely rocky to begin with, but he had gotten rid of the most troublesome stones over the years. To stumble upon one after he'd gone through the effort of clearing it was a rare event. Dispelling the rock was a painstaking undertaking, but Bari and his workers did not cease until nearly every pebble was removed from the land.

The region in which the land lay was somewhat of a valley surrounded by mountainous wilderness. Although water was plentiful enough in the immediate area, there were dry seasons when very little (if any) rain fell. During this time of year, the land was too dry and the weather too hot to produce crop. To have ported in water from the lakes or river would not have proven profitable. So, there was no farming in those intensely dry summer months.

During the summer months when sowing did not occur, Bari prepared equipment for the next planting season. He repaired equipment that appeared to be on the brink of failure. He replaced any items that look beyond the point of repair. He added new items to his inventory as he saw the need. He made repairs to his barns and storage sheds during that time. He also tended more to his flock of sheep and herd of cattle. He accomplished his shearing during that time and made his sales of wool and overly mature livestock. He examined his seed to make sure it was still suitable for planting the next season's crop. He also purchased additional seed for new products he wanted to yield in the upcoming season. He made all the necessary preparations for the impending planting period, so when the short window of opportunity for planting and harvesting was upon him, he'd be prepared to begin the process all over again.

Bari fished a great deal more during the agricultural off–season as well. He had his preferred sites around the local area where he knew he would almost always do well. He knew exactly which bait and tackle to take to each area and achieve the best harvest. He could lure in a specific species at about the size he desired based on the bait he fished with, the depth at which he fished, and the time of the fishing season. He knew the right time of day to start and how long the peak bag times lasted. A good catch was as guaranteed as one could get when Bari engaged in the craft of fishing.

Most of Bari's male workers would take part in his fun–laden fishing trip; even though they were by no means obligated to do so. It was not a working trip that mandated their presence. It was more of a male–bonding, team–building, fun–for–all fellowship event from Bari's perspective. It created camaraderie amongst his workers. It also allowed the workers a chance to relax and engage in friendly competition with their employer. They spent a great deal of effort in trying to bag more fish than Bari. They would even join forces at times to try and outdo his fishing ability.

Their occasions of success were extremely rare. Upon tallying the final creel amounts, Bari almost always wound up with the superior catch. They were amazed at how hardly anyone ever left the fishing location with more fish than Bari. They would each keep what they caught; but in cases where some caught much more than others, they would share amongst those who did not bag enough to make the trip worthwhile. Even Bari would share from his bounty. It was an unwritten fishermen's creed to share the wealth and leave no one without.

On occasion, Bari ventured out from his frequented fishing locales and sought a more diverse variety of game. This generally entailed a trek to seaside and casting of nets or setting of hooks in deeper, larger bodies of water. Fish from the ocean had a different taste and texture than those of the freshwaters in the local area lakes and streams. They grew much larger as well. The greater size meant a greater degree of difficulty in catching them, but the greater the challenge, the greater the experience.

A few of the workers in Bari's employ would accompany him on those outings. The journey to the ocean and back required four days' travel. The men spent two days in getting there; a day of fishing and preparing the fish for the trip back; and a day to get back. The return trip was a bit of a struggle. They were forced to make the trek back without any stops or detours and they rested only enough to ensure their animals were not overworked to the point of injury. Bari used his finest horses on those trips for obvious reasons. He would rest the animals well before the trip and upon returning in concern for their overall health. He also watched them closely along the way to make sure they did not become overly fatigued with the stressful labor.

They really had no choice in exerting themselves far beyond what was normally required of them on those return trips. An expedited trip back was paramount in maintaining the freshness of their catch. Sure, they had means of preparing the fish for travel, but it still would not keep for very long and they could ill afford to allow all that labor and investment to be for naught.

Bari procured the services of commercial fishermen once they arrived at seaside. He'd developed a relationship with a couple of brothers who worked for their father as deck hands. Bari and his crew would charter the boat for the entire day to allow for a full day of fishing. They almost always fared well on those trips. He and his companions brought back plenty of fish and in many varieties. They sifted out their favorites and kept those to themselves. They often caught enough to sell some at the local market and used the proceeds to pay for the trip. Of the remainder, they shared some with close friends and relatives (upon returning home). They kept the balance for their families' consumption.

It was always a great trip. All who took part in the sea bound excursions anticipated making the trek. They enjoyed it even when they did not bag a sizeable amount of fish. Just getting away and being among fellow gentlemen outside of a work environment was relaxing in itself. It afforded them opportunities to share treasured tales of their past. They became more acquainted with each other's varying cultures. Some told amusing (and sometimes amazing) fish stories of other trips of which no one could verify legitimacy. If the story sounded questionable, everyone else would challenge the integrity of the story teller. Regardless of their trustworthiness or lack thereof, the stories would always end with a hearty round of laughter.

The thrill–seeking seafarers indulged in their fair share of virile competition as well. The one who snared the largest fish was honored by the rest as the master fishermen for that day. Each of the other anglers had to begin or end each verbal remark with, "sir" to him for the duration of the trip home. There was also a prize for the one who caught the first fish. Everyone else had to respond to his every command until they caught a fish of their own.

They also had gamesmanship among those who were veterans among them. The veterans would hustle to get to their most favored location on the boat. For some reason each of them had what they considered the best fishing spot on the boat. Getting to the "right" spot didn't involve superstition of any sort. It was just a testosterone–activated territorial fascination with them. It all added to the thrill of victory they sensed as they began their quest of man against fish.

The menfolk even had pranks that were playfully acted out on the newcomers. Anyone who had not previously experienced a fishing trip with them was lauded as prince of the vessel on the morning of the ocean outing. At breakfast time, the person was fed well and given a mock crown to wear onto the boat. They fed the prince things they knew would cause queasiness once they were afloat for any extended amount of time – as if being on the water for the first time wasn't enough to nauseate them.

Once the waves began rocking the boat, they watched the prince to see if he would eventually head for the side of the boat to heave his undigested cuisine into the ocean. If he did, he would often lose his crown while leaning over the boat's side rails to cast his gourmet breakfast overboard. They would all have a big laugh and inform the prince that he was demoted to fish feeder, because he had lost his crown and was seen offering food to the fish. It would often take the prince a while to figure out that they'd tricked him. Some never got it by themselves and had to be offered hints until they came to the realization that they'd been duped by their cohorts. The gang all had another heaping round of laughs once the ex–imperial finally realized the prank. They would then console him to the point where he could enjoy the remainder of the outing.

There were rare occasions when they arrived at their ocean–side destination and the weather would not permit a venture out onto the water. On those occasions, they would spend a portion of the day shopping the local fish markets for prepared seafood. Of course, prior to making their selections from the fish market, they enjoyed a day on the town. Only after a time of dining and relaxing would they make their way over to the market. They each had an eye for fresh fish, so it was no problem for them to determine which products had been on display for too long. They could determine by the condition of the eyes and the firmness of the flesh how long the fish had been on exhibition.

The local long–term vendors had grown accustomed to their visits and often pointed them to the back to choose from their freshest stock as soon as the visiting fisherman arrived at their stations. The band of occasional ocean-goers would purchase enough fish to take back to their families and have the merchant prepare and pack it securely for their journey home. But again, they made certain to take time to enjoy themselves for the day prior to embarking on their seafood shopping spree. Their animals still needed their rest and the men still needed their leisure time.

They would spend a portion of the day touring the surrounding areas. Some would visit the local worship house during the morning hours. Worship houses weren't nearly as formal as the temple in which they worshipped. In those houses, there were simply readings from the holy books and discussion on the readings of the day. Those present would listen to the one who read from their sacred books while elaborating on the meanings of its writings.

On one particular trip there was not much reading, but rather a great deal of discussion. It seemed there was a young man who read from their books the day before the fisherman arrived and claimed to be the great one their sacred books said would one day come and restore their country to its glory days. Bari and the portion of the crew who joined him could not follow the conversations surrounding the issue. There was too much back and forth quarreling between those who believed the young man at his word and those who didn't believe him. So, Bari and his men departed and sought something else to pass away the time.

The men who had not accompanied Bari and the others to the worship houses weren't interested in what was being taught in there. They were more attuned to the wineries and public bath houses. They ventured to the hillside area where the great philosophers gathered to debate various topics. They also visited the places where women made their living serving male travelers who desired to stop and refresh themselves. Those guys did not have wives and the associated commitments of marriage. They had a separate set of objectives than Bari and the others in that respect. Still they were all loyal workers and companions to each other, despite key differences in their choice for personal gratification.

The fishing party had their favorite pub, which they frequented for lunch on those weather–inhibited trips. Regardless of how they split up and spent their mornings, they would all reassemble in the early afternoon and share a meal together at the pub. They would lounge for hours and eat and reminisce over the memorable moments of past fishing trips. There were more than enough interesting stories to get them through the meal "hour." Some of the stories, even though they were true, were unbelievable to the newcomers.

It was an amazingly good time for all of them, including the local pub members. They sat and ate and chattered until it was time to go pick out their selection of fish at the market and begin the trip back home. Bari always paid for the meal after debating (jovially) with his workers for the right to do so. The men would at least convince Bari to allow them the privilege of leaving gratuity. After the debates ended, they left the pub with a hearty, "So long!" on their lips and a handsome tip on the tables. Everyone in the pub moaned at the group's departure. Bari's crew brought extra life to the already lively place. No one wanted to see them go, but knew from past visits that their stays would be short-lived.

Bari not only paid for lunch, but he also financed the entire trip on those weather-weary occasions. Although the workers offered to contribute, he insisted upon taking responsibility for all expenditures. The workers always made certain to express their sincere appreciation for his contribution towards the outing. They never allowed him to feel like they were attempting to take advantage of his kindness. They slipped in payment for food or supplies, whenever the opportunity presented itself. They would share house specialty snacks they'd brought along with them. Any special dishes prepared by their wives (which Bari had grown fond of over the years) were sure to be in their possession and a portion was offered to their beloved employer. They would also sneak in a surprise purchase of some special item to present to Bari and Yrma once they returned from the trip. Keeping it concealed until they returned home was always a challenge, but they often succeeded in securing it from his view.

The arrival home made for a most delightful setting. They were always greeted to hugs and kisses from loved ones who congregated at the anticipation of their arrival. On the following day, they would all gather on the portion of the property designated for celebrations and commence to having a feast. The workers who'd stayed behind would have already prepared a fatted calf for the feast – roasted on open fire and seasoned to perfection. Each of the families would bring their favorite side dishes to compliment the roast. There were also several types of breads and desserts to accompany the many dishes and the roasted meat. Everyone in Bari's family and employ were invited to the feast. Of course, they would often invite others outside of that domain; but Bari never objected to that.

Bari would begin the festivities by blessing the food and giving thanks for a safe trip and the blessings they all enjoyed together. He often gave a speech centered on being grateful for what he had accomplished in life and the relationships he had formed among the attendees. He would give an account of the latest adventure and share some humorous events encountered by the men during the trip if there were any. There was almost always something amusing to share with those who were left behind. He carefully talked around any dangerous encounters they may have had in an effort to avoid alarming the lady folk and children. He felt there was no reason to jeopardize anyone's opportunity of making future trips with them.

Once he completed his opening speech and offering of thanks, Bari performed the ceremonial carving of the roasted beast. After that, he and the men would serve the women and children. Only once the others were waited upon would they join in on the meal. Once the females and little ones were provided their first serving, it was every man for himself. No one was considered above or beneath the other. Bari's laborers, his foremen, his distinguished guests, and even Bari himself were all among equals. Just as on the excursion they were all brethren. If any of the women desired seconds once the men were done with their initial duties, they were self–served. The younger kids were assisted by the elder ones or an adult who just happened to be nearby. Of course, some adults were specifically sought out by their own child or those with whom they were familiar. They gladly obliged the children's requests.

Bari would give the fishermen the following day off to recuperate. The remainder of his workforce was allowed to report late the next day for a half–day of light duties. It was a break from tradition and a show of humility and gratefulness. He really saw strong value in letting others know how much he appreciated them.

He wasn't concerned that there may be work accumulating for the workers. They all deserved the rest period. It was an excellent way to enjoy the leisure of their off–season. They were all aware that the term was a short one and they would soon be remarried to fulltime labor and business as usual.

The children finished their meals as quickly as the adults would allow them. They were eager to make their escape from the watchful eyes of the older clan. They had their games laid out and ready to begin as soon as the dining activities were complete and they were granted their freedom. They would eventually move their party out among the scattered trees or into one of the open fields, as secluded from adult supervision as possible. Once there, they pretended to be one of their favorite adults or one of the heroes from the narratives they often heard from the grown–ups. They challenged each other to wrestling matches, throwing competitions, foot races or one of several other imaginative, competitive events. They ran, played, laughed, and did what's normal for kids.

In the absence of the younger bunch, the adults enjoyed music and dancing and shared just as much laughter as the juveniles. They also reminisced in the narratives of legends of their cultural past. The men had competitive games they played as well. Their games were more skill–oriented than the kids'; nonetheless they were just as competitive and imaginative. The difference was that they required not only strength, speed, and agility, but also strategy–a component not yet very well comprehended by the younger group. The elders competed just as hard as the children and those who won an event basked in the glory of victory as much as the kids and in some cases more so.

The women often sat and carried conversation on various topics. They shared their finest crafting ideas and talked about the humorous calamities of their male counterparts. They chatted about botched dishes the men had attempted to prepare on occasion. They made mention of their husbands' clumsiness in caring for the newborns. They shared recipes for new dishes they had created via trial and error. The older wives gave helpful advice to the younger ones on making their marriage and family life the best it could possibly be during both times of prosperity and times of scarcity.

After a period of alienated fellowship, the men and women would come back together and join in music, song, and dance. All who were musicians gathered their instruments and played favorite melodies. Someone would strike up a song and the others would soon join in. The musicians would pick up the melody and change their tune to match. Bari and Yrma would bring out the finest wine and the festivities would hit their peak. There was lots of laughter and celebration of life. It was always a peaceful, gentle hoot of a party. No one ever got unreasonable in their consumption of fermented drink or their display of delight. It was an excellent culmination to the offseason activities.

When the rainy season finally returned, Bari and his crew again directed their efforts toward farming the land. Farming was hard work. Even with the softening effect of the rains, it took a bit of effort to work the soil. The summer heat and lack of humidity had made it dry and brittle far beneath the surface. Weeds were plentiful at that time, because they grew during the summer months when nothing else would remain in the fields. Bari didn't trouble with controlling the weeds during the off–season. He wanted to give himself and his workers a break from that for a while. Besides that, the weeds and grass prevented erosion of the soil. Rich soil was a valuable commodity in that region. He needed something to keep the soil from washing away when the rains did finally fall at the end of the dry spell. So, despite their troublesomeness at other times, the weeds did serve a purpose during the dry season.

Bari and his workers spent a little time ridding themselves of weeds as they prepared the soil for the next planting of crop. The weeds were turned under the soil and chopped up when the workers cultivated the soil. Even in that the weeds served a purpose as they died and became fertilizer for the next generation of crop. The weeds did not totally go away during the planting season, though. Once the soil was prepared and the seed sown, some weeds were still able to somehow make their way back to the surface. There was constant work in keeping the weeds under control. One would not know it, however, by observing Bari's fields. He and his workers took special care in keeping those fields looking and producing their best.

There were exceptions where Bari and his workers did not even try to remove or control the weeds. There was a weed growing amongst the fields where he planted his wheat that the local farmers referred to as "tare." The tare looked exactly like the wheat during its maturation phases, so there was no way to tell the two apart. If Bari and his workers had tried to remove those weeds they would have run the risk of discarding good wheat plants as well. However, if he let them grow to full maturity, then he could easily tell them apart. The tares would have absolutely no substance at that point. They bore no fruit (grain) whatsoever. At the point of full maturity the workers could easily discern the difference and separate the tare from the wheat without risk of losing good crop. Thus, the workers just waited until harvest time and gathered the wheat with the tare. Then they could divide the two and make use of the wheat. They would gather and burn the tares so they would not multiply their seed into the next season's crop.

Bari really enjoyed working the land and maintained a healthy immodesty towards his profession. He was extremely self–effacing in most cases (except during times of friendly competition, of course), but not in the case of his farm work. He knew he was an excellent farmer and everyone around him did as well. He was not shy about making decisions or giving advice regarding cultivation. He knew the business and wanted to make sure each of his employers and customers was aware of that. Their awareness of his horticultural excellence was the key to his ability to retain great employees and market his goods at their highest (albeit fair) market value. It was also how he maintained his status as the first choice among those who desired his product.

So, he took his job extremely seriously. It was apparent that his workers did as well. They took ownership of the success of his annual harvests. A good yield was as important for them as it was to him. Their pseudo ownership was not seeded in covetousness, but merely a byproduct of their desire to do well by Bari. They were fully aware of how well Bari compensated them as workers. Compared to neighboring homesteaders, they were paid a lot more. Not only did Bari pay them higher wages, but he also treated them better than most other business owners. His workers were very aware and appreciative of that and showed their appreciation to Bari in the proficiency in which they performed their duties.

Should you have ever passed by Bari's farm during planting season, you would know professionals had worked those fields. Each row of vegetation was in order and perfectly positioned. Each plant was the proper distance from the other. The crops grew green (or colorful in some cases) and appeared in perfect health. They glistened in the morning dew and stood tall against the heat of the noonday. There was very little sign of wilting by evening and they were again inflexibly vertical by the next morning. Even passersby who knew absolutely nothing about farming would admire those meadows. One did not need occupational expertise to see that the fields were managed extremely well.

When harvest time arrived there was a short window of opportunity to gather the entire crop and get it into storage for family provisioning or off to market for profit. Harvest time was the hardest working time of the year for Bari and his crewmen. He had the regular workers whom he employed year round. They were very proficient in what they accomplished; but harvest time required extra help in spite of that. When the harvest was ripe, his usual staff of laborers was just too few.

So, Bari would seek out and hire supplementary workers for the duration of the harvest season. If he felt he needed additional workers after the first hiring, he would go out and hire even more. When the work was done, he would pay them all equal pay whether they started near the beginning of the harvest season or in the middle or near the end. That was his policy and he made sure everyone knew it prior to entering into his employ. Although his regular staff knew the policy and agreed with it, some of the new hires were confused by it. Some felt since they worked longer they should have been paid more. In the end, however, they were more than satisfied with what they received in the way of payment. It was just what Bari had promised and it was more than adequate for their rendered services.

Bari simply wanted to reward each of them evenly for their assistance in making the harvest a success. He knew that some would perform light duties and others would do very laborious work. He knew that some would be eager to work and some would just be fulfilling a commitment. He knew that keeping up with each of their tasks, their times, and their commitments would be hard work in itself. He knew he could manage that, but even if he decided to do so, there would still be some who felt they deserved more than others at payday. Rather than allow the opportunity for the appearance of showing favoritism of one employee over the other, Bari made an arrangement at the onset of their employ and remained committed to that agreement. It was the simplest and most effective way to make sure the harvest was tended to and every worker received a just reward for their efforts. Some may have felt as if they were overpaid, but none could ever gripe about underpayment. It was Bari's simplistic plan to a guaranteed satisfied employee and it worked tremendously.

A bit of the work Bari required of his workers was indeed challenging; but not only did he treat them fairly and pay them well; but he also worked just as hard as they did – if not harder. He didn't join in the vigorous labor to flaunt his abilities or outdo anyone. It was just his demeanor. He had an impeccable work ethic and he expected the same of his hired help. He felt the best way to get the quality work he expected and needed from them was to lead by example. He worked hard right alongside them. He felt that if a leader could do something to assist in furthering the group's goal, then they *should* do something and do it to the best of their ability. Bari was not a fan of authoritative figures who just bellowed out orders to others when they were capable of accomplishing some tasks on their own.

Bari never had the opinion that at some point one has achieved greatness and could just sit back and watch everyone else do the work it required to maintain that distinction. He never had a desire to sit as lord over others and be catered to. He did not feel his progression to the top was a reason to stop contributing to the efforts that gained him that success. "Everyone can be a contributor," was his signature mantra and he sang it often.

Bari believed in the honor system when it came to dealing with people. In fact, his pet peeve (if it may be referred to as such) was a display of dishonesty in folks. He could not tolerate association with deceitfulness. He could not hide the anguish of having encountered a dishonest person either. If, when executing a transition, he found that the person was dealing with him fraudulently, he would walk away from the conversation. He wouldn't entertain another word—regardless of the person's counter after having been exposed of their deception. If it were a purchase, the person could offer him the product at half price, but he would not buy it. In the case of a sale of a product, the person could offer him twice the market rate, but he would not sell it. Some felt he cost himself more than a few favorable opportunities for the inflexible policy of honesty, but he would not budge on that one principle. He felt that business should only be done with trustworthy business associates. He believed if one was willing to compromise in that area, then they would compromise in any area. To Bari, there were implications that deeper risks accompanied engaging in business with such people.

Bari would often loan money to his fulltime workers. When doing so, he never required a written receipt. He trusted they would repay their debts and they almost always paid him back. The only times they did not make restitution was when they requested more time to repay him and he forgave their debt. If there were ever a case when they simply could not recompense the monies by the mutually agreed upon time, they would come to him and make him aware of their circumstances. He would forgive the debt and never mention it again. Most of his workers still attempted to pay back the debt at a later date (on multiple occasions), but he would refuse every offer. His response was always, "I've casted that debt into a sea of forgetfulness," referencing an extract from their religious books. He felt that a forgiven debt should stay a forgiven debt. He would have wanted the same if it were he indebted to another.

Bari stood firmly on that principle of his, and he held those under his authority to the same standard. There was one case where Bari had forgiven the financial advance of one of his workers who could not pay, but found that the worker was unwilling to forgive a debt of another worker who could not repay him. Bari was furious that the worker would not show another the same leniency he'd shown the worker. He viewed it as pure hypocrisy. He rescinded his forgiveness of debt and required the servant to work it off to him before he received any further pay. If the worker was unwilling to do so, then Bari would have had him placed in jail. The worker paid back the debt and learned a hard but valuable lesson. It was Bari's way of teaching the worker that if one desires forgiveness;

they must be willing to forgive. Forgiveness was essential to life for Bari. He felt life absent of forgiveness was not worth living.

Bari had achieved high status and enjoyed a pleasant life. He knew that and those acquainted with him were aware of it as well. They also recognized he wasn't just surviving off of his family's good name. He could have easily survived and prospered solely from the reserves from his grandfather's accomplishments. Anyone with any amount of influence would have offered him a high–paid position of perceived importance if he desired such a thing. He could have easily taken advantage of political favors offered on behalf of notoriety of his kinsmen as he had often observed of many of his peers. Many of them held governmental offices or obtained jobs out of political favor and just lived by the accomplishments of parents or others in their families.

Bari chose to make his own way. He certainly was offered a jump start by having been born into a prosperous family; but he decided to build on what he had been given rather than just nibble away at it until it was completely depleted. He managed his own business. He went to and fro conducting his own barters. He transported his own crops and livestock to market. He did it all on a very regular basis. It was rare that he sent others in his stead. It wasn't that he felt his workers were untrustworthy. They had proven themselves more than reliable on every occasion he'd afforded them. He just felt that he wasn't exempt from the hands–on, hard work required to have and maintain success. It was that attitude that made him as well–off as he was, both with his finances and with the level of respect he commanded in and around his community. He was a living testament that people who command respect from their actions never have to demand respect from their lips. He proved that one can win over people's high opinion simply in the way they handle their personal responsibilities. People sincerely respected him for the honesty he conveyed in business, the integrity he displayed in his religious beliefs, and for his exceptional work ethics.

Hard work was the nucleus of Bari's life six days out of the week. He worked vigorously and continuously in the fields and around their home. He worked his way through assignment after assignment, never considering the level of effort required to maintain it all. He moved about from house to field to barn and back again. It was a never ending cycle. It wasn't an arduous task for him, though. It was just a way of life in which he took great pleasure. He went out each day looking forward to that day's challenges as well as its successes. He enjoyed the feeling of exerting his body nearly to its maximum level of endurance. One might suppose that the feeling was comparable to an Olympian completing his or her workouts during training. It made them look forward to the next gaming event with expectation of success rather than with fear of failure.

It was not until the seventh day of the week that Bari operated outside the norm of his rigorous work routine. The seventh day was a day of recuperation for him. He allowed his body its essential rest time. Their culture incorporated the restoration concept in every aspect of their lives. They believed strongly that one should not allow deterioration to develop in any facet of their being: ecologically, socially, physically, or spiritually.

Every seven years, they forewent preparing the soil for planting season. The seventh year was the time to allow the earth to recuperate from the previous six years' exertion. They would harvest anything that grew on its own, but they did not work the soil during the seventh year. They also released anyone indebted to them of their fiscal obligations every seven years. Even personal infractions were forgiven according to the seven-year pattern. The forgiveness of monetary liability and other wrongdoings was granted under the same recuperation principle. Relationships, just as the environment and finances were equally important in their perspective that incorporated recuperation of one's total being. In some cases, even lawful infringements were forgiven via this pattern of restoration. It was an amazingly effective method for rejuvenating love, respect, hope, endurance, and many other elements of life that sometimes require refurbishment.

On the seventh day, there were no tasks to complete and Bari did not have to maintain any schedules. Anything that may have begun on the previous day could wait until the following day. He allowed his workers to rest as well. He afforded them the same time to recoup as for himself. They would have to present a very strong case if they were to perform any tasks on that seventh day. About the only allowable case was an animal straying too far from the fold and requiring retrieval.

Beyond that occasion, no one in the Weshuan communities worked on the seventh day. It was that way by choice for some and it was a part of the religious laws and customs for others. Their religious restrictions simply did not permit them to perform manual labor on the seventh day of the week. It was set aside for honoring their God and performing their religious practices as well as relaxing and recuperating. If Bari caught any of his personnel working on that day, he would make them stop and leave the task undone until the next morning. If the religious leaders caught any Weshuans working on that day, they would punish them. Punishment could be anything from a punitive fine to a public flogging. They took the law very seriously. Bari was a bit more lenient in his dealing with offenders than the religious leaders. Not all who worked for him were Weshuan; hence, they did not all fall under their religious jurisdiction.

Bari and Yrma would pray together and have breakfast as on the seventh day just as any other day. Yrma took the time to prepare their meals on the day prior, however; so, there was no labor involved beyond serving the meal. After breakfast, the two of them would study the books of their religion. They always invited the hired help to partake in the studies. They had a library built onto their home for the purpose of study. Most of the workers appreciably joined in, but there were some who did not. Again, not every person in Bari's employ was reared under the same religious convictions as he. If he had them as regular employees, it was because they had good work habits and had all–around good ethical values. Bari did not hold it against them or treat them any differently if they chose not to join in the religious studies or follow in its practices. It was purely their choice to take part or not.

Bari and Yrma's religion required study and obedience to what they understood from their study. They took the seventh day of the week to really concentrate on those studies. They read and memorized things on other days, but on the seventh day extra attention was given to study of their religious books. After a few hours they would hold discussion amongst themselves and share with the workers who were present what they understood from the writings. They did their best to dispel any misunderstandings. There was a lot to remember and understand about their religion and they endeavored to know and understand it well. They both felt a personal conviction to understand as much as they could about their religion and to share what they understood with the others.

The fundamental reason of their study was to learn to show love for their God in all they did and learn to love everyone they encountered as much as they loved themselves. That was their goal in achieving complete comprehension of the writings in their religious books. They studied out of a desire for a pure heart, a clear conscience and sincere faith. They felt if they studied their books with that intent and lived their lives to that effect, then even those who did not partake in their religion would respect it nonetheless. They felt others would then admire their belief system because of its sheer moral principles–if for no other reason. The principle of their religion was to mature spiritually to a point where they would love unconditionally. Despite what others were doing or had done or might continue to do, they were to learn to love them without restraint. Bari and Yrma understood that principle of their religion well and sought to live by it with every fiber of their being. Their commitment to do so was very attractive. There were a number of workers who studied with them and who followed their practices and principles simply because of the gentle influence Bari and Yrma's principled life had on them.

Bari never claimed to know every letter of those books; but he understood the principles quite clearly. He understood them and his understanding was reflected in his lifestyle. There were certain actions that Bari's religion required its followers to perform and he executed those faithfully. But then again, everyone in his ethnicity completed those acts. They performed them without protest and without omission. They made an effort to let others know they were performing those acts as precisely and as often as they should do them. Those acts were the signature mark of their religion for anyone who might question what they believed in. No one who witnessed performance of those religious acts need question what they believed in.

Those acts illustrated to others how Bari and his people worshipped the God they believed in; however, the rituals were not the foundation of their belief system. The principles those acts demonstrated were the nucleus of their belief system (the principles of unconditional allegiance to their God and unconditional love for fellow human beings). Everyone who completed the acts did not necessarily understand and follow the principles of those acts. Many performed those acts to let others know what belief system they belonged to. Bari and Yrma completed the acts because they understood and wanted to follow their principles. They took extra effort in ensuring that their lives beyond the religious acts followed the principle of those acts. They incorporated the principles behind their religious acts into their relationships and their business associations and their everyday interaction with people. That's what made their religion not just acceptable to others and not just admirable, but also attractive.

On certain days, in an act of duty to his religion, Bari made his way to the temple to worship and pay tribute. Worship was simply acknowledging that he believed there was a God and recognizing the sacredness and sovereignty of that God. As with any religion, those who believe in a thing will perform some form of sacrament as an outward sign of that belief. There may be several acts that constitute those outward signs. Some are more liturgical than others. Some are performed regardless of where one finds themselves. Others are performed in the sanctity of a designated place of worship. Those performed publicly are often arbitrary. Those performed in a designated place are often more delineated than others. In Bari's case, the acts of worship performed at the temple were extremely defined and presented very meticulously. There were a fair number of well–defined steps to acknowledging their God during temple worship.

Beyond worship, the further objective of Bari's visit to the temple (to pay tribute) served a threefold purpose. First of all, it symbolically signified his gratefulness to his God for sustaining and bestowing kindness upon him. Bari was just offering a token of thanks by giving back a portion of what his God had blessed him with. Just as he showed appreciation to his workers for all they did for him by offering bonuses and gifts, Bari honored his God with gestures of gratitude via the tribute. It was one of those acts that were deeply engrained into his cultural rearing. For as far back as his written religious history went, his people had been honoring their God with that tribute.

Secondly, the tribute was used to sustain the religious body in place to manage operations of the temple. A small portion of that tribute provided food and necessities for the clergymen who maintained the temple and conducted the worship services. Terms were embedded in their laws and traditions requiring that each male citizen bring a certain percentage of whatever he produced (crop, livestock, etc.) to the temple so that a portion of it could serve as provision for the priests and temple workers. The priests and their workers were not allowed to own property or engage in a profession, so they relied solely on tributes from the other adult males of their religious community for their families' provisioning.

Finally, the tribute served as a remissive payment for any wrongdoings (intentional or unintentional) they had committed against their religious beliefs or their fellow citizens. Although Bari was a good man, he knew he was not perfect. He would pay tribute for his wrongdoings as well. Their law resolved that certain acts against the law and other citizens could be reconciled by rendering of various tributes at the temple. No portion of those tributes was to be retained by the priests or their workers. Those would be offered as a sacrifice for the accompanying transgression. Those tributes were burned and the wrongdoer's loss of the assets was considered payment for the wrong they had committed against another or society at large. The principle was that no wrongdoing ever happens without a cost to someone and the wrongdoer should ultimately bare that cost. It's the same logic that seemingly most legal systems operate from nowadays.

There was a caveat to paying tribute for a wrongdoing. In some cases, even a tribute would not grant forgiveness. In other cases, if the wrongdoing was severe enough, then tribute alone was not adequate compensation. If it were an offense such as murder or infidelity, then the law required capital punishment. One could not contribute their way out of such an offense.

If someone committed a homicidal act (or some other wrong doing) purely by accident, then there was a stipulation that went along with the tribute. The family of the deceased or aggrieved person could enact the "eye for an eye" clause. That clause allowed the family to carry out the same act on the perpetrator as committed on their loved one. That article allowed the offended party to do so without facing judgment for their retaliation.

The only source of saving grace for the person who'd committed the wrong unintentionally (if the family showed no mercy) was if they could make their way to a "safe city," then they could remain and reside there un–avenged by the family members. If the guilty party ever left that safe city, then they were again at the mercy of the family of the one whom they had shown offense.

Within Bari's culture, there was little or no room for granting mercy to those who had wronged another aside the seven year principle. Some even ignored that principle and sought vengeance indefinitely. Relatives were compelled with the greatest zeal imaginable to avenge the wrongdoing of a family member regardless of how the wrong came about. In fact (for those intentional crimes), the law even appointed the closest male next of kin as the legal bounty hunter. Of course, the law would not protect those who sought vengeance beyond the seven year mark. Given the emphasis placed on vengeance, it was in the best interest of the perpetrator to get to and remain in the "safe city" for the balance of his or her life when the offense was of an unintentional nature.

The consequence of their action, despite its unintentional nature, was in many cases a seven year sentence at minimum. In cases where families refused to forgive, it became a life sentence. Hence, one might consider the city a prison; but if they were to do so, it would equate to that of a minimum security facility. People could live a normal life as long as they remained in the city. No one could enact the eye for an eye rule within the safe city gates. The guilty party could send their tribute to the temple by another to obtain forgiveness from a religious standpoint. Beyond that, the guilt was present at least for the seven years, but in some cases for the rest of their lives or until the person(s) seeking to exact revenge passed away.

There were six such communities in Weshua's vicinity available to those who had accidentally caused death or serious injury/wrongdoing to another. The cities were strategically dispersed along the region where Bari lived and conducted his business. They basically followed the pattern of the main waterway in that region (although they were not immediately adjacent to it). There were three safe cities on the east side of the river and three on the west side. The idea of placing them spread apart and on opposite sides of the river was to allow the accidental offenders a chance to get to a place of refuge before becoming a victim of familial retribution. Regardless of the area in which they committed their crime, they should have had fairly immediate access to a safe city.

Of course, upon reaching to the city, they still were required to face trial. The religious leaders would come to the city and hear their cases. Each offender was required to have at least two witnesses present for trial if they were to claim amnesty. The religious leaders would consider the credentials and reputation of their witnesses then hear and determine the validity of their story. If the jury (or judges – they were one and the same) determined that the death or other offense was in fact caused by accident, the offender was allowed to remain in the city unscathed. Otherwise, they were sentenced immediately. In cases where death was involved, the guilty offenders were executed at once. The power possessed by the religious leaders was acutely alarming.

Provisioning for those who lived in the safe cities was often bequeathed by the families or close friends of the perpetrators. In some cases, they were provided for by the priests or other good–hearted persons living in close proximity. There were no major cities nearby, but small settlements were sprinkled about them. The cities operated under the rule of the priesthood, so there were no internal authorities. This aspect of their structure had its advantages and disadvantages. Those within the city never paid taxes, but they also never owned anything. If there were disputes of any sort, they were settled by the religious leaders. If a resident of a safe city committed a misdemeanor crime while there, they were excommunicated and left at the mercy of avenging family members of their original victim. If the offense was a felony or the same as the reason they were in the city, then they were executed immediately.

The cities were purposely positioned far from the main cities. They were mostly in the mountainous regions. The rationale for their placement was twofold. One reason was to minimize the desire of the inhabitants to return to their home towns. Leaving the mountains meant they had to travel a single road in and out of the city. That made them extremely vulnerable to anyone awaiting an opportunity to enact the eye for an eye rule upon them, should they decide to leave the city. As one might guess, those holding pungent grudges against the offender would camp out and wait for their attempt to leave the city. This offered an opportunity to avenge their slain or otherwise offended family member.

The other rationale for positioning the cities in those strategic locations was to make sure they were not located anywhere near the city of the temple. The religious leaders felt those guilty of murder or other serious criminal acts should not reside near such a holy place. They did not take into account the inadvertent factor of the crime. They still considered the persons unclean and thus stationed them as far from the holy temple as possible. Bari's people showed an astonishing amount of respect for and great pride in their temple. Nothing of the sort the safe cities were comprised of, in their opinion, should be positioned close enough to possibly defile it.

Bari and Yrma conducted recurrent excursions to the temple for the sake of performing worship and offering tribute. Although some of their workers worshipped at the temple just as Bari and Yrma, the laborers made their trips to the temple separately. This was not based on religious beliefs or decrees against fraternization or anything of that nature. Bari and Yrma just decided to make those trips on their own. They saw these voyages as opportunity to spend time seeing sights and enjoying each other's company. It was quality time together outside of the day–to–day norm. It was Yrma's version of the fishing trip Bari and a portion of his workers took during the farming off–season. It was her chance to get away from the monotony of household tasks and everyday responsibilities as well as have uninterrupted companionship with the love of her life.

She would also have time to herself, since the greater portion of the worship effort was the man's responsibility. The male was designated as spiritual leader for the family as much as he was their physical provider. So the male was the one elected to participate in the temple activities. In fact, women and children were strictly forbidden from certain sections of the temple where men acted out their religious duties. Yrma's presence in the inner portions of the temple was impermissible. So, she mainly went along for the sake of an extended outing with her beloved Bari. She did take part in the publicly available worship service, but that was the extent of her religious experience during the trip.

There was an area outside of the temple (referred to as the courtyard) where the women and children could gather and listen to a lecturer teach from their religious books. There were also other males who had not been officially "adopted" into their religious circle who stood around and listened to the teachings. They were recognized as foreigners and were not allowed inside the temple, either. Persons who listened in the courtyard could offer their own monetary contribution towards the benevolence of others, but were not required to pay tribute as were the temple worshippers. Those monies collected in the courtyard were allocated to financially assist the less fortunate. Yrma gladly listened to the teachings that went on there and happily gave out of her abundance. She could definitely see where the monies could be put to good use. Besides that, the good feeling of offering to the needy was a perfect compliment to the joy of receiving good teaching. The undertaking did not occupy much of her time, though. For that reason, Yrma planned ahead for what she would do while Bari was inside the temple partaking in the time–consuming rituals of their worship service.

The time they spent at the temple and traveling to and fro was an opportunity for much–needed vacationing–not just for Yrma, but for Bari as well. They really needed the time to break away from the everyday stresses of life. They worked hard each day, both she and Bari; so they deserved time to themselves. Although Bari's fishing trips to the sea were breaks from his day–to–day duties, those excursions still required intense labor–both physically and logistically. He was just as exhausted from his fishing trips as he was from a normal day in the fields; hence extra day off for him and his companions upon returning from seaside.

So, the young couple incorporated a great deal of leisure time into those temple visits. They took pleasure in the quality recess period. They had earned the right to take their time, so they moved at their own unhurried pace. They relished in the opportunity to let others prepare the meals, clean the clothing, fix up the bed, and fetch their items while they just enjoyed each other's company. They didn't care to have it that way always, but on the occasion of retreat, they thoroughly enjoyed it. They had earned the privilege to sleep in for a few days. They had earned a right to leave the cares and concerns of everyday life in someone else's capable hands and just enjoy the relaxation and rejuvenation only attainable from a pleasurable vacation.

The two had to journey a great distance to get to the temple; so there was no reason they should try and make the trip in a single effort. It would require day and night travel and a need to carry a great deal of provisioning along. It would have then been no different than Bari's fishing trips. But they did not want the trip to the temple to be hectic and tiresome like the oceanic excursions. So, they chose to break up the journey and make stops in several of the towns along the way. That was their way of making a bona fide vacation of each temple visit. It afforded them time to relax along the way. It presented the occasion to thoroughly appreciate each trip. It also allowed Bari the opportunity to be refreshed and rejuvenated when he entered into the temple to perform his worship duties.

While making their way to the city of the temple their focus centered mostly upon getting there and taking part in the worship ceremonies. So, although they did not rush themselves, they didn't partake in very much exploration on the initial segment of the trip. Bari wanted to perform his religious duties before any intense leisureliness. It was just the order of things for him. He always made certain business was concluded prior to taking leisure. That way if any complications arose, he still had the time and resources to work around those impediments.

Since it was such a long trip to the temple, Bari did not transport his tribute. He feared he may lose or damage it along the way. He just didn't feel he could maintain a high quality tribute along the journey to the temple. He would much rather exchange monies for a tribute when he arrived at the temple. Then he could present the tribute unblemished during worship services. He showed great reverence for the practice of giving and wished to make the best offering possible. Offering tribute meant a great deal to him. In fact, it was engrained into his religious convictions. He would have felt he was doing his God a tremendous disservice to not offer his best tribute in the exact manner in which they were required to offer it.

So, Bari had need of exchanging monies for the tribute he desired to make in the temple once arriving into town. There where resources available in the temple specifically for that purpose. Those who did not have exactly what they wanted to offer as contribution could exchange monies and obtain their desired tribute. Their religious laws and customs made stipulation for such exchanges to be readily available at the temple. The temple workers were required to keep those items on hand for the sole purpose of meeting the needs of parishioners who'd traveled afar to worship at the temple. Bari knew the resources would be there for offering tribute, so he did not inconvenience himself and Yrma with transporting his own.

He wasn't a bit concerned with the probability of needing to barter from a market vendor or individual when he arrived at the city of the temple, either. Although he could find the same items elsewhere; he would pay a handsome price for them. The marketplace was a terrible place to try and barter for such items. The vendors there knew the demand for objects of tribute. They knew people would esteem religious value over cost and pay the exorbitant price regardless of the inherent unfairness. Therefore, the vendors' prices were way above the actual worth of those items. Bari wasn't concerned about that, though. The exchange rate for each item of tribute was already set at the temple. He knew what to expect from the temple workers. He would simply make the exchange for a tribute upon arrival at the temple and go about his business.

Bari and Yrma made their journey to the temple on foot. Bari owned beasts of burden which they could have ridden and forced to transport their belongings, but he and Yrma both chose to walk. It was a tradition they'd developed for themselves over the years. It presented a humbling effect; which they both felt was a characteristic they should continue to hone. It kept them from cultivating conceit or depicting haughtiness. They desired to never flaunt their success among the populace. They never wanted to create an atmosphere where someone felt inferior to or venerated them. They wished to go unnoticed and just blend in with the crowd. They found that approach generated genuine greetings and honest opinions from those they encountered during their travels.

Making the trip by foot also allowed the animals to be available for the hired help while Bari and Yrma were away so as not to place an extra burden on the workers or the remaining animals. Had they taken the animals away, it would have required a shift in the rotation. Such a shift would have meant extra coordination and extra care by the workers. It would have created a logistical encumbrance. It was an added burden that Bari and Yrma just did not wish to place on their workers if they could avoid it. Hence, they chose to travel on foot.

The trips to the temple would have been more strenuous on the beasts than a normal day's work at the home front and Bari was well aware of that. Temple visits were not like the quick fishing trips that Bari and his workers made during the off season. Each day on the trek to the city of the temple would have been tougher than a day's work back at the homestead and their animals would not have had the opportunity of daily rotation out of the work schedule as when back home. It was another reason Bari and Yrma chose not to bring the animals along. There was just too much added stress.

Bari and Yrma did not regard their hired help as property or slaves as most of the business people in their region and culture. Most 'owners' relegated their employees to indigent servitude. Since their employees were so poverty-stricken and could not survive without employment (regardless of the terms of employ) the business owners treated them as literal slaves. They determined their employees living quarters and conditions. They imposed their beliefs upon the employee slaves. They determined the amount of rations to be issued to the workers and when they should or should not produce offspring. Some of the male owners even assisted in the female slaves' reproduction process.

Bari and Yrma did not make requests of their employees that they were not willing to fulfill themselves. They did all they could to make their workers feel like family. The consideration they showed by leaving the animals for them to use in completing their chores was just a diminutive fragment of the equation. They shared in their workers' celebration of memorable moments such as births and marriages. They assisted them in getting through moments they wished to forget such as deaths and major illnesses. They contributed their physical resources (when needed), including manual labor. When their workers built new homes or added on to and repaired their current dwelling place, Bari was present with tools in hand. Bari and Yrma truly made their employees feel as if they were part of the family.

The workers viewed Bari and Yrma as extended family as well. They made sure the two were invited to every milestone event of their lives as well as those of their children's lives. The employees' gestures were not made out of duty–bound respect for their employers. They were not looking for gifts or to obtain special favor, either. When they invited Bari and Yrma to an occasion, they would not allow the two of them to contribute monies or bring any items of greater value than gifts offered by common guests. They simply wanted Bari and Yrma to feel welcomed to share in the celebratory moments of their lives. They had a genuine desire to include Bari and Yrma as part of their familial community.

Most property owners, although they knew a trek such as the one to the temple was hard on their animals and more importantly their workers, were not as considerate as Bari and Yrma in that regard. The other proprietors often flaunted their possessions without any consideration of the welfare of the beasts or the inconvenience to their workers. Even though most had fewer animals in their rotation than Bari, other owners would still ride their animals and carry as much provisioning as possible. The animals were so burdened down with the owners and their belongings that the risk of injury due to overexertion was much higher than normal. The trips back to their homes bore an even greater risk, because the owners often brought home more merchandise than they left with. There were often times when the owners had to purchase a different beast during their travels, because they had overworked their own to the point where the animal could go no further.

Not only was the trek itself problematic for the animals and the workers, but it was also impractical for the owners. The owners had to carry along an entourage to protect both them and their belongings from would be bandits. Of course, that meant more workers pulled away from the normal daily business routine back at their homesteads, which meant a more difficult task of maintaining business for both man and beast while the owners were away.

It was really senseless for the owners to cause such an inconvenience to so many, just so they could boast their accomplishments to the world. They could never make use of all the commodities they transported during those voyages and they certainly could not justify the inconvenience to their employees. Not only that, once those owners got to the city of the temple, it was impossible for them to pass through the city gates with all the goods they carried with them. In those cases, the owner had to have their entourage unload everything at the entry of the gate, then load it all back on once the animal passed through the gate. They had to repeat the process on their way out of the city.

It really was an insensible way to conduct their travel and all just to impress others. So, rather than be such an inconvenience and burden to their workers and animals, Bari and Yrma chose to travel on foot – as humiliating as that was to most well–to–doers within their culture. They took only bare necessities, which Bari carried on his back or in a small two–wheeled cart he would pull along. Although Yrma never grew weary during those trips, she would sometimes ride in the cart as a form of amusement. Bari never grumbled when she did mount the cart. He could barely feel the difference in the small amount of weight she appended to his load.

They were not one bit concerned about the amount of effort or time it took to make the trip by foot. They would break as often as they desired and linger at a location as long as necessary to recuperate for the next segment of their journey. They would dine and refresh themselves at taverns along the way. For that reason there wasn't a need to pack very much water or provisioning. They would load up with just enough food and water to get them from one portion of the trip to the next. It would take more time overall for them to make the journey, but that was of little significance to them.

On one particular trip, as Bari and Yrma entered into the city of the temple, they noticed palm branches lying at the entry way of the city and all about the streets. The branches had been trampled upon as if several people had just entered through the city gates. The fact that they were palm branches meant that the townspeople were welcoming a very influential figure into the city. Because they were still in place and the green leaves (although trampled and broken) had not yet begun to discolor, Bari and Yrma knew that the event had occurred most recently. Apparently, someone of pronounced importance was currently visiting the city of the temple.

For Weshuans, it was customary to welcome notable guests into their cities by the laying of palm branches (and occasionally clothing) in their pathway. It was a way of honoring their presence. The incoming guest would walk over whatever had been laid in their pathway. It was a sign of adoration as well as ultimate respect for the visitor. It was the "red carpet" treatment so common within today's global culture that's often presented to movie and music stars or royalty and high–ranking government officials.

Yrma audibly pondered who the important person currently passing through could have been. Bari nonchalantly disregarded it as perhaps another well–known regional politician whom the local politicians were attempting to woo into showing their city political favor. So often the local politicians would expend great amounts of effort and capital to basically bribe higher ranking regional politicians into granting a request. The request was usually something that was either against the rules or out of the norm. It usually only benefited the local citizens and most often made it appear to the constituents that their local political leaders held clout among their superiors. Bari had witnessed the act on several occasions and despised it greatly. He felt certain the collection of debris at the gates and along the streets was a sure sign of such activity.

Bari and Yrma walked over the debris and through the city gates and made their way into the city. There were remnants of the branches scattered all along the streets. Bari thought aloud, "This person must be really important. I've never seen so much rubbish in the streets in my entire life." Eventually the amount of refuse would begin to diminish, but there were traces of the celebration throughout the city. They noticed the trail all the way from the city's gateway to the courtyard of the temple. Whoever it was must have sought the temple as their immediate destination. Bari thought out loud again, "I guess whoever the politician was; he came to pay tribute for all the wrongdoings our locals have talked him into." They both chuckled at Bari's "tongue in cheek" statement, but they knew that their local politicians were capable and guilty of seriously immoral undertakings. Their names often riddled the local news in connection with scandals of all sorts.

2 BETRAYED

Bari and Yrma sauntered into the courtyard together. They came to the point where they would wish each other well via a spirited kiss and go their separate ways. Yrma headed toward the side skirts of the temple square to seek out any teaching that may have been taking place. A gentlemen surrounded by commoners was lecturing on a topic related to their religious writings, so she gently pressed her way into the crowd. As always, she would get close enough to hear, but not to be noticed by the orator. She did not wish to be summoned to answer a hypothetical question or to quote a verse from their religious books. Those who stood closest to the speaker were often called upon to assist the teacher. They would reiterate or elaborate on the point of discussion or verify what was written in their books coincided with the speaker's account. Some listeners made certain they got close enough to be chosen for such duty. They wanted to show how well–acquainted they were with the books of their religion and the principles they projected to the readers. Yrma was well–versed in their religious writings (perhaps just as much as anyone there), but she did not wish to attract attention by flaunting her knowledge. She only wanted to take in and assess what was being taught to the masses.

After separating from Yrma, Bari moved quickly towards the temple. Service would commence soon and he wanted to be prepared for it. As always, he greeted passersby along the way (some of the faces were familiar; some weren't); but he did not allow any conversations to become more than a crisp, hardy greeting. Again, Bari was a purpose–oriented man. Once his mind was fixated on a task, he would not stop until he'd completed it. His sole purpose for coming to the temple was worship service. He was intent on accomplishing that before carrying out any other task.

Bari arrived in the temple prior to service with ample time to examine the merchandise available for tribute. He didn't care to be rushed through the process of seeking out a tribute to offer before entering into worship service. He knew there would be a great deal of commotion surrounding the exchange process. He allotted himself time for waiting in the overcrowded lines for his opportunity to make an exchange. There was always a flurry of events taking place at the exchangers' tables. Many other parishioners who came from remote locations chose to acquire their tribute once they arrived at the temple just as Bari.

It just seemed logical to everyone that they should purchase the item (or rather exchange it for its monetary worth) upon arrival. If they waited until they got to the temple, they could get their tribute in excellent condition, versus trying to keep the item in good form along the extended journey. There were so many opportunities for their tribute to be lost, damaged, or stolen on those road trips. It did not matter whether the trip was made by foot or by animal some form of mishap was bound to occur if one chose to journey such a distance with tribute in hand or onboard. So the majority of those who visited the temple from afar chose to exchange monies for their tribute upon arrival.

Bari awaited his turn at the exchangers' tables, and then appraised the selection. He surveyed each article very carefully. He was not at all pleased with the choices. The items weren't nearly as well kept as he had witnessed in the past. There were several noticeably abysmal markings and imperfections. He thought to himself, "I would never use something so disgraceful to offer as tribute – neither to my God nor to my worship leader. How can this temple worker expect such a thing from me?"

He made the exchanger aware of his displeasure with their selection and made it clear that he preferred to purchase his tribute from a local vendor instead. He felt certain he would find a better selection than that offered at the temple. He knew he would pay a higher price, but at least he could get a presentable tribute. Before he turned away, he pronounced to everyone present his repulsion of the items being offered as tribute.

The exchanger responded to Bari's comments with an expression of annoyance and progressed to his next customer as if the encounter had never taken place. Bari was even more appalled when the worker didn't attempt to mitigate the issue or at least defend his honor. Bari reasoned within himself that either it was not the first time the exchanger had been confronted about such a poor presentation or he was just apathetic in regards to the mediocre service he rendered to the parishioners. Bari resolved that it must have been a combination of both. He felt certain that he wasn't the only one to notice such poor offerings. He couldn't believe he was the first to broadcast complaint regarding it, either. He surrendered a deep sigh of disgust then turned and moved towards the exit of the temple.

Bari contemplated the freshly occurred course of events as he walked along. He thought about how incredibly dispassionately the exchanger just went on about his business. Tribute was a very solemn affair in Bari's culture. All of what took place in the temple was a serious matter. He recollected the stories of how his grandfather was able to so easily assemble that band of fighters to expel the entire army of Kreges from their land for degrading their temple and disregarding their religious principles. He considered it very bold of the money exchangers to take the approach they had in committing comparably the same act.

In Bari's mind, this was just as insulting as the acts of the Kreges – maybe even more so. At least the Kreges could offer the excuse that they were not fully aware of the hallowedness attributed to the temple and the services rendered therein. Those exchangers could not claim such naivety. They understood every aspect of the holy place and its practices. They knew the routines regarding their religious processes were very precise and performance of their duties required detailed attention in every aspect. The practice required the utmost humility and extreme accuracy in presentation. The objects they used in the worship experience were to be prepared a certain way, maintained a certain way, and displayed a certain way. Those who wished to take part in the worship services had to follow specific instructions in doing so. Those who conducted the worship services had to manage the sacraments with acute precision. Even the attire they adorned was to be crafted and worn to absolute specifications. Every action and every item involved in the service had to be managed meticulously.

Everything they said or did in the temple had to be offered in strict adherence to the instructions written in their religious books and according to their laws and customs. Any deviation from the mandatory statutes stipulated in their laws and customs was totally unacceptable and completely unforgivable. There was a time when deviation from those prescribed processes meant instant removal from temple service and punishment along with it. It did not matter if the infringement was accidental or purposed. It mattered not if it was carried out by a worshipper, a temple worker or a worship leader; the action was to be punished to the fullest extent of the law. If the infringement was severe enough, the punishment could have been death! That's just how significant temple worship was to Bari's people.

Under no circumstances would Bari begin his worship experience with a tribute that was not offered according to specifications. It would nullify any positive effect the worship experience might have otherwise had on him. The entire ceremony would then have been meaningless. He would have left the service in the same Spiritual condition in which he came – if not worse. He would not have felt as if he'd presented a deserving tribute to his God or his religious leaders, such that his God would have felt his gratitude and the religious leaders would have sensed his sincere endorsement of their governance. He did not consider such a tribute satisfactory imbursement for his leaders' services. He would not have felt absolved of any wrongdoings he may have committed since his last visit. He would not have experienced any Spiritual fulfillment whatsoever. He would not have felt as if he'd grown any closer in his relationship to his God. He would have just gone through the motions of a religious ceremony rather than have grown in his faith or improved in his relationships. "How could they attempt to demean something so meaningful?" he thought to himself.

Bari began to feel an agitation he'd never experienced before. He began to feel as if his temperature was rising rapidly. It literally felt as if his blood would soon begin to boil. He felt light–headed, although not in the sense of drunkenness. He felt like something was overcoming him. He certainly had felt anger in the past, but the agitation Bari felt on that occasion was noticeably different. The offensive behavior of the temple workers bothered him far more than anything ever had prior to that occasion. It went beyond his emotions and found its way to his soul. That vexing of the soul was much more dangerous than any normal emotional agitation he'd felt in the past. It was the type of agitation that made "the priest" Mathes become "the warrior" Mathes.

Bari was disgusted beyond measure. He expected inferior products of the sort when shopping out in the marketplace where thieves and hustlers thrived, but not there–not at the temple. Although he knew the marketplace could produce a much better grade of merchandise, he also knew it was teeming with dubious characters trying to obtain something for nothing. They were trying to take advantage of anyone and everyone that came along. They watered down their wines. They loaded their scales with undetectable weights so the reading was incorrect and they could unsuspectingly overcharge the buyer. They reduced the amount of dye in their purple linens so fabrics faded after having been washed only once. They performed the bait–and–switch routine when packaging products for their customers. Customers paid top price for top quality, but wound up finding an inferior product in their possession once they had traveled great distances to their homes.

Vendors in the marketplace were constantly scheming to take advantage of either folks' ignorance or their innocence.

Bari knew their tactics well and expected that type of behavior when he went to the marketplace. In fact, he seldom purchased items for himself from there for that very reason. He mainly visited the marketplace because his wife was awed by the many different spices, fabrics, trinkets, and other oddities from distant lands. She could easily look beyond the deceitfulness of the not–so–trustworthy vendors. She outsmarted and outlasted the marketers' attempts of treachery on most occasions. She argued and bargained until she got the price of an item within her desired range.

Bari never wasted time endeavoring to influence vendors to charge what the products were actually worth instead of inflating their prices. If he did decide to purchase something, he'd just pay the advertised price. Yrma, on the other hand did not view negotiation as a wasted effort. She loved the challenge of a good barter session. She considered it comparable to a competitive sport and enjoyed the challenge. She emerged as victor more often than not. In fact, her winning percentage was quite lofty.

The highlight of the trip for Yrma was strolling through the market and admiring the innumerable commodities from diverse regions of the world then negotiating a reasonable price for the things she desired to take home. She took her time and combed over every inch of that marketplace to discover what new items were at her disposal. From end to end and from table to table she patiently sifted through each piece of merchandise. She made note of prices and condition of each item of interest. She would then back track, performing the entire process in reverse. She wouldn't purchase anything on the first pass. She feared she might notice something of better quality or the same item at a lower price in a different area. She would even examine a section a third time if her notes from the first two passes failed to show which item was best valued.

Yrma felt as if she was in a fantasy world when entering the marketplace. She absolutely adored it. There were people from all surrounding areas who came to barter there. The vendors consisted of traders who'd traveled the world over and returned with every item of interest they could place their hands on. Only a small percentage of the vendors were local residents. The same was the case of the consumers. Many came to sell and many more came to buy.

Sometimes Yrma thought the people were just as interesting as the merchandise. Their stories were intriguing to say the least. Some of their appearances were equally intriguing. Some of their stories were questionable. Some of their appearances were *quite* questionable. Yrma wasn't at all bothered by their appearances, however. She was always eager to join in conversation with them. She loved to indulge in the stories of their cultures, their struggles, and their accomplishments. She favored the folklores they offered in explanation of the origin of some of their products. Some of the stories were unbelievable. The full impact of their dialogue was comparable to reading a novel with the characters standing right in front of her. Her trips to the marketplace were chock-full of blissful moments.

Of course, Yrma would only converse with other women. It was not culturally correct for women to interact with men outside of their homes unless they were immediate family: husbands, brothers, or sons. Their culture did allow the amount of conversation required to greet someone or to exchange information concerning the products, but that was the extent of inter–gender communication. It was just improper for females to hold conversations with males beyond a greeting or barter.

Not only was it unacceptable behavior, but Yrma also did not feel at all comfortable keeping conversation with men if Bari wasn't nearby. So many people knew Bari and knew she was his spouse. She feared it would give them the wrong impression of the wife of such an honorable citizen. So, she sought out other women to exchange dialogue and seek interesting stories with while on her marketplace excursions. The number of fascinating narratives she encountered was astonishing.

The current trip would produce a very interesting lady with a most intriguing story; however, the story had nothing to do with marketplace items of interest or cultures and practices of foreign lands. Yrma was sifting through articles when she heard a lady in a very excitable voice recounting her story of a recent meeting with a stranger at the well. (The well was a common meeting place in the northern country.)

The lady was one that most would refer to as "non–culturally–correct" regardless of which culture one had in mind. That was certainly the case for their mild-mannered culture. Not only did the lady converse openly with men in public but she was extremely fond of them and apparently they were equally fond of her. Well, they at least had a seasonal fondness of her. She had been married five times and was currently in an intimately close relationship with a man to whom she was not married. Again, her promiscuity was very taboo for the mild–mannered lifestyle promoted within their culture. All of that changed for the lady, though, after a happenstance meeting with the stranger at the well in the northern country.

The fact that the stranger (who lived in the southern country) had an extensive conversation with a citizen of the northern country was an intriguing story within itself. Although the two regions had a vast number of similarities they had just as many irreconcilable differences. Among the similarities was the fact that the northern country had a temple city just as the southern country in which Bari and Yrma made their routine temple visits. The second temple was built after a dispute among the leaders of the regions. Somehow the leaders could not resolve the dispute, so some leaders in the northern region decided they wanted nothing more to do with the southern region. They didn't even want to worship in their temple. So, they built their own. Years later, there was a great regional debate centered on which of the two cities' temples was the most appropriate place to worship.

Both temples were associated with very notable figures in their religious history. The southern country's temple resided in the city nicknamed after the most renowned military leader in their history. He was a great warrior turned king. He was also devoutly religious and a phenomenal psalmist. The temple was built by that king's son who became a legendary king in his own right. The son was known as the wisest and wealthiest king of all time. When he decided to build the temple, people of royalty travelled from near and far to donate lavish materials towards its completion. They presented the son with the finest lumbers, metals, ivory, and precious stones with which to construct the temple. They even sent their most skillful craftsmen to assist in constructing the temple. They did so, because they all wanted to be acquainted with the legacy of the son who proved to be a great and honorable king. The temple was completed after a number of years of construction and properly named in the son's honor.

The north side temple wasn't birthed through such an affluent legacy, but its history was intriguing enough. Its greatest claim to fame was that it stood near a well which was produced by one of the region's three most notable religious founding fathers. The well was very popular even beyond the area of its northern country locale. It bore a strong religious significance of its own. As a matter of fact, the well in the northern country received more religiously inspired visitation than either of the two temples. Many who frequented the place felt the water it provided was hallowed in some way.

Over the years, the two regions came to despise each other because of the debates over their respective temples. Eventually the debates grew to include other nuances of differences in their regions. In time, they disputed over everything. They disputed over governance of certain areas of land. They disputed over ownership of bodies of water. They disputed over ownership of certain historical and religious artifacts. There were numerous disputes, but the other debates seemed of little or no significance compared to the debate as to which temple was the best place of worship. That debate had become so intense it caused an austere schism between the two regions. Northerners would have no dealings with the southerners and vice versa, because of the dispute. In fact, they would not even greet one another in passing.

Despite the dispute, northerners and southerners alike still visited the well to gather water. It seemed the serenity factor of the well overpowered the disconcertedness generated by their disputes. Amazingly, there were no conflicts there, even with the dislike shared between the two regions. The well visitors simply ignored one another as they took their turns drawing their water. Perhaps the well itself had a calming effect on them. Then again, maybe they just felt the sanctity of the place just trumped greatly over their full–bodied disputes. Regardless, the well in the northern country received considerable visitation. People came from all directions and all areas to draw water from the man-made crater.

The well's popularity was such that almost everyone from the surrounding area went to draw their drinking water from there. Others would make a trek there to drink from the well as part of their religious or cultural fulfillment. Still others who visited the well were travelers stopping to collect water to refresh themselves and their animals as well as lay claim to having viewed such a famed site. The place had the attractable influence of an amusement park or an nth wonder of the world. No matter how many times people had heard of it or read about it or even observed illustrations of it, they still wanted to go and physically experience the well for themselves.

The well was indeed a magnificent draw. There was rarely a passerby who did not make it a point to stop and visit the site. The cavity was slightly less than one hundred fifty feet deep and hewn into solid rock. Its water was supplied by an underground spring. Most wells in the area were sourced by still water – an underground pool so to speak. Because the water that supplied the main well was moving, it stayed cooler and never had a stale odor or aftertaste to it. The locals referred to it as living water. Where water from the other wells would just sustain and refill, the water from the main well seemed to actually renew and fulfill. It wasn't magical or mystical. It was just a much better grade of water than that which was drawn from other wells in the area. Because of the water's superior quality, however, many would dispute that there *was* an element of mystique to the well and its contents.

The well had survived for many years despite several wars and governmental overthrows having transpired in the region. Other prominent landmarks had not fared as well during such altercations. The well seemed to be immune to whatever took place around it. Often when there was conflict, the overcoming enemy would destroy anything that stood to hold the community together. Anything that represented the community's religious beliefs or cultural heritage was destroyed or rendered inoperable and unusable. Even the temple in the southern country had once undergone destruction and required reconstruction after approval from the then overruling government. So many other notable landmarks were destroyed as well. For some reason, however, the well withstood the test of many skirmishes and still remained a favored attraction for travelers afar and a main source of drinking water for those in the immediate area.

Men often visited the well early in the morning as the inaugural task of their daily chores. They gathered water for their households or their businesses or both. Women who were married never had to visit the well, because their husbands managed that task for them. Single women would go to the well in the middle of the day and make their withdrawals. Doing so aided in keeping with their cultural tradition of maintaining separation of genders (other than immediate family) in public places.

There were some instances when male and female were there at the same time, but it did not complicate things. Those occurrences often happened when passersby stopped during the midday to refresh themselves. In those cases, the females would allow the travelers to draw their water first. It was a cultural courtesy. In the cases where the travelers had no means of gathering their water (if they had no pail), the female would draw the water for them and offer use of their utensils. That was another cultural courtesy they offered to strangers. It was offered to all but those from the southern country. The dispute between the two regions invalidated that act of civility – except for the occasion of the lady at the marketplace.

The lady Yrma encountered at the market excitedly addressed on–listeners with a story of her most recent visit to the well in the northern country. She had stumbled upon a stranger from the southern country who was sitting near the well when she was about to draw her water. The stranger asked her for a drink of water. There were already two oddities to the story the lady presented to the listening crowd. The first was the fact that the male engaged in open dialogue with an unrelated female in a public place. The second was, again, northern country residents and southern country residents absolutely did not openly communicate with each other, even when visiting the well at the same time. So, this already made the story interesting to the lady's enthusiastic listeners who were both northerners and southerners.

The lady went through her story, which was fairly uneventful until she came to the part where the stranger began to discuss her troubled past. She had not provided him any information; nonetheless he knew her history as well as she knew it. He gave historical accounts of her actions that only those closest to her should have been aware of.

After he revealed his in depth knowledge of her past (along with several words of wisdom) the lady knew there was something special about the stranger. She determined within herself that he must have been a prophet. So, while she had his attention seized she sought to find out from him once and for all which temple was the most appropriate temple in which to take part in worship service. She had grown woefully weary of the debates. Some of her family members in the southern country would not even communicate with her because of the dispute and she wanted desperately to come to resolution on the matter.

After discovering the stranger's high level of intellect and mysterious wealth of knowledge, she decided she would pose the question to him. If the stranger responded with the southern temple as the preferred place of worship; then she would go there, reconcile things with her family members, and begin worshipping at the southern temple. She decided if he said the northern temple was best, then she would ask for some form of proof to convince her family and beseech them to come and worship at the northern temple. After the stranger's display of such wisdom and understanding, she felt that if anyone had the solution to this age–old quarrel, the stranger should have it. She was shocked at the stranger's response.

The stranger informed the young lady that their form of temple worship was no longer the key factor in their religious fulfillment. He made it clear to her that neither the temple at the northern site or the southern site really mattered in the worship experience. He offered his rationale and it made perfectly good sense to the woman. He made it clear that coming together to worship was important, but not so much *where* she chose as her place of worship. He made her realize that she should be more concerned with *how* she went about the act of worship. He told her that the sincerity of her worship (not the vicinity) was the key component.

The listening crowd was quiet for a moment, but then exhibited harsh reaction to the woman's delivery of the stranger's assessment. It seemed they totally disregarded the principle being taught in the worship aspect of the conversation. The majority of the crowd felt the temple and the rituals that took place in the temple were absolutely essential to their religious culture. It had been the focal point of their relationship with their God for many, many years. Hence the intense debates and schism over which temple was the best location to conduct and take part in the services administered there. The stranger's valuation was a deadening blow to both sides of the debate. Both sides were rendered winless and their arguments useless. The woman thought they should have been glad to have such a neutral resolution, but instead neither side was pleased with the stranger's ruling.

A slight murmur began to materialize amongst the listeners. The small crowd showed signs of revulsion towards the woman for her commentary and eventually became hostile. The lady tried hard to make them see the stranger's perfectly logical principle, but they were deaf to her plea. As clear as the logic in his message was, they still could not get past its nullifying effect on their strong cultural and traditional ties to their hallowed religious practices at each of their respective sacred meeting places. They did not evaluate the quality of worship they were participating in. They were much more concerned with the patterns they had developed and the traditions they had established and were upholding in those institutions. They still held the magnificent structures in which they worshipped in high regard. The rest of the stranger's logic did not seem to matter to them. They were not willing to just minimize the temple's significance at the suggestive comments of a total stranger. It was also impossible for them to release the struggle of years of debate as to whose temple was holier than the other without either side having the pleasure of claiming victory. It seemed each party expected to one day emerge as victor of the dispute; so neither wanted the argument to result in a draw. Apparently, either would rather have lost the battle than have it end in truce.

It was easy to see how they could get so attached to the places of worship they'd erected in the two regions. Yrma could attest that the temple in the south country was a magnificent sight to behold from an external view point. All who viewed it marveled at its stateliness. And although neither she nor Bari had ever visited the northern temple, Bari often suggested to Yrma that it was undoubtedly built in the same lavish style and constructed of the same materials. He suspected it was built to the exact same specifications.

Yrma never had an opportunity to view the inside of their temple, but Bari had described it so often and in such detail that she had a vivid image of it plastered in her mind. He'd often repeated to her each of its dimensions and she could recite them without flaw. She knew the sanctuary of the southern temple where they worshipped was nearly thirty–six hundred square feet in area and over six stories in height. The building was erected out of the finest stone. The interior (the walls, the floor, and the ceiling) was made of unflawed cedar wood. There were winding stairs that climbed from one chamber to the next. There was an inner room behind the sanctuary purposed for the priests and their helpers only. That room was about twenty–four hundred square feet in area. The interior there was also made of cedar. Its walls had brilliant carvings of flowers and buttons. Within that room was a smaller room reserved specifically for the high priest. It was about twelve hundred square feet in area. It contained precisely displaced consecrated ornaments. There were carvings in those walls as well. The walls and the floor in that room were overlaid with gold. The laudable structure was truly magnificent; and Yrma and Bari felt certain the northern temple was no less impressive. That was why the crowd of worshippers from both regions had such a hard time with the directive to not place so much emphasis on their places of worship. They really felt special when they attended worship services at those temples. Association with such an esteemed edifice produced a great bit of pride in the people.

The majority of the listening crowd illustrated their displeasure with the message presented in the woman's public address. As the clamor grew, so did the distaste for the freshly introduced perspective on their religious practices and holy places. In a moment's time they were flinging small pieces of half-eaten fruit, vegetables, and bits of barley loaves at the female orator. Had the protest gone much longer, they would have most likely picked up stones to cast at her. Such a thing was not uncommon when the majority felt someone had spoken in blasphemy against components of their religion.

It was perhaps the first time since the schism that southerners and northerners agreed in a public discussion concerning the temples. Their conformity was to the woman's detriment. They all viewed her as an enemy of the temple (either of them) and a threat to their religious practices. It looked as if the small crowd was about to exact renegade justice on the woman until Yrma pushed through the assembly of listeners and took hold of the lady's hand and led her away from the imminent danger.

Yrma guided the woman through a few sales booths and eventually to the other side of the market. Once there, she attempted to convince the lady to not tell the story in public anymore. The lady replied that she did not understand the attitude of her audience. She had told the same story in the streets of her home city in the northern country and many appreciated the outcome. In fact, many of her townsmen sought after the stranger and questioned him more on topics of their religious practices for which they had lingering unanswered questions. He convinced them that there was a much better way for them to obtain their religious fulfillment than what they were currently practicing in and around their temple. The way he taught made the worship experience for their God as well as their relationship with each other a personal one. As it was, it was a very impersonal worship experience and an even more impersonal relationship. The northerners were so pleased with the stranger's teachings, they asked him to stay and teach them more. He did so for a few days.

Yrma was moved by the woman's enthusiasm, but still attempted to explain to the lady the significance of temple worship to Weshuan culture. She tried to make the lady understand the structure and forgiveness and obedience factors of the temple practices from a male's perspective. Yrma did not indicate that she fully agreed with it, but she understood it and did all she could to make the lady comprehend it as well.

She educated the lady on how faithfully Bari and she made those treks to the city of the temple so that they might meet their religious obligations. She reminded the lady that it was not just tradition she was up against, but passionate pride as well. Yrma expressed how those within the temple felt there was nothing greater on earth than their position and status in that place. She pointed out how those who visited the temple to worship took ownership of the magnificence, beauty, and holiness the structure portrayed to the outside world. Yrma simply wanted the lady from the northern country to see the influence the temple had on the lives of those who had placed so much stock in it for so long. Yrma wanted the lady to see that she should not have expected such an abrupt change to be readily accepted by a community so deeply rooted in the tradition and pride that the temple represented for them.

The lady was not at all persuaded by Yrma's homily. She wanted nothing more than to share what she considered really good news. In fact, she felt it was the best news she'd ever heard. For her, it meant there should be no more separation of family and friends on the day of worship. She felt it should also have meant no more bickering over territorial ownership of articles and landmarks in and about the two regions. It meant that women could have an equally representative part in their religious experience as did men. The lady felt that several other freedoms would result from the revelation brought about by the stranger. She had no intention of discontinuing her dissemination of the good news she'd just received from that young man at the well.

Yrma could sense the lady's strong desire to continue in sharing her story with anyone who would lend an ear. She did not want the lady to incite another disturbance, though; so, she pulled her further aside. She quietly inquired of the lady the stranger's purpose for making such a profound declaration regarding their worship practices. She also asked the lady what would become of the old way, if everyone adhered to the stranger's new way. Yrma asked one question after another. The lady could not answer all the questions Yrma hurled at her. In fact, she could answer very few. She wasn't concerned with the questions, however. She didn't feel she needed any further answers. She fully comprehended the stranger's statements. They made perfect sense and left her feeling a new sense of religious fulfillment. She felt a Spiritual freedom that she had never felt before.

Yrma convinced the lady to leave the market and go share her story elsewhere, but not before securing all the information she could relating to the woman's encounter with the stranger at the well. Although Yrma was left with many unanswered questions, she thoroughly enjoyed her conversation with the lady and felt a high level of concurrence with the responses. Yrma witnessed a full–fledged sense of freedom in the lady. Although she could not completely understand why, Yrma felt a bit freer herself. She also felt a newly developed curiosity for the stranger and his refreshing outlook on their religious practices and beliefs.

Yrma bade the lady farewell and continued with her shopping; but her mind was tingling with uncertainties. She had to forcibly convince herself to concentrate solely on shopping again. Slowly she moved the entire ordeal with the lady and the stranger and the belligerent crowd to the back of her mind and focused again on the task at hand. She was back on her mission to find the finest merchandise at the fairest prices. She would do it; because she was the best at such. Bari could attest to that.

Even though Bari could barely tolerate Yrma's rigorous shopping routine (almost a religious ritual in itself); he did appreciate her astute ability to barter with those scoundrels at the souk. She would get the finest commodities at the best price and as a businessman Bari truly admired and appreciated that. He also had as genuine an appreciation for the cultural draw of the marketplace as Yrma. Although he loathed the amount of deception that took place there, he was compelled to agree with her that the marketplace was absolutely fascinating in that regard. There were a plethora of interesting artifacts from around the world.

Bari felt the products could basically sell themselves just based on the level of curiosity they induced in the consumers as they browsed about. That was why he could not understand why so much scheming took place amongst the traders there. He saw no reason for the merchants to be misleading when conducting their transactions. In his expert opinion, they could have made handsome profits without the additional archness; but for some reason they chose to connive. Obviously they were not satisfied with just making a fair (albeit very healthy) profit. They wanted even more. It seemed the roots of evil beneath the "love of money" tree ran deep into the unhallowed grounds upon which the marketplace stood.

For Bari, it became a task to find a good honest deal there, despite the variety of offerings. Hence, he had come to expect to be cheated when he visited there. Even when he was not clever enough to see it in time (which was very rare) or when he gave in out of disgust (which was quite common), it wasn't overwhelming for him; because he expected it in that place. The majority of the vendors there just had a manipulative mindset about them. Instead of honest, hardworking businessmen, they had become dishonest, indolent thieves. He had almost given up shopping there on his own. He'd resolved to leave the bargain hunting and bartering at the market to the wife.

Bari did not expect to encounter the same school of thought at the place of worship that he often experienced at the marketplace. He did not expect to be forced to shop around and find a decent product at a fair price at the temple. There wasn't supposed to be a selection of inferior merchandise there. Every product should have been presented at the highest quality and available at the proper rate. There was not even supposed to be a profit made there. The rate was based on the amount of property a person had accumulated from their labors or what they were obligated to give based on the wrongdoing they sought atonement for. Somehow the exchangers had concocted a way to coerce the people into feeling obligated to give more for their tribute. They were giving more and receiving less. It seemed to Bari that the exchangers' tables in the temple had become a spin–off of the marketplace. It was no longer a chamber for honest exchanges. It too had become a den of thieves.

Bari absolutely loathed dishonesty. Those who conducted themselves dishonestly (in business or otherwise) made him sick to his stomach. In fact, it was a common occurrence for him to depart the marketplace with his stomach in knots. It was a nauseating, heart–throbbing experience for him. He wanted so much to tell them to keep their goods each time he visited there, but he certainly didn't want to deprive Yrma of her furthermost pleasure: sifting through and accumulating what she considered treasures of the world. The merchants tugged at his stomach while his wife tugged at his heart.

Being pulled in opposite directions was a terrible feeling. He was beginning to get that feeling now and he wasn't even at the marketplace. He was still in the temple, which was supposed to be a place of absolute serenity. Tranquility was non-existent on that visit. His heart wanted so much to go through the worship ceremonies, but his stomach was sick from the dishonesty demonstrated at the exchangers' tables. Marketplace déjà vu was all he could feel on that visit.

Bari wanted to enter into where the high priest performed his ceremonies without a tribute and ask him why the selection, the service, and the exchange rate were so deplorable. That was virtually impossible, though. Not only was the high priest unavailable for dialogue with the common worshippers, but it would also have been extremely unorthodox for him to have gone to worship service not bearing a tribute. Such a thing would render one dishonorable in the sight of the religious leaders and temple workers. Even the other worshippers looked down on such an act. Those who chose not to make the tribute (according to their religious laws and customs) were viewed upon as impious. They were relegated to worshiping externally in the courtyard with commoners rather than in the areas deemed sacred and available only to conforming, contributing individuals.

It was a catch twenty–two situation for Bari. On the one hand, he could ignore his personal convictions and just give according to the commonly accepted practice. That would appease the religious leaders and all those who frequented the temple and blindly adhered to the habits formed there. It would require a personal compromise, but he would be allowed to worship as everyone else and would preserve good rapport among all. On the other hand, if he decided to go against the grain and give contrarily to practice, he felt he would be condemned by the religious leaders and shunned by his peers.

After mulling over the decision for a moment, Bari resolved to bear the risk of rejection and go with the option that seemed most in line with his knowledge of their religion principles. He would seek out a better selection from a local vendor–outside of the marketplace–and give a tribute according to those standards. He would not relegate himself to presenting his tribute by their terms. He knew he risked losing amity amongst the leaders and fellow worshippers, but he would have peace within himself and he felt "peace with self" was a much more valuable commodity than "acceptance by others." He did not wish to barter away his inner peace.

Now, bear with me as I reiterate the source of Bari's frustration. It is not my intent here to belabor the point; but there is a need to make certain the readers fully capture the magnitude of his anguish. As stated before, it was the normal approach when making long journeys to attend temple worship that parishioners wait until they got to the temple to obtain the gift they wished to offer as tribute. A parishioner could have owned the tribute at his home that he wanted to take to the temple. Bringing that tribute and presenting it would have been the ideal thing to meet the requirement. However, in order to make sure the tribute did not get damaged in transition, the parishioner would much rather obtain a tribute when he arrived at the temple. So, he took that tribute, before leaving his place of residency, and sold it to a neighbor or friend. He received whatever the two agreed was a fair price.

The parishioner should have then been able to take that money on his journey and present it to the exchangers at the temple for the exact tribute he sold back in his hometown. There should not have been any questions. There should not have been any negotiations. The practice made the exchange an even one. No value was lost by the parishioner and no profit was gained by the temple workers. It was fair for the journeyman and it was fair for the workers at the temple. The exchanger did it as part of his temple duty, so it should not have mattered to him what the parishioner offered for the tribute. The variation in the amounts given by parishioners from different regions would have easily offset the temple workers' cost for maintenance of the local tributes.

It was a flawless system as it was designed from the beginning. The exchange rate was set based on whatever it would cost to produce and maintain the tribute at the parishioner's place of residency. Everyone knew the rate was based on the contributor's local economy. That meant the exchange rate on a specific item might be one amount for a person from one region, but a different amount for a person from another region.

The workers should never have counted monies the parishioner brought in to exchange for tribute – at least not in his presence. It was set up as an honor system. The exchanger should have just received whatever monies the parishioner offered and exchanged it for the tribute. To the journeyman that was one of the benefits of waiting until he arrived at the temple to obtain his tribute for offering during worship service. It meant he would not have to gripe at what he was paid for the tribute on his end. He could just receive what was offered and give that amount to the exchanger for the same tribute during the exchange. The purpose was to make the worship experience as pleasant and meaningful for the parishioners as possible. The original process even made the trek to the place of worship more inviting.

Everything that was provided to parishioners in the temple should have been offered free of charge. The temple workers were authorized to receive provisions to live by; but they were not to make gains from their efforts. A predetermined portion of the vows that were made by the worshippers to honor their God were to be sufficient provisioning for sustaining the temple and its workers. That was understood by the temple worshippers and it was supposed to be understood by the temple workers.

Somewhere along the way, the exchangers (and perhaps other workers in the temple) saw an opportunity to make a profit beyond the provisioning that was designated for them. The exchangers no longer paid heed to the general rule. They set prices on the tributes based on the temple workers' cost for producing and maintaining the tributes. They then tacked on a bit more for incidentals. The supplementary fees somehow continued to grow with time. So, they decided to charge a little more for the tributes than their worth. Eventually they would offer a lesser grade of tributes, while still overcharging for them. The practice totally desecrated the system. It strongly resembled the business that went on at the marketplace. It seemed that the culture outside of the temple was having a strong influence on the ethics inside the temple. That was the exact opposite of what should have taken place.

That is why Bari, after making such a long journey (on foot at that) was so frustrated with what he'd just experienced at the temple. The purpose of temple worship was to renew faith in and faithfulness to his God as well as rejuvenate his spirit of what society had drained from it. Temple worship was supposed to build them into better individuals who might offer a positive influence to those outside the temple. It was to be a sanctuary from the cold and harsh environment he faced outside of there. Now, one of the things he sought most to escape from within society was greeting him face–to–face within the temple. He now wished he had taken his chances with maintaining his own tribute along the tedious journey rather than expecting so much from the temple workers and receiving so little.

Bari felt his worship experience would have been so much more meaningful if he could have given tribute as he had purposed in his heart. The temple workers were (whether unknowingly or not) trying to force him into grudgingly offering a tribute that did not meet his standard and did not fulfill his established commitment. Bari felt if he had managed his own tribute, he could have worshipped and contributed with a sense of fulfillment rather than just give out of necessity. His visit would have been a cheerful event. He knew if he had given the inferior tribute they wished to force upon him, he would have been choosing and giving a poorly kept tribute. He would have been constrained to worshipping in anguish and emptiness. His offering would have become something given strictly out of practice, but otherwise meaningless.

Bari concluded that it would be better to not worship at all in his current frame of mind. What a terrible predicament the temple workers had pressed upon him. His entire worship experience was ruined due to their inconsideration of the prescribed principles of the tribute. The frustration mounted with each second he recounted the event. He did not realize it, but the spiritual agitation was escalating quickly. He found himself leaving the temple with no intent of making future visits. The actions of those within contrasted the original practices and principles far too much for his taste.

As Bari made his way out of the temple, he passed a young man who was just entering the building. The young man moved with purposed. It was as if he came to do more than just worship there. It appeared that he came to perform a specific task. The young man had quite a host of admirers hovering around him and a dozen or so men who appeared to be traveling with him. The twelve were discussing the magnificence of the temple and its adjoining buildings. They were mesmerized by the splendor of the edifice. It seemed everyone who came into the temple left with a very similar dialogue centered on its incredible architecture. It truly was a splendid sight.

The crowds and the attention shown to the stranger made Bari feel the man must have been renowned among the locals, but he wasn't familiar with the face at all. He had not seen him in the area before. He had not seen anyone who resembled the young man, such that he might recognize a familial resemblance of some sort. That was a bit baffling to him. Bari did, however, recognize two of the men travelling alongside the stranger. They were the fisherman's sons whom he chartered the boat from on his annual seaside fishing expeditions.

He would recognize the two of them anywhere. He had spent many days at sea with those two. Neither of them noticed Bari in the transitory encounter. They were deep in discussion with the rest of their party who were still admiring the impressive architecture. Bari did not beckon for their attention. In fact, he did not pay them much attention at all. He was far too frustrated for idle conversation. He continued past them on his way out of the temple.

Bari wondered why the stranger had such a large entourage travelling with him. He glanced at him as their paths were about to cross. There appeared to be nothing terrific about the young man at all. He looked extremely average to Bari. His skin was a little on the dark side just as many of the locals. He had matted wooly hair the same as most in the region. He wore the same everyday clothing as they. He had no grandeur about him that would attract individuals to him. There was nothing about his appearance that they should desire to be around him. Nonetheless, Bari could feel a special aura of eminence about the gentleman.

When he came face to face with the stranger, Bari gazed into his eyes and for some strange reason the strong feeling of distress went away. He mustered up enough congeniality to greet what appeared to be an important stranger in town. The man greeted Bari back twice as congenially and it seemed instantly Bari was liberated of his disappointing encounter at the temple. He no longer had that unpleasant, unfulfilled mindset. In fact, he was experiencing a greater sensation than anything he had undergone in any of his past temple visits. Amazingly, now, his temple experience was inverted from its original state. The term "amazingly" fits here, because he had not partaken of any liturgical formalities that were normally associated with temple worship service. All he had done was to greet the stranger and receive a most pleasant return greeting. It was incredible. He felt revived within an absolute instant.

Bari wanted to turn back and see what would be the young man's business at the temple. Even though his clothing didn't indicate it, Bari felt certain he would be the teacher for that day. For some reason he felt the individual was well–qualified to make presentations at the temple. He wanted to see if the stranger would offer a discourse during his visit. He just knew the young man would have an outstanding message and he zealously wanted to hear it. He had completely disregarded that he should bring a tribute along with him – according to protocol. He wasn't even thinking on those terms. He just wanted to hear what the stranger would have to say. He seriously contemplated following him back into the temple to discover his purpose for being there.

Bari mulled over the idea momentarily and even made a slight turn in that direction, but ultimately decided against it. He remembered Yrma was waiting for him at the market and he didn't want to have her wait much longer. Although he was certain that she would not have opposed to having extra time to spend at the market, he also knew she expected him to be punctual and would worry if he'd been too tardy. She probably would have made another pass through the aisles searching through a few more items to make certain she hadn't overlooked any irresistible bargains; but she would have worried nonetheless. Bari realized that he had consumed a great deal of time looking over the tribute offerings. Besides, he had already made his determination to not worship on that day. So, he resolved that he would take the pleasant sentiment the stranger had bestowed on him and enjoy the moment in his solitary trek to the marketplace.

As he walked away, Bari took notice of evidential commotion from within the temple. He turned around in time to catch a glimpse of the exchangers running for cover. He saw items being tossed to and fro as tables landed on their side. Bari heard the stranger's voice as it echoed through the temple, "You've made this place a den of thieves!" The young man's tone wasn't nearly as congenial as the smile Bari witnessed when the two of them greeted one another. All he could make of it was that the stranger was scolding the exchangers for such a lousy offering of service at such an exorbitant cost to the parishioners.

The stranger wasn't just politely asking them to cease in their dishonest activities. He forcibly demanded they stop, and then evicted them from the temple. Bari thought to himself with complete satisfaction, "Good! Give them what they deserve." They were taking advantage of the people who came to worship instead of meeting their needs as they were entrusted to do. Bari felt certain they deserved punishment for such an offense. It was unforgivable from his viewpoint.

After witnessing the cleansing efforts of the stranger, Bari felt he could now consider his trip to the temple a very good experience. He was extremely gratified by his witness of an authoritative figure remedying the impurities that were taking place at the exchangers' tables. Well, he assumed the man was a figure of authority. "Who else," Bari thought, "can make such great demands of temple workers and not be reprimanded on the spot by the religious leaders?" Anyone of a lesser position would have been carted off to prison if not executed on location. He briefly wondered where the stranger got his authority, but didn't dwell on that for long. It really didn't matter to him. He was just glad to witness the purification that had just happened right before his eyes.

Bari's resentment invoked by the awful temple experience had totally dissipated at that point. The brief encounter with the stranger completely lifted his spirit. He was no longer weighted down by the disappointment and anguish he'd felt inside the temple merely moments before. Watching the stranger correct the inappropriate activity in the temple offered Bari hope of coming back to the temple and worshipping in a meaningful way. He was no longer concerned about being hoodwinked by the exchangers. After having faced the stranger's wrath, he felt they wouldn't dare attempt that again.

Bari scurried over to the marketplace to reassemble with Yrma. He presented the narrative of his most recent experience.

His account of the event left her in awe. She was amazed first at the awful impurities in the temple service and secondly at the emotional outbreak of the young priest. They were still making assumptions on the young man's title and level of authority. They could think of no other title to bestow on the youthful stranger. He came into the temple making demands and offering reprimands and restoring liturgical order. They knew only a priest could take such authoritative measures in the temple.

The only puzzling remainder to the equation was that priests were very noble in appearance and never showed outward emotion. Not only that, they were rarely chosen to such high positions until years and years of service at the temple. Questions danced around in their minds such as, "What kind of priest is this and who gave him such authority and *how* did he even get to be a priest at such an early age?" Bari determined that he must have been barely thirty years of age. Again, they were both still assuming he was a priest. For him to display that much authority in the temple without suffering admonishment, they felt certainly he had to be a priest and not *just* a priest, but a *high* priest.

Yrma thought for a moment, then recapped in her mind the story she'd heard from the woman at the market. She wondered if the stranger was the same as the one the woman spoke of. She shared the story with Bari. Bari felt for certain that it was the same person. He recognized the authoritative characteristics of the priest even though those qualities were not manifested in his attire and outward appearance. Bari was certain that the stranger had the authority to make such a statement to the woman at the well concerning the temples and activities that took place in the temple. He had just witnessed the stranger's abrupt takeover of operations at their temple and not one other person of authority there questioned him. "Certainly the leaders heard him throughout the temple if I heard him so audibly outside," Bari thought aloud. "It had to be the same person."

The only problem he had with his theory was that if the stranger was a priest (and assumedly a high priest), then what would he be doing at the well talking to a woman – especially a woman of the character Yrma described in her intriguing story. The question posed a threat to Bari's theory; but he was convinced that the stranger was a very high ranking priest nonetheless. He didn't dwell on the questions around what type of authority the young man had and how he obtained such. He just took pleasure in the thought of having him there to restore to order the disorder he witnessed at the temple that day.

Bari had the notion that there was soon to be a changing of the religious guards. After what he had witnessed, it was evident that a change was necessary. If the stranger had not come when he did, Bari's religious responsibilities would have been a daunting task from that day forward. He would've had great difficulty returning to the temple to perform his religious duties if he could have returned at all. He felt there must have been many others who felt the same as he.

But now, Bari felt comfortable with going back to the temple. After that episode, he was certain that things would operate as they should with the new high priest in charge. He did not want to go back, however, until things settled and the place was returned to orderly fashion. He knew it would take some time for the temple workers to get accustomed to doing things decently and in order again. He and Yrma agreed that he should wait and return to the temple on the next trip. They decided, nevertheless, that he would not keep the money he'd brought along to exchange for his tribute during that trip to the temple. Instead they would use it to purchase food and necessities for any unfortunate citizens they might encounter along the way.

Bari had, as always, transported a considerable amount of currency. He never entered the temple without a substantial contribution. It was his intent to offer exceptional tributes. He didn't do it to be noticed by the temple workers. He wasn't seeking favoritism or recognition from the laymen or from the leaders. He didn't do it to be forgiven for some terrible wrongdoing he had committed, either. He really had done very few things that were considered wrong by their law. According to their law, he was a very good man. He simply had been remarkably prosperous in business and life in general. For that reason, he wanted to offer a tribute that was commensurate to his prosperity. So, he always brought a large sum of money that he might obtain an exceptional tribute. Now that he wouldn't be offering tribute on this occasion; rather than just dump those monies off on one person or family and run the risk of its misappropriation, he and Yrma decided they would seek out different people along the journey home and offer financial assistance to them.

Out of the goodness of their hearts Bari and Yrma made the decision to distribute the monies, but that was not the only reason. There was a universal law in their culture that required those who had more than they needed to use a portion of it to take care of those who were lacking in their basic necessities. That law was enacted to help those who could not help themselves. In fact, it was more than just law; it was encased in their religious beliefs. They felt that if a person were to have pure religion and to be blameless before their God then they must assist those who could not help themselves. Bari and Yrma knew the law well and lived by it dutifully. They would often give out of their abundance to elderly or widowed women and fatherless children. They never flaunted the act of giving to the needy. They just inconspicuously offered of themselves. They knew that boastful exhibition of their giving would nullify its gratification effect as well as its religious purpose.

So, they dutifully gave without flashy exhibition; but during that trip Bari wanted to go above and beyond the call of duty. In fact, it no longer felt like it was a duty to give to those who were in need. It now felt more like a privilege. He couldn't understand why he felt that way that time around. He just felt honored to share out of his abundance. Maybe the interaction with the stranger had something to do with it. He certainly felt invigorated after their brief encounter at the temple.

Bari wanted to take that emotional ecstasy experience beyond the temple and far beyond those courtyard gates. He did not want it to be an isolated occurrence based on a single event. He wanted to experience it on a daily basis and not just during periodic visits to the temple. He felt the best way to maintain that sentiment was to take what he could not contentedly offer at the temple that day and offer it to those who could not or would not come to the temple. He felt he would have other opportunities to offer in contentment at the temple. Yrma shared his sentiment. The two of them decided they would spend the majority of their time journeying home helping those in need.

In his initial act of giving, Bari dragged Yrma hastily back towards the temple. She could scarcely maintain the pace he set for them. Bari was intent on returning; because he'd heard of a widow woman who never departed the temple area. Even though she could only enter a certain area outside the temple, she stayed there day in and day out. Rumor had it that she stayed there and constantly fasted and prayed throughout the day and into the night. Those who were attentive to her prayers said she rambled on about old prophecies concerning a priest that would come along and clear up the misunderstandings of temple teachings and clean up the impurities of temple operations.

She had made it known that she would not leave the temple until the priest had arrived to complete the task. Many thought the old lady was just senile and ignored her. Others would offer occasional provisioning for her welfare. They hoped that there was some validity to her babblings. Apparently, Bari *wasn't* the first to notice the awful service at the money exchangers' tables and perhaps beyond those tables; even though few others ever complained about it. It's amazing how long the people stared directly in the face of the impurities of their leaders and acted as if the corruption didn't even exist.

Bari located the elderly woman and offered monies to her that equaled one month's provisioning for an average family in their region. He just reached into his money bag, pulled out a few coins, and offered them to the woman. He made no attempt at being precise in the amount he offered to her. It was a substantial amount for a single offering. It would meet her needs for quite some time.

Once he had met the needs of the widow woman, he and Yrma went quickly on their way. Neither he nor the old woman discussed the turning of tables or the apparent authority of the young man Bari had just encountered at the entry way of the temple. Perhaps she had not heard the commotion. Perhaps she had not even noticed the stranger as he made his way into the temple. She was nowhere near the entrance at the time of his arrival. At any rate, they did not exchange dialogue regarding the event. Bari just greeted her with blessings, placed the money in her hand, and moved on. As she thanked him for it, she went on her way as well, leaving the temple behind her.

Evening was approaching and Bari wanted to make it to the next major city before nightfall. He had lost a lot of time in the temple with the array of events that occurred within. Now, he felt he needed to hasten before night fell upon them. He wasn't concerned about himself, but he did not want Yrma traveling during the night. Night travel was very dangerous outside of the city area and they would have to leave the heavily populated area to get to their next destination. There were numerous menaces lurking (of both human and beastly nature) in those unpopulated zones.

There were a number of routes to take in getting to the next major city in the direction of their home, but the shortest was about seventeen miles in the northeast direction. It would take the average person about five hours to travel there by foot. They were well–conditioned and could push themselves to make it in four. It was the fastest route, but it was also the most dangerous. If they traveled in daylight, there was much less chance of encountering peril. They could get there just before dark if they made no stops. After a long deliberation with himself, he decided they would take the short route at a hurried pace. He offered his plan to Yrma and she agreed to the route and to the pace as well.

They were well on their way as evening drew closer. They had walked and shared occasional conversations at a quick and even pace. Between the discussions, Bari recounted the incident at the temple with the stranger again and again. The episode just resonated in his mind. He kept wondering to himself from whence the young man originated and how he rose in rank so quickly. Bari pondered at the impact this newcomer might have on temple worship. In some cases, he wondered to himself. At other times, he and Yrma wondered aloud. They were extremely curious of the effect the stranger would have on their religious culture.

They wondered aloud, "Will he change some other aspects of worship service? Are there background issues that are not presented to the everyday worshippers that also need addressing? Will he allow women and children an opportunity to worship as the men instead of leaving them segregated and less involved as is currently the case? Will people who are not born into our religious culture be granted permission to participate in every part of the worship services unlike it is at the present time?" He and Yrma wondered out loud about many things. They talked and talked until the sound of voices and footsteps interrupted their dialogue.

Bari noticed the on comers before Yrma heard them. Once he stopped talking, Yrma became aware of them, also. There was a group of men approaching from the rear at a fast and steady pace. They appeared to be seriously mission–bound. Bari could not determine if that mission involved overtaking unsuspecting travelers or not. Since he and Yrma had kept a faster than normal pace themselves, he deduced that the company must have been on a much faster pace than normal to have caught up with them. Such a pace had to be purpose–driven. He was a bit suspicious of the nature of their velocity of travel.

Anxiety began to creep in. Bari was well aware of stories of bandits who traveled that road and robbed its travelers along the way. That's why he contemplated so strongly before settling on the shorter, but potentially dangerous route. There were countless tales of badly injured and even dead bodies found along that road. In fact, the road was known as "The Way of Blood." In most cases, the incidents occurred at night, but every so often there were stories of attacks taking place in broad daylight. He shuddered at the idea of becoming a statistic on the Way of Blood. He tried hard to maintain his composure so as to not cause alarm in his wife.

Routinely, he would not have traveled that road, even in the daytime. Again, the only reason he took it was because it was the shortest distance to the next major city and it would have afforded him the opportunity to get to an inn so that his wife would be indoors before nightfall. There was an inn at the end of the Way of Blood where it intersected with the main road – the road he probably should have travelled (he thought to himself).

Normally the Way of Blood was heavily traveled during the daytime; so he expected to see an abundance of passersby. It was not the case on that day. On that particular day and at that particular hour, the road was barren except for Bari, Yrma, and the party rapidly approaching them from the rear. It was almost as if it was a setup. It was as if it was pre–planned or maybe even preordained that Bari and his wife would be there at that precise location at that exact hour. "What a weird feeling!" he thought. Again, he shook the thought from his mind and tried to appear unmoved by it.

As the fast–approaching party got closer, Bari began to get a little more concerned about the possibly ensuing situation. He wasn't afraid of confrontation. Bari was an immensely masculine young man and could handle anybody in a fair fight. In fact, he could probably handle any two men in a fair fight, but he knew well that bandits did not fight fair. They did not fight as singles or pairs, either, but rather as groups. He knew if the group approaching them was of the sort, he'd be faced with a dilemma. They were traveling in numbers and he was just one. They would have weapons and he had none.

He did own a dagger, but he never considered bringing it along. He didn't expect to be in a situation where he would need a weapon to defend himself or Yrma. He never expected their lives or wellbeing to be in danger. He thought to himself, "Who would possibly want to harm a respectable young couple and a hometown hero at that? And no one should want to hurt a beautiful lady such as Yrma." He was now wishing he had not given people the benefit of the doubt regarding that matter. He knew if they attempted an attack, they would have no concern for his laudable status. They would not be appreciative of Yrma's fairness, either—well, beyond a momentary pleasurable event. He knew they would have no concern for how he and his wife fared during an altercation. He mentally scolded himself for opting to take that route and for not bringing his weapon along.

Bari maintained his composure. He did not want to say or do anything that would alarm Yrma. That would just make matters worse. If she felt any reason to be alarmed, she would cling closely to him, which would place her more into harm's way. That would make it more difficult for Bari to counter the attack; because he would have to stay in defensive mode such that he might better protect her. It would ultimately make them both more vulnerable. So, he gave no indication that he felt evil was lurking even though he was strongly aware of its presence.

Bari tightened the knot on his coin pouch and tucked it away, deeply beneath his cloak. He still had a substantial amount of money left, which would make him a prime target for the assumed assailants. He did not want to give any indication that he was anything more than a common traveler. He wasn't dressed eloquently and didn't have an animal trailing him with an accumulation of prized possessions; so there should have been no reason for anyone to believe he carried a large sum of money with him. He tucked the money away tightly, so they wouldn't hear the coins jingling in the bag. Bari knew it was not a good time to attract unnecessary attention (if ever there was such a time).

Bari motioned for Yrma to go ahead of him. That way he would be between her and the oncoming travelers. He felt it was the best thing to do as her gentleman protector. In that position, the presumed bandits would have to get past him to get to her. If he couldn't defeat them all, he could at least retain them while Yrma ran for safety. He felt she wouldn't need much time to place distance between her and the probable attackers. She had enough athleticism about her to escape the inherent danger. Bari would just have to make certain he postponed the reputed ruffians long enough to keep them from chasing after her immediately.

After strategically planning his counterattack, Bari began to compose himself. He straightened his back and spread his broad shoulders as much as he possibly could. He walked gingerly enough that the gold coins would not rattle in his pouch, but deliberately enough that the oncoming party would discover no timidity in him. He looked around at the men to determine which might be the strongest. If they should attempt to overtake him, he would go after their strongman first and hope to discourage the others by outdoing their best.

They walked past with their heads down. He greeted them, but to no reply. He slowed his step and pulled his wife back to his rear. He looked her in the eyes as he positioned her behind him, just to let her know he was taking precautionary measures. He then looked back forward to see if the men would double back on him. Before he could turn enough to face them, they were already upon him. They recognized his defensive maneuver when they noticed how he placed Yrma furthest away.

It was a brilliantly planned attack from a military perspective. They knew he would be more concerned with the safety of the lady than with his own. Their moving in front then doubling back was to place him in a less defendable mode while they positioned themselves to make an offensive move. By the time he repositioned himself for defense they were already executing their offense. Apparently they had done this a number of times. Either that or they had studied war under very well–trained military staff. It may have been a combination of both.

Bari screamed out an order to Yrma to make an attempt to escape the perilous scene. Subsequently, he attempted to execute his defensive plan. He felt he could still hold them off long enough for her to get away and make it to safety. He made certain that she heard him, but she appeared to have not. She braced herself and made an attempt to assist him in the counterattack. She threw rocks and screamed and attempted with all her might to aid her beloved husband.

Each of the bandits had concealed clubs with which they attacked Bari. The clubs were roughly sculptured, so that each impact left cuts and scratches upon contact. After a couple of blows in the same area, the clubs were tearing flesh from Bari's body. He had ceased from trying to persuade Yrma to run away and was now countering with ferocious swings. He made contact on several occasions. He caught the club of one attacker and twisted it sharply back against the man's wrist. The bandit screamed as he felt the ligaments in his wrist being severed from the previously attached bone. He heard his bones crack at the strength of the farmer's grip. Bari threw him to the ground to block the path of another oncoming attacker. As that attacker tripped over his fallen comrade, Bari hit him in the back of the neck with the bandit's club he'd confiscated in the previous maneuver. He hit the second victim hard enough to make sure he stayed on the ground. The blow was almost critical. They would later discover the bandit was paralyzed from the neck down.

Bari fought with warrior–like precision. He turned and dodged and countered. He really did everything that a well–trained soldier would do. The DNA of Mathes showed true in every movement, although Bari never realized he possessed such skill sets. Nonetheless (in spite of such a heroic effort), with all the strength and cleverness he mustered in repelling them and with all the pain he inflicted upon them he could not sustain his defense for very long. They held a clear advantage over him. There were just too many of them and they were coming too fast. They were also all armed and he only had the one club he had wrestled from the unfortunate attacker. After a while, his countermeasures lost all effectiveness.

The bandits beat him until he was senseless. By the time they were done, Bari was literally half dead. In fact, he was perhaps more dead than alive. It appeared he was not even breathing although his eyes were still open. They stripped him of his cloak in search of any valuables he might have on his person. It seemed as if they were certain he did have something. They were determined to search until they found it. They removed every piece of garment he wore (excluding his undergarments). They located the money pouch and took it from him. They took his cloak and outer garments as well. They left him lying there virtually naked and better than half dead.

They caught and bound his wife, gagged her mouth with rags from his torn garments, and carried her away. It was getting closer to nightfall now. By the time they got to their intended destination, it would be night; so, concealing her would not be an issue. Chances were they would sell her off as a slave or worse. The practice was common in those remote areas. Women were very unsafe when unaccompanied by a male companion. In this case, having an accompanying male did not increase Yrma's degree of safety.

The bandits prepared a makeshift stretcher for their badly injured comrade and four of them carried him off. They patched up the wounds of the one with the shattered wrist as best they could, but he was obviously in a great deal of pain. They would eventually give him cup after cup of strong liquor to help him to cope with the excruciating pain. He was so drunk by the time they moved on that he could not walk alone. He required support of one of the other bandits to keep pace with the group. The rest of them dressed their wounds (Bari had certainly left his mark) and they all departed the scene.

The bandits left Bari to die in a very shallow ditch along the roadside. They were not a bit concerned for his welfare. They never even looked back at him as they walked off into the same direction from which they'd come. They didn't discuss the incident or its outcome. They had already divided the monies amongst themselves and drawn lots for the usable clothing they had taken from Bari. It was very easy for them to detach themselves from any guilt or pity surrounding the incident – even with the serious casualties their group suffered during the altercation. It was just another day's work for the band of thieves.

Bari lay motionless as he watched them walk off with his money pouch, his clothing, and his most prized possession. Had they not taken his wife, he would have counted it a victory to have repelled them as well as he had–despite the injuries he'd suffered in the process. He really had provided a tremendous challenge for the gang of criminals. It was a valiant contest having been one against so many. It would be a long time before they recovered from the injuries he had inflicted upon them. It was obvious that the one of them might not ever recover. If anyone had witnessed the brawl, they would have crowned Bari as champion. With Yrma gone, however, Bari concluded that he had suffered a most terrible defeat.

He lay there baking in the evening sun. No one came traveling along the road. He saw that as extremely odd, since this road was usually not so barren. He felt like someone should have passed by during the time he spent lying in that ditch. It seemed as if he had been there for an eternity. He toggled back and forth in and out of consciousness, so he'd lost track of time. During those moments when he did regain consciousness, he could barely move his aching body. The best he could muster was to gently lift his head and move it from side to side and even that was agonizingly painful. Still, he fought through the agony and attempted as best he could to survey the area.

After fading in and out of consciousness a few more times, he could not clearly recall the event as it played out. After a certain point, he could not remember how Yrma fared in the ordeal. He wondered what had become of her. He looked for his wife through blurred, bloodshot eyes. He did not see her. He didn't see any residue of an apparent struggle that would indicate her welfare or lack thereof. He saw no blood stains—outside of those in the immediate area where he lie in excruciating pain. He deduced that they were his own. He did not see any of her clothing lying about. There were no strands of hair left behind. There were no overlooked pieces of separated jewelry, either. His crude forensic assessment of the area left him without any clue of what might have become of her as a result of the confrontation. He could not determine if the assessment was favorable or not.

He tried desperately to better position himself to further examine the scene. He placed every ounce of strength that remained in his body into each attempt. After several tries at rising up from the ground produced naught, he submitted to the pain and frailty of his body. A feeling of utter helplessness overtook him. He laid his head back speculating what would happen next. It was getting dark, now. He did not expect any help to happen along before nightfall. Once nightfall would finally come, he knew he could expect wild dogs to come along and tear him apart. He was confronting a situation he never imagined he'd be faced with. He began to pray silently for his God to intervene and rescue him. It was his only alternative at that point.

Bari just laid there in desolation. He scanned the area, occasionally, looking up and down the road hoping someone would happen along. Eventually he did see someone coming from a distance. It was a priest. It wasn't difficult to determine that it was a priest despite the approaching nightfall. The person was still adorned in full religious regalia and riding a beast of burden equipped as that of a cleric. Apparently, the priest was leaving the temple after his duties for the day. He must have had urgent business somewhere, because priests rarely left the temple in uniform and certainly not that close to nightfall. Bari's heart began to thump with excitement. He tried to beckon the priest, but he could not formulate the words. The thrashing he had undergone temporarily rendered his larynx inoperable. He could only marshal enough noise to produce a muffled groaning sound.

Bari hoped to make eye contact with the priest as he passed, so he could make the priest aware of his innocence as a victim. Otherwise, the priest might have guessed him for a bandit having failed in his attempt to rob someone else. He felt the religious leader should be able to look into his eyes and discern his guiltlessness. He anticipated that perhaps the priest might even recognize him from previous visits to the temple where he'd often worshipped and offered tribute in the past. Although priests very rarely interacted with commoners (almost never), Bari felt as often as he'd been there and as much as he'd contributed to the temple, certainly the local priests must have at some point sought to discover who was the generous giver. He felt the clergyman would surely recognize him. He didn't take into account the disfiguring effect the thrashing had on his face.

Bari had presented handsome contributions in his long history of trips dedicated to worship and giving tribute at the temple. Despite his attempts to be inconspicuous in making those donations, he felt certain that someone must have been keeping an unofficial account of them. He paid notice to how they lauded the ones who flaunted their high-value tributes. He'd done all he could to be unnoticed in giving them; but now he hoped the ecclesiastic had at least once peeked out from his inner sanctuary to determine who the generous giver was and perhaps offer a special blessing upon him. "Perhaps they *do* notice those of us who aren't a part of their elite cliques." Bari thought. He could only hope at that point.

Bari's hopes began to diminish as he watched the priest guide his animal hastily to the other side of the road long before reaching the area of the ditch occupied by a battered, bloody, and almost lifeless body. Initially, he determined that the clergyman may just have been moving to the other side to call out to him once he got closer. Bari understood that a priest could not get too close to what might appear to be a suspicious situation. Their laws and traditions prohibited it. It did not matter how badly the person needed help, it was forbidden for a priest to get close to anything that had the potential of being an unholy setting. If there was human blood, death, or other apparent uncleanness, the priest could not intervene – at least not to the point where they were required to make physical contact. That meant they could not get close enough to offer help. The assistance would have to come from someone else. As Bari rationalized why the priest was moving over he thought to himself, "Why is it that these men are charged with our overall welfare, but they can't lift a finger to help us in the time of our most desperate need? What a useless regulation!"

Since he was in such critical condition, the priest had to stay a certain distance away and send a helper to tend to the lifeless body – if such was the case. Until determining if the body was dead or alive, the priest had to approach with caution and check for vital signs from a distance. That meant he would have had to call out to Bari and wait for a response. Then he would at least know Bari was still alive. Once he did that, he could have gotten close enough to determine the degree of his injuries and decide what type of help to seek for him. Bari listened for an appeal to offer help or at least an inquiry of confirmation to whether he was alive or dead. He never received the proposition. Instead, all Bari heard was quickening footsteps of the animal as they became more pronounced, then fainter and fainter and fainter...

The priest was not positioning himself to offer help to the perishing parishioner when he guided his beast to the other side of the road. He was positioning himself on his high horse to move forward, in spite of the apparent need of the frequent temple worshiper. Bari couldn't believe that a person with such a great appointment to care for the souls of people could ignore his immediate and desperate need and just move along as if he did not exist. He wondered how many other times that had occurred, even if the situation was not as grave as his. He wondered how many times the religious leaders had simply moved forward with their personal agendas, despite the apparent need of their parishioners. He could feel the anguish he felt against the exchangers returning; only that time, it was magnified a hundred fold. He felt within himself that regardless of what their laws and traditions governing his situation attempted to accomplish, the priest's actions could not be justified and they could not be forgiven, either.

After a moment, something dawned on Bari. If the presumably holy man could allow the exchangers to soil the sacredness of worship by exploiting visitors in the temple, surely he (though being a priest) could pass by without offering an ounce of compassion. Bari felt that certainly the priest had to be aware of the conduct of those money exchangers. The priests were responsible for everything that took place in that temple. Bari could not believe that the religious leaders were that unobservant. He felt even if the stranger hadn't made the ruckus he'd made during his visit, the leaders still had to be aware of the impurities in the exchangers' procedures.

Bari deduced that the priest must have ignored the impure actions of the exchangers just as the cleric had ignored him as he lay alongside the road in that considerably feeble state. Logic convinced Bari that if a person's religious beliefs convicted them to be honest in diminutive situations, then it would also cause them to be honest in significant situations. Likewise, he reasoned that if their moral aptitude permitted them to be dishonest in insignificant circumstances, then it would allow them to be dishonest in major circumstances as well. Bari was no longer taken aback that the priest had totally ignored his physical need, if he so easily ignored his spiritual need. His infuriation with the clergyman intensified and more speculation entered into his mind. He thought to himself, "This is entirely unforgivable."

As Bari pondered over what he perceived as uncharacteristic behavior for a clergyman, he also ascertained that it was very odd that the priest could travel the Way of Blood without escort of any sort and remain unscathed by the bandits. Sure, priests were well–respected around the city. People cleared the front row seats for them when they came into a place. They announced their names and titles as they made their way to the front – just as they did the politicians and other public figures. They always provided them the choicest cuts of meats, freshest breads, and most colorful fruits – even at the marketplace where there seemed to be few who were honorable. The priests were highly revered among the respectable clan in high society as well. They received invites to the weddings, the parties, and the political gatherings of the uppermost members of society. Everyone from the top of society to the bottom respected the priests.

That was the case within the city gates. In the present case, however, they were outside of those gates and far from the city. Everyone out there was treated the same regardless of their social status. They were all regarded as targets. The only scenario that spared someone from being hunted out there was if they were bigger and stronger than the hunter.

The worst of the worst hung out in that region. They were not respectable people. They were not compassionate people. They were not reasonable people. They were bandits. Bari knew that bandits didn't respect priests any more than prisoners. A target was a target to those ruffians and the more humble the target the more coveted the prize. The priest should have been an attractive trophy for those types.

Hence, Bari wondered to himself: "Why did the men who attacked me and Yrma not attack the priest as well?" It was a logical question. Certainly they must have crossed paths somewhere along the way. There were no side streets or byways to the Way of Blood. There were no bushes or rocks to hide in or behind while someone passed by. It was a straight, un–camouflaged route. There was no way the priest could have bypassed those bandits unnoticed.

They had to have seen the priest and they must have known that he would be an unarmed and easy target. "Even if they felt he had nothing they could use on his person, they could have sold his beast for a handsome profit," Bari continued in his mind. It didn't take the mind of a seasoned philosopher to figure that something was out of the ordinary with that situation. He had an uneasy feeling about the entire development. Now, not only was his life hanging by a string, but so was his reverence for those who supposedly tended to his faith. His anger evolved into disgust. He was quickly losing respect for the entire lot of the priestly order.

Bari rested his head back on the ground and gazed upward at the darkening sky. For a few moments he just laid there. He was numb to the physical effects of the pain at that point. He was almost anesthetized to its mental effects as well. He was at the point to where he didn't care which way things progressed from there. At that juncture, it did not matter to him if he lived or if he died. He stared into the sky until he was about to fade away once again until he heard more footsteps. His desire to live began to creep back. He mustered enough strength to lift his head and see who it was that time. As his eyes focused in on the oncoming figure, he recognized by the attire that it was an assistant to the priests. The assistant did not cross over to the opposite side of the street as hastily as the priest. Surely he had recognized by now that a body laid in the shallow ditch just to his left.

Bari experienced the return of a modest ray of hope. He presumed that the mind–set of the lowly assistant might differ from that of the high ranking priest. Bari felt since this person was not a high ranking official (who could not relate to one with infirmities), then the assistant might stop and offer help. He felt maybe this one was more in tune with the needs of the people, since assistants interacted with common folk much more than their superiors. He thought maybe priests didn't understand how to meet a person at the point of their needs, since they never experienced the realness of life encountered by the average person. Even if they had experienced a commoner's life in their past, Bari felt they had since been so far removed from those experiences that they could no longer relate to them. He thought perhaps they were just too far above the situations that people dealt with to really understand what they were going through.

He thought to himself, "Maybe the assistant doesn't oppose to unholy situations as much as the priest. Perhaps he can relate to my circumstances. Maybe he can overlook the potential impurities and come close enough to meet my need." He began to feel good about the probabilities, now. He thought again to himself, "Maybe there is hope yet for our religious leaders" as he waited to hear encouraging words and a helping hand from the priests' assistant. The assistant continued to walk on the same side of the road as Bari until he got almost to the point where Bari lay. He passed over to the other side as he fixed his eyes upon him. It seemed almost that the intent was to recognize him, before moving past him.

Bari saw the face of that one. It was a familiar face. He had seen him earlier at the temple when he expressed his disgust in the service of the exchangers. The assistant had given him the same look as the exchanger had in response to his objection to the poor service. There was a "How dare you question our integrity?" expression on the assistant's face then. It seemed to Bari the assistant now had a "Serves you right!" look as he passed by his almost lifeless carcass. With that exchange, Bari's hopes were shattered worse than before. Several scenarios passed through his mind. "What is really going on here?" he wondered in agony. The suspicions danced about in his head as he faded again into unconsciousness.

Bari began to regain awareness one more time. He felt as if his body had begun to play tricks on him. It seemed as though he was lying in a bed rather than in that ditch on the side of the road. He didn't feel the protrusion of rocks against his body. He didn't smell a dusty scent in the air anymore. He opened his eyes. It was dark. Night had fallen and he knew that it would now be just a matter of time. He listened for sounds of wild dogs howling, growling, and sniffing about. Surely his scent had made its way to their nostrils by now. He listened frightfully, but heard absolutely nothing. His eyes began to adjust to the darkness. Suddenly, he realized he was no longer lying in the ditch by the roadside. The dark sky he thought he was staring up into was the loft of a building. He *was* in a bed!

Bari moved to get out of bed, but found he was still very weak and extremely sore. Still, he made an attempt to rise up. He was able to lift his torso into the upright position; however, the exertion left him a bit dizzy. He sat still for a moment allowing his body time to regain its equilibrium. After recouping his stability, he pulled the covers away and swung his feet over the side of the bed then onto the floor. He supported himself with his hands and pushed himself up onto his feet. He wasn't able to maintain his balance once he stood and overturned a small table with bandages and ointments resting upon it. He tumbled to the floor resulting in a loud thud that reverberated throughout the building.

An older gentleman rushed in to see what had taken place. He found Bari fumbling around on the floor attempting to recover from the fall. With concern in his voice he screamed out, "Are you okay?" As Bari sat up he responded to him, "Where am I and how did I get here?" The old man hurried over and helped him back onto the side of the bed. He steadied Bari with one hand and reached with the other for a cup of water from another table that Bari had not managed to overturn, yet. The courteous gentleman had him sip a few swallows of water and clear his head before he made any effort at holding a conversation with him. He then explained to Bari his whereabouts.

Bari ascertained that he was in the inn he was trying so desperately to reach with his wife before nightfall. If only he could have gotten there on his own. He suddenly felt a terrible sense of failed responsibility. He began to internally fault himself for the acts that had recently occurred en route to the inn where he now lay helplessly. "How could I have chosen to take the Way of Blood with my wife traveling along?" he thought. "I should have stayed the night in the city of the temple. I could have easily avoided all of this." He began to feel that there was no way Yrma would forgive him for his poor judgment call – if she was even alive to do so. He felt he would never be able to forgive himself. His emotions continued in a whirlwind of a downward spiral. He silently scolded himself, "This is unforgivable."

The innkeeper saw the disgust in Bari's face and looked down to him with accommodating sympathy. He began to explain to Bari how a do–gooder traveling in from the northern country had seen him alongside the road (almost dead). The do–gooder placed Bari on his beast while he walked beside him. He brought Bari to the inn and immediately begun to nurse him back to health. The do–gooder cared for Bari for two days, but had to depart at that point. He left money for the innkeeper to continue the tending until he recovered fully. The do–gooder also promised to come back through and pay any additional costs, should the innkeeper incur any. The do–gooder had given Bari another chance at life.

Bari was deeply moved by the innkeeper's story of the do–gooder's kindness. He was overwhelmingly grateful. He broke down in tears. All the emotions of the recent events coupled with the innkeeper's narrative just completely besieged him. The innkeeper stood back and let him have a moment to release it all. He didn't try to comfort Bari with meaningless clichés. He didn't try to take Bari's mind away from the situation with wayward conversation. He just gave him time to process it all. It seemed as if he understood exactly what Bari was going through. It was as if he had witnessed such a scene before.

Once Bari regained his composure, he relayed to the innkeeper the story of his demise. He went into every detail of the physical struggle with the assailants. He fully explained how an unknown enemy had come into his presence and within an instance claimed the thing in life that mattered to him the most. He never made reference to the large sum of money that was taken from him as he painstakingly recounted the events. He did not make mention of his strong suspicions of the impure leaders' involvement. He never complained about having been stripped of his clothing. He didn't discuss the leader's lack of concern over his physical wellbeing while exposed out there on the roadside. He never commented on any loss of respect for them. The only loss he acknowledged to the innkeeper was that of his exquisite escort.

Bari described Yrma to the innkeeper and asked if he had seen her. Bari's voice almost transitioned into song as he illustrated her attractiveness. He gave every perceivable detail possible. He mentioned everything that an on–looking male would notice about her. It almost embarrassed the innkeeper to listen as Bari described her. The older man could almost feel himself lusting after her in front of Bari. He did everything he could to not allow it to show on his face as Bari unsparingly provided each detail of Yrma's appeal.

Unable to respond verbally, the innkeeper just sadly wobbled his hanging head. Not only was he challenged with fighting off salivating over Bari's racy description of his wife; but he was also wrestling with the pain he felt from Bari's loss. He was a very compassionate man and would have felt sympathy for anyone who had suffered injuries as Bari. The means by which Bari had suffered the injuries, however, really pulled at his heart's string. He was so overwhelmed that he had to sit down. He was feeling faint from the array of emotions that Bari's story invoked in him.

Bari continued the conversation and indicated that he wanted to begin the search for his wife immediately. He asked for clothing and a few items of sustenance for his journey home. He promised to come back and repay the innkeeper for his kindness. He did not take it lightly that the innkeeper had gone through such trouble to ensure his welfare. The innkeeper might have easily let him die while still having accepted the monies the do–gooder left for his caretaking.

The innkeeper politely refused any further payment. The two of them had several exchanges on the matter. Bari was strongly insistent with his offer of repayment; but the innkeeper was equally resistant. He would hear nothing of the sort. He told Bari that the do–gooder had left more than enough money to cover his expenses and had even committed to providing more if necessary.

The innkeeper was just as honest a man as Bari. He would not dare overcharge anyone for services. Besides that, caretaking was not a service he rendered in expectation of payment. He would have done the same even if the do–gooder had not offered compensation. He could never walk away from someone with such a visible need. He would not have been able to forgive himself. The innkeeper's degree of compassion for his fellow man left Bari was deeply moved. He thought to himself, "The religious leaders could learn a lot from this guy!"

The innkeeper brought the clothing requested by Bari. He had several articles that were left behind by former patrons. He held onto them for various reasons. In some cases, he suspected the customers would request them on return trips. In other cases, he doubted they would return; so he collected them for a while then offered them as charity to the needy.

He sized Bari up perfectly and presented articles he felt were of use. He even had a perfect pair of sandals and a staff to assist Bari on his journey. He also presented the provisioning Bari would need for the trip. Bari accepted the articles with gratitude. That is, all but the staff. He did not want to give the appearance of weakness to anyone who might be observing him along the way.

The innkeeper insisted that Bari stay a few days more so that he might completely regain his vigor before restarting his journey home. He could tell by his slow movement and heavy breathing that Bari really shouldn't travel just yet – especially alone. He had recently dressed some of Bari's wounds and knew that they might reopen if he overly exerted himself. He talked quickly while Bari pieced together the items he intended to take on his journey. Although he talked fast and at a high tone, by the time he finished the last sentence of his plea, Bari was staggering out the back door and offering expressions of gratitude to the innkeeper.

Bari's journey home was excruciatingly painful. It was as emotionally painful as it was physically. He often had to stop to keep from falling faint from the pain and fatigue. Time and time again he muttered to himself, "I should have listened to the innkeeper." He also had to hum spiritual songs to himself to minimize the psychological effect of the sadness the ordeal had wrought in him. It was all he knew to do to deal with the pain and the anguish of what he was experiencing at the time. Still, he pressed forward. He was determined to get home and discover a plan of action for moving forward.

He finally reached his homestead and rushed into the house. His initial thoughts were on the safety of his wife. The painful effects of travel that wreaked havoc in his body were of little or no concern. He could block that out mentally while he concentrated on the welfare and whereabouts of his beloved mate. Nothing else really mattered at that point. Corrective measures could be sought for loss of anything else, but if the companionship of his wife was irrecoverable, then Bari felt he too would be lost forever.

He looked for signs of Yrma having returned to their home. He checked the kitchen, but there was no sign. He checked the bedroom and still no indication. He checked the visitor's quarters and there was no evidence. He checked every inch of that house for a single clue of her return. He could find none.

Bari's workers came rushing in behind him. Community members began to trickle in to see what had taken place. Word had gotten around that he'd returned without Yrma and that he appeared as if he had returned from battle. By now, everyone was wondering what had happened to them. The neighbors were quickly filing into the house in search of answers. They came in quietly and stood waiting for his oral report. Most that looked upon him were appalled at his appearance. Some didn't even recognize him. His face was bruised and disfigured tremendously. His head had been shaven so that his wounds might be tended to. Even if he might experience complete physical healing, he would never look like himself again. Many felt that odds were against him ever experiencing spiritual healing.

The workers and neighbors may have been correct on their assumption regarding Bari's spiritual healing. He had already resolved that several of the actions having recently taken place were simply not forgivable. They weren't forgivable by Rhomine civil laws. They weren't forgivable by Weshuan religious laws. They most certainly weren't forgivable by Bari's personal convictions. In his mind, there was absolutely no way restitution could be obtained for the loss he had just experienced at the hands of his trusted religious leaders. And since they could not recompense his losses, whatever penalties they had forthcoming could not be avoided, either. Someone had to suffer greatly just as he had suffered greatly. Someone would have to lose something dear just as he had lost something so dear. He felt it was the only way he could establish a balance for the acts against him. The eye for an eye rule suddenly began to make sense to Bari.

The workers and neighbors continued to surge in. Some came to show sincere concern and offer to their assistance. Others came to get the gossip surrounding the recently occurred events. It seems to always happen that way when bad things happen to someone. Either way, the on lookers arrived in droves. Parents came in covering their kids' eyes, so the kids wouldn't be frightened by Bari's appearance. Women burst into tears. Many wanted to console him, but were afraid to touch or come close to him. They felt that he was in enough pain without their interference. He looked so war–battered that some even feared if they got too close, he might have a mental breakdown and attack them. They watched in careful attentiveness as many murmured and pointed in his direction. The majority of the crowd treated him as if he was a freshly captured wild beast.

Bari ignored the gasps, the whispers, and the horror–filled gazes. He was non–responsive to the offerings of condolence. He waited for all of them to get their questions and comments out then he told his story to the inquiring crowd. He wanted them to know what happened so they could assist in locating his wife. Just as with the innkeeper, he left out the intricate details of his unfavorable encounter at the temple. He left out information regarding the lack of compassion displayed by the priest and the assistant who both left him to die in the ditch. He didn't include any of his insinuations surrounding the impure leaders' probable involvement in it all. He wasn't looking to start a religious revolt (he still was not his grandfather). He just wanted to restore his life to normalcy.

Bari mentioned going back to the city of the temple and seeking information on Yrma's welfare and whereabouts. Some of his closest workers and friends insisted that he rest and let his body heal a bit more. They beseeched him to let them form a search party and go in his stead. He reluctantly agreed to their proposition. He was in a great deal of pain and some of his wounds had reopened and greatly needed attention. Had it not been for the open wounds, he probably would have ignored their advice and went on the repeat journey, anyway. He could feel himself giving out, though. He knew he had lost a sizable amount of blood and that his body needed time to replenish and repair itself. He supplied the men with what they needed, including his best animals, and bade them farewell.

He waited a few days while his wounds were attended to by some of Yrma's maids. They had the proper touch. They also had medical aides (salves and herbs) that the innkeeper did not possess in his crude medicine stockpile. After a bit of attention and time, Bari got much of his strength back and his wounds were healing well. All he needed after that was good news from his search party. His workers had long since left for the city of the temple to inquire of Yrma's whereabouts, but he had not yet received any report from them. Bari could not handle the suspense of not knowing what they had learned about his missing wife. After having heard nothing, he decided he would go and search for her himself. He felt he could make it without incident, now. He packed a few necessities along with a bag of money – and his dagger. The ordeal that befell him before would not come about as easily a second time.

8 ENRAGED

Bari had been traveling for quite some time and was beginning to feel the effects of the journey on his body, again. He sorely wished he had chosen a good animal for his own use as he had done with the workers and friends he'd sent out a few days earlier. He hadn't recovered nearly as much as he thought previous to starting the present trip. He had muscle–aches, joint–aches, bone–aches, and aches in areas he could not pinpoint where the pain was coming from. Despite the amount of pain, however, he felt a fresh, hot bath was all he needed to bring some much desired relief.

He noticed a small bloodstain on his left arm near the socket of his shoulder. He would have to replace the bandage at his first stop. He would also need to apply ointments to aide in the healing of the remaining wounds. He brought some of the salve along at the command of Yrma's maids. There were just a few small, nagging open wounds left. He could sense that the others might need redressing as well. Despite all of that, he was not one bit repentant for having left home before reaching full recovery.

He was nearing the inn where the do–gooder had taken him on the day his entire life changed for the worse. He fought off the vivid memories of the attack: the tone of the voice of the band leader as he barked out orders to the others; the screams of those he had repelled with his counterattack as he inflicted pain upon them; the pain of each stroke of the bandits' clubs that hammered against his body with the force of full–strength swings; and the terrible feeling of not knowing the well–being of his wife. Tears formed in his eyes. The anger in his heart intensified several times over. He no longer felt the pain in his body. His mind was now occupied with not only the idea of locating his wife, but also the opportunity of exacting revenge on the vagrants. He wanted nothing more than to pay back those who had ruined his life and betrayed his faithful allegiance.

Although he never thought he would ever have use for it before, Bari was now eager to invoke the "eye for an eye" imperative. He understood the reason for it much better now. He now realized that there were lawless people who would inflict great measures of pain on others if they felt there were no repercussions for doing so. He was sure that knowing the law would permit the same actions against them would deter many (although obviously not all) from infringing on the wellbeing of others. Bari understood fully that laws are for those who won't abide in honesty and good will. He was aware (now more than ever) that the law provided the consequence that would dissuade many who would otherwise harm another and feel no remorse in doing so.

Since Bari was not the lawless type, he would never take advantage of someone, regardless of their position or disposition. That's why he never before considered there was personal value in the "eye for an eye" law. He held the philosophy that retaliation could never bring about good. He felt that going back and forth avenging each wrong would only increase the pain or prolong the disagreement. Wars would never come to an end. Friendships would never mend again. That was his thought process before. Now, his mindset had changed considerably. He was now thinking that it was easy to discuss forgiveness until you're the victim of an unforgivable act. Now, not only did the "eye for an eye" rule make perfectly good sense, but he was also prepared and eager to make use of it.

Bari stepped into the building. He walked slowly to the innkeeper's station. He wasn't walking gingerly because of the pain, although the pain had increased to a point where he was more than ready to gain relief. He walked without hurry to allow time for his eyes to focus to the dim lighting inside. He ignored the pain and walked as upright and masculine as he possibly could. He did not want to give hint of his weak condition to any of the patrons inside. He knew that would make him a prime target, should there be any criminal types lingering; and he felt certain some of the sort were loafing about the place.

He went towards the check–in counter. His intent was to seek a hot meal and an even hotter bath then give attention to his remaining wounds. He would spend the night there and rest up for the next leg of his journey. He could sleep off the effects of that day's travel and give his body the opportunity to rejuvenate itself. He felt that he could have made it further even with the pain and small sign of blood, but there was no use in running the risk of night travel. He knew he was an easy target in his current condition, despite having brought his weapon along. He also knew he could not get anything accomplished in the city of the temple during the night had he continued to journey anyway. All businesses would be in recess for the evening by the time he arrived at the city. He knew he might not even find a place to sleep in the inn there. It was nearing time for census and there was never room in the inns at the city of the temple that time of year. Therefore, Bari saw no need to pass up a good night's rest at his present location.

The innkeeper recognized Bari's scarred face immediately. They greeted one another with a hug and a kiss on the cheek as was their custom. The innkeeper led him to the back so they could discuss matters in isolation. Once they got into better lighting, he noticed the small bloodstain on Bari's arm. He immediately turned to get supplies to tend to it and any of Bari's other needs. Bari held him up and stated that he could tend to those later. The innkeeper saw that he was in much better condition than when he left to go home. He agreed to allow him to tend to his own wounds in his own time.

Bari asked the innkeeper if the do–gooder had passed that way again. He wanted badly to offer his gratitude to the one who had saved him from probable death. The innkeeper told him that he had not seen him since the incident. Bari asked question after question attempting to determine the whereabouts or the identity of the do–gooder. The innkeeper could not offer any useful information. Although he was aware that the do-gooder came in from the north, he did not know the direction in which he departed the inn. Bari finally conceded and ceased the barrage of questions.

Bari sighed and then inquired again about his wife. The innkeeper remembered his story from the initial visit and sadly shook his head to the second query. His countenance changed as he dropped his head. He truly was a man of great compassion and it hurt him fiercely to listen to Bari recount the incident. It was almost as painful for him as it was for Bari. Bari placed a hand of consolation on his shoulder and thanked him. He had a flashback of the Bari of old. Even though he was in great need of consolation for himself, he still possessed the wherewithal to offer comfort to someone else in need.

Bari offered once more to pay the innkeeper for the compassion and care he had shown before. Again, the innkeeper rejected his offer. He had no intention of extorting more money for the already rendered services. He didn't even request the initial payment from the do–gooder. Nonetheless, Bari assured him that the offer stood if ever he desired or needed it. He ended the conversation with a request for a room and a place at the dinner table. The innkeeper called to an assistant to prepare the room and he told Bari he would send up medical supplies later. Bari politely refused and told the innkeeper that he had brought along supplies of his own.

Bari freshened up and replaced the necessary bandages. He would apply the salves later as he felt their scent might annoy other patrons during dinner. Not only that, they may have given indication of his wounded condition. He gathered himself and headed downstairs. He felt totally recharged when he entered into the dining hall. The aroma was enlightening. The smell of roasted meat and fresh–baked barley loaves filled the air. Each table was garnished with freshly cut flowers and bowls of dried figs. There were very few empty chairs in the place. Noise filled the room as every patron attempted to talk over the other; and it seemed everyone was talking about the same sequence of events.

As Bari zoned in on the discussions, he learned that a stranger had entered the area and was wreaking havoc among the religious community. It seemed the stranger was not only putting the teachings and practices of the religious leaders into question, but he was also leaving the law makers and well–educated clan speechless in public debates. He challenged a lot of their traditions and practices and the townspeople were very intrigued by lack of response or retaliation from the leaders. Not only did they have inadequate replies to most of the stranger's challenges, but in some cases they had no response at all. The entire room was alive with chatter about the activities of the stranger.

Bari filtered through the noise while he made his way around patrons and to an empty table. As he sifted out the conversations, he found one side of the argument was that the newcomer was a saint; a prophet; a man of great authority; and the next ruler of the people. They felt that he was the one to come whom the old books of prophecy spoke of. Some even felt he was a reincarnation of one of the great religious leaders of Weshua's ancient glory days. They felt the stranger would restore their province to the times when other countries feared their military might and revered their legislative intellect.

On the other side of the debates, Bari could hear that some felt the visitor had no esteem for people of authority. They felt he had no respect for Weshuan law or for the closely adhered to religious customs of their people. Some felt that the actions of the stranger were criminal. They thought some of the words he spoke were sacrilegious. They felt if he continued on the path he was travelling, he would surely wound up face–to–face with an executioner.

Bari didn't know what to make of it all. After a few moments of hearing arguments back and forth, he began filtering it all out. He went to a dark corner of the dining hall and took his seat. He sat and looked aimlessly in alternating directions as he waited for service. A young lady brought him a cup of wine and a dinner tray. All patrons were served the same dish (except on special occasion), so there was no need to take his order. She placed the plate in front of him as she bent down slightly to offer a soft–spoken greeting in his ear. With all the noise, she had to get close so he could hear her over the others. The sweet smell of her perfume pacified Bari's violently active mind. The aroma had an absolute soothing effect. Coupled with her intense attractiveness, it almost made him forget his recently developed troubles.

She was a beautiful young lady. Although she would have looked striking in sack cloth, she made herself even more appealing by wearing a sparse outfit. Well, the outfit was skimpy for their modest culture. Most women there covered themselves nearly from head to toe with loose fitting clothing of drab shades of colors. The young lady, abandoning tradition, wore a colorful, snugly fit, and low–cut dress that barely reached past her knees. She asked Bari if he would like anything else. Bari's eyes were drawn down towards her protruding cleavage whose display became exaggerated by the angle of her leaning posture and the missing portion of her dress' neckline. As he struggled to make his eyes focus on her face, she offered a most inviting smile. Her eyes seemed to sparkle in the dim lit room.

Bari tingled with hormonal excitement. He experienced an internal current of yearning that nearly intoxicated him. His mind took him to a place where gentlemen deny going and unruly men boast of having been before. Every inch of his body desired to know her (in the biblical sense). For a moment, his flesh grew weak, but his will remained strong. Once back in a respectable frame of mind, he shuddered at the idea of what had occupied his thoughts and caused the sensation that occurred in his body. He then (less than politely) refused her offer. In fact, he was borderline harsh, which was a reaction that had never before manifested itself in him.

In times past, Bari would have respectfully rejected the proposition while complimenting the young lady on her natural beauty. He would have done so in a manner that would have been flattering enough to promote a sense of self-esteem and offered without any judgmental temperament. He simply would have pointed out that he admired her as a beautiful young lady. He would have encouraged her to consider using her beauty to the advantage of finding a good husband and a steady lifestyle versus what she presumably had at present. For him to have made such a statement would not have been considered chauvinistic considering the reserved values of their time. It was just how things flowed in their society. Women sought to marry at a young age and to begin a family as soon as possible. She seemed to have strayed far from the norm.

Although he was speculating, it seemed (by their standards) that she obviously lived a less than desirable lifestyle. It appeared to Bari that she was allowing her sheer beauty to be taken advantage of by men with no morals and absolutely no interest in her other than the momentary pleasure they procured from her. Before he'd grown so insensible, he would have at least discussed those matters with her even at the risk of being totally embarrassed by having been wrong in his presumptions. He would have delighted in having his instinct proven faulty in that case.

Again, Bari's demeanor had changed somewhat. That time he didn't follow his compassionate instinct. He didn't even consider providing encouragement on that occasion. Instead, he shunned her away as one would a stray, mangy dog attempting to befriend, in hopes of obtaining a morsel of meat. There was no intent to hurt; but he certainly did not want to give the impression that he wanted her extended company–at least not in the way she seemed to indicate by her smile. Bari could have denied her apparent offer in a more gracious manner, but for some reason he didn't on that occasion. It seemed Bari had begun losing his commitment to a nonjudgmental, forgiving, caring demeanor. The young lady smiled at him again (the second time in a more respectful manner) and proceeded to the next patron.

Bari began his meal as he continued to block out the clamor around him. It all sort of blended together in a muffled reverberation. He did not care to pick up on any of the conversation, although the crowd was quite lively with chatter. Following their conversations was the farthest thing from his mind and he certainly wasn't interested in joining in with any of them. He was retreating into a trance of solitude. Despite the immensely crowded, noisy, and closed–in atmosphere, he managed to make himself feel invisible to the crowd around him.

All of a sudden, Bari heard a single voice which seemed to stand out among the others. Either the voice was decibels higher than the rest or it was exceptionally familiar. He determined it to be the latter. He recognized the voice as that of the leader of the band of thieves that had attacked him a few days ago. Bari came out of his reverie and looked around for the face of the person who owned the voice. Eventually, he would discover it. He did not recognize the face, because he never saw the bandleader during the attack, but he was absolutely certain of the voice. That voice had echoed through his mind over and over during nightmare after nightmare. He had no doubt that it was the leader of the malicious clan. He heard the principal offender barking out instructions in the background and the words and tone of the culprit remained etched in his mind.

Bari's newly developed character almost coerced him into drawing his dagger and planting it in the man's chest as he sat at the table. He'd resolved that he would have felt no remorse in doing so. His remaining bit of reasonable intuition, however, calmed him to the degree that he could think through a plan that included following the bandleader and gathering more information on the whereabouts and wellbeing of his wife. Her safety was far more important than his revenge. Besides, there would be plenty of time later for achieving vengeance.

So, Bari focused his efforts on the chief of thieves and those who surrounded him. As he did so, he immediately recognized the face of one of the men in their party. It was the priest's assistant! Bari was certain of it. He remembered the light altercation with the assistant at the temple and he definitely recalled the encounter with him along the Way of Blood. That was the last face he saw before passing out in the ditch. The assistant's face was one of the images that resurfaced in Bari's nightmares along with the sound of the bandleader's voice. He knew with an unquestionable degree of certainty that the man sitting a few feet from him was the priests' assistant.

Bari wondered to himself, "What on earth is the priests' assistant doing in a place like this? Those priests are always condemning parishioners for frequenting or even visiting these places!" The priests never offered pleasant commentary about the types of people who went to those places, the people who worked in them, or the owners of such. The religious leaders made it appear that there could be no good found in the patrons of those pubs. Now Bari was witnessing one of their clan functioning as if he was right at home there. Bari didn't doubt that there were other religious elites in the place as well. He continued to wonder, "How can they have so much hypocrisy that they condemn something in which they partake and obviously with some degree of comfort?!"

The countless speculations that percolated in Bari's mind just before he passed out on the roadside then began to melt down to conclusions. It seemed his encounter with the thieves along the Way of Blood was directly linked to his dissonance with the money exchangers and the priests' assistant at the temple. He strongly considered that other such occurrences along the Way of Blood were linked to other disgruntled parishioners' verbally expressed dissatisfaction with the service at the temple. "How heretical is that?!" he thought. Not only did the religious man refuse to offer assistance in his time of despondency, but he was also directly linked to the hurt Bari and his wife had most recently fallen victim to. The idea of it all was beginning to make Bari sick to his stomach. He wondered how many more of the religious leaders' actions were centered upon pretense and impurities.

Bari completely lost his appetite. He convinced himself to continue consuming the meal, however; because he understood that he would need his strength to keep watch on the perpetrators and, if necessary, directly challenge them. He knew they would not spend very much time at the inn. Those types never stayed in one place very long. He intended on following them whenever they departed the building. He felt certain they would either lead him to Yrma or at least provide him with information of her condition and location. He determined as soon as he obtained the information he needed, he would take eye for eye from each of those who'd contributed to his afflictions.

Bari was starting to feel the side of his grandfather that many had already seen in him. Of course, if anything would bring Mathes out of him, his current quandary would certainly do it. The actions of those before him were beyond the point of wrongdoing of one party to another. What they were taking part in was degradation of the religious principles his people believed in and the temple of their God at which they expressed those principles. It was total disregard for their most revered customs and beliefs. "This," Bari thought, "is utter hypocrisy." Something had to be done about it! It was totally unforgivable.

Bari considered, for a moment, acquiring the innkeeper's assistance in bringing the criminalist clan to justice. He felt he could trust the innkeeper and that the congenial businessman would be eager to aid him. The innkeeper had certainly proven himself an honest man in Bari's eyes. He had also displayed great concern in the matter. Bari wondered, however, what burden he would be placing on the owner of the establishment in asking him to take part in his attempt to right the wrong.

After mulling over the idea for a while, Bari decided against seeking the innkeeper's assistance. He preferred to continue his efforts in solitude. He decided to observe the group long enough to gather the information he needed to draw the authorities into the matter. He felt that something would be done if he could bring to light the crimes that were being committed by the supposedly holy men. He knew, though, that his evidence would have to be substantial. No one would take likely to a common citizen (even one as admirable as he) bringing accusations against such men of influence. Many would not believe that someone who (in the public's eye) held to impeccable moral standards could commit the acts Bari intended to make known. Bari decided he would collect as much information as he possibly could before seeking legal action or enacting his own renegade justice. While conducting his investigation, he would continue to seek information on the condition and whereabouts of his wife.

Bari went back to consuming his meal and his drink as he continued to survey the actions of the party of interest. He glanced over from time to time just to be certain that he had identified the priest's servant correctly. He also wanted to build and store a mental caption of the bandleader for future reference. Bari had just as much intent in repaying him as he had in settling with the others. Although the leader was wise enough to not have any blood on his hands, he was just as guilty as the others. In Bari's mind, the leader was most guilty. He felt that some of the others would not have gone as far in their actions had they not been coerced and led by someone capable of greater evil. It was evident that the band leader was capable of significant malevolence.

Bari kept close watch on the two criminals. Despite the many attention grabbers in the room, he was completely focused on the words and actions of those two. He could hear their conversation above all other chatter in the place. Nothing else could draw his attention at the moment. The drunken laughter and the bitter arguments of those who had taken too much drink could not do it. The clatter of dishes being placed upon and removed from the tables could not compete for his attention. The attractiveness of the female servants wasn't enough to deter him. He was absolutely focused on following the discussion of the delinquent duo.

Bari examined their every action as they talked, laughed, and carried on like bar rats for quite some time. Eventually they completed their meals (along with more than a few rounds of drinks), bade each other good night, and rose to go to their rooms. The bandleader was so intoxicated, he could barely walk. The priests' assistant wasn't in a much better state. They had racked up a healthy tab for their evening of food and drink. It was much more than the average patron from those parts could afford. The priests' assistant paid the bill without once complaining about cost and even left an exceptionally higher than average tip as he rose from the table.

Bari noticed the activity of the assistant as he stood to make his way out of the dining hall. As the man was placing the money on the table, he motioned with his head to someone across the room. Bari followed the path of the assistant's line of vision to see who it was he had beckoned or at least acknowledged before departing the eating chamber. It was the young lady who had waited on Bari when he entered the room. Bari's attention shifted to the young lady who was looking in the direction of the assistant as he got up to leave the dining hall. She nodded back to him as he walked towards the door.

Bari's attention remained with the young lady as the assistant left the dining room. She continued what she was doing for a moment. She then progressed to another table and cleared it of used dishes and glasses as well as any tips that were left behind for her. Finally, she went and cleared the table where the assistant and his party had supped together. She picked up the tip, emptied the table, and then made her way to the door. It didn't take much mental effort for Bari to figure out the purpose of her timely departure. He felt a bit of pity in his heart for the young lady, but it was hurriedly overwhelmed by the anger and resentment he felt towards the priests' assistant.

His emotion of antipathy for the spiritually impure piercingly overwhelmed his spirit of sympathy for the spiritually impoverished. Such is often the case when detestation builds the way it had in Bari. His disdain for impure leadership caused him to make no effort reaching the lost, even though he had the aptitude and provisions to work around the encumbrance. He instead concentrated his efforts on combating their impurities and failed in his responsibilities towards helping someone in need. Bari had gotten to the point where resentment was overpowering nobility. He was developing a pure hatred for those religious phonies and it had overcome any desire he would have normally possessed that would compel him to do good to anyone.

Bari arose to retire to his room. As he walked toward the door, he brushed up against another patron. The man had also been drinking and was heavily intoxicated. He turned and shoved Bari aside in retaliation. As he watched Bari to see if he would counter, he noticed the scars and bruises on his face. "What got hold of you?!" he barked out through slur and saliva. He began to taunt Bari as the group of patrons sitting around him folded over while laughing at Bari's misfortune. The drunkard continued, "Watch where you're going before I give you a few more trophies to take home." Bari's hand twitched visibly as he did all he could do to hold back from retrieving his dagger and inserting it deeply into the inebriated individual's abdomen. The man taunted him even harder about the twitching. Bari knew he could not draw negative attention to himself if he expected to be in position to continue investigating the whereabouts of his wife. So, he politely begged the man's pardon and left the dining room.

Bari didn't sleep much that night if any at all. Most of the darkness was spent calculating how he might go about searching for his wife and securing his revenge. A great deal of time was expended on internal debate as to whether he would continue trying to discover enough wrongdoings of the priestly crowd to bring them to justice or just exact his own judgment on them. He recognized the fact that it would be more genteel to carry his case to the courts and let them deal with the offenders accordingly. Gentry, however, was the furthest thing from Bari's mind. Although justice could be carried out in the courtyard, satisfaction would better be delivered by his own hands. He wanted badly to right the wrong himself.

Not only was Bari stirring all night about obtaining his revenge from the religious counterfeits, but he also spent time sulking that he did not respond to the drunkard's challenge in the dining hall. Bari no longer had the mindset of walking away from confrontations. His peaceful disposition had been altered substantially. He was angry at the world and at that moment he felt like challenging the whole world. He felt he needed to send the message to every person that he was not their marionette. It seemed lately that everyone wanted to lead him by strings into whatever direction they chose for him. He felt he had given the impression that he had no other choice but to follow when he bowed to the patron's challenge in the dining hall. He sorely wished he had silenced the big whiskey–filled windpipe.

Just before daybreak, he found himself staring at the ceiling while still contemplating his next move. As he mulled over what would happen next, he listened for signs of stirring in the hallway. He wanted to be up and out when the priests' assistant departed the inn. He decided to prepare his belongings and head down to the dining hall for breakfast at sunrise. He left everything lying on his bed neatly packed and ready to go. If he were required to make a quick exit, he would just run back upstairs and grab his bags then be on his way.

The dining room was again fairly crowded despite the early hour. The noise level was not nearly as high as the previous night, though. Bari supposed that was because alcohol was not served with the breakfast meal. Their laws prohibited consumption of fermented drink before a certain hour. Of course, not all vendors followed the mandate, but the innkeeper was a respectable businessman. He did not place profit over principle. It would have been easy to fiscally manipulate the local authorities and get a "waiver" on the regulation, but he chose not to do so.

Bari surveyed the room and took a different corner than before. He still made sure he was able to survey the entire dining hall. In the new position, however, he was able to monitor the window as well. From his latest vantage point, he could see everyone who entered the dining hall and everyone who left the building. He was determined not to miss the departure of the vagrants, regardless of which direction they decided to travel when leaving the inn.

The young lady came again to wait on him. She greeted him with a warm "Good morning!" and the same respectful smile with which she parted his company. She didn't make any suggestive gestures on her second visit. She was merely seeking acknowledgement as a fellow human being. Her greeting was as respectful as if she was presenting it to her own father or the high priest himself.

It was clear that on this visit she wanted to be part of a meaningful dialogue instead of just the topic of the pointless discussion she normally encountered during her work shifts. Most types that frequented the place were far from what she would deem respectable. Their conversations were almost never suitable for a lady. If the discussions were ever centered on a woman, it was only because they were boastfully reminiscing over how many they had been with. Their conversations almost never showed respect for the female gender.

The young lady sensed an ambiance of respectfulness for the counter sex with Bari. He did not seem like the average brute that frequented the inn. It almost made her feel respectable to have someone reject her mischievous although discreet offer, even if the refusal was a bit harsh in nature. The rejection of mischief offered the opportunity to engage in meaningful conversation. Those moments were very irregular for her; so, if she sensed the presence of one, she embraced it. As a matter of fact, she didn't just wait for such a moment to come along. She desperately sought after them during her brief playful encounters with the male patrons who visited the dining hall.

She offered a warm greeting, but Bari did not tender a return salutation. She spoke again, suspecting that he was not fully awake, but again to no response. She realized after her second greeting attempt that he must have judged her character based on last evening's exchange. Although he shunned her away the night before, she still sensed something different in him than in the others. She realized that he wasn't interested in her business offer and respected him for that; but she didn't think he would place self-righteous judgment on her because of it. She just didn't feel like he was the condemning type.

All night she had pondered on telling him her life story. If she couldn't tell it all, she would at least convey as much as she could while performing her dining hall duties. She wasn't seeking anything, but acceptance. She thought if she could tell him her story, he might be sensitive to her plight. Perhaps he would offer encouraging words she longed to hear. If he did offer a lead on a way out of her current situation and into a better one, she would have considered it a bonus; but she wasn't seeking that. She just wanted to share her plight with him. She thought something good would have come from her next encounter with Bari if she could have just opened up to him at that instance.

Now she thought otherwise. Apparently he really wasn't different than the other pseudo–religious types that often paid a visit to the inn – many for more than just a room and a meal. Just as they, he saw no more in her than the terrible thing he felt she had become since her arrival at the inn. Like them, he had no idea of where she had come from or where she wanted so badly to go to. She wanted terribly to see that he was different from them, but apparently he was not.

She reluctantly categorized him with the rest of the low–life sorts that came into the inn to relieve themselves of their miserable lives outside. They all came in pretending to be righteous, but proving to be otherwise. They were righteous only by their own standards. The only difference she could see in their self–righteousness and Bari's was that they exploited her and then condemned her. Their condemnation may have been hypocritical because of their sharing in the unrighteous act, but it was justifiable. He condemned her without justification – only on suspicion.

She politely placed his plate before him and went about helping others as she fought back tears of disappointment. She briefly stepped out of the room to recompose herself as she was desperately losing the fight. Bari's rejection grieved her more than the others' hypocrisy.

Bari was too engulfed in his own circumstances to realize the damage he had caused the gentle creature. He was totally oblivious to what had just transpired between them. He had no intent of hurting her feelings – no more than he did of exploiting her beauty the night before. Her first impression of him was correct. He really was different from the others. He simply was too focused on righting the wrongs that had turned his personal world upside down to notice even the least measure of her dilemma. He currently did not have the capacity to show compassion. Vengeance had cornered his attention and it had fully masked the deep–seated humanitarian character that dwelled within him.

Because she did not know Bari's state of affairs, the young lady just felt the shunning was disapproval of her very being. It was a rejection that she had felt many times before, but again, she thought she had sensed something different in Bari. She was not trying to build a relationship from the initial offer of purchased companionship. That was merely a means of survival. With that she was seeking to maintain her existence. Now, she was seeking acceptance of who she was, not what she had become. It seemed to her that Bari was that ray of hope for nonjudgmental acceptance. He may have very well been her last hope.

The young lady's current lifestyle was definitely not one of choice. She didn't just step into the situation, she was propelled into it. A terrible tragedy had befallen her, leaving her to believe she had nowhere to turn but onto the path she now traveled so reluctantly. She followed that path each day with a heaviness of heart. It was a terribly burdensome weight. The hardest part of the struggle was masking her disappointment in self from the patrons. She had to conceal it from her employer as well. It was a tremendous burden for someone so young to have to bear alone.

She was the only daughter of a once prominent businessman from Bari's own hometown. Her father and mother were slaughtered by another set of bandits on the very road upon which Bari was assaulted brutally. After the attack, the bandits had their way with the young lady and sold her off as a slave. The outcome of the horrific event ultimately situated her as "property" of the innkeeper.

She had no other family members to search for her and take her in had they found her. In her culture, women who had no father, no husband and no sons were considered widows. They were basically wards of the State (so to speak) or they became property of someone. The State in that case was not a governmental body, but rather the general public. It was her local community. Since those from her local community were too busy wolfing at each other over who would control her father's affairs, no one had the time or the desire to discover her whereabouts and condition.

The innkeeper, being a just man, decided to do what their unwritten law required of them. He purchased her from the bandits and took her in. It was an act of kindness focused on preventing a much worse situation befalling the young lady. Thus, she "belonged" to the innkeeper. She was his property according to their law. Fortunately, the innkeeper was a fair owner. He provided her room and board for her services in the dining hall. His intent was to provide her shelter and safety until she could find a husband who would normalize her life again. He was unaware of the extra monies she brought in with her nightly transactions outside of the dining hall. He certainly would not have approved of such activity.

But then again, she did not approve of it either. She had never planned on embarking on such an unflattering profession. She certainly did not plan on maintaining it as an incessant occupation. Her intent was to one day walk away with her freedom not ever being the property of or requiring assistance from anyone again. She took the approach of "any means necessary" in securing the funds to acquire her independence. The more disgusted she became with the requirements of her trade, the more disciplined she became at putting away revenue for procuring her freedom one day. Through it all, she longed for the day when she would finally take her walk of liberty.

Since Bari seemed to have been uniquely different from most other men she'd met, the young lady instinctively looked to him for that father–like acceptance that she had been missing for so many years. The innkeeper, although he meant well and treated her most fairly, lacked the characteristics of a father as she had known them. She remembered her father as a strong, business–savvy, emotionally aware, and rugged, yet gentle man. She witnessed each of those same qualities in Bari. The innkeeper was business–minded enough, but he was lacking in the other characteristics. He was hardly the rugged type. His build was short and round. Besides that, he showed very little if any emotional awareness. He would never be able to sense when a woman needed to talk or desired a hug or just wished to remain to herself.

As the young lady observed Bari, she quickly realized that all the qualities she once witnessed in her father manifested themselves in Bari. The characteristics presented themselves so profoundly that it caused her to desperately long for a conversation with her daddy. She wanted badly to just sit and talk with him. She wanted to hear his manly voice. She wanted to test his wit and wisdom. She wanted to share her story of pain so that if he did nothing but sit and listen, she would have a captive, sensitive ear. All she wanted from Bari was to act as a momentary placeholder for her father. When Bari denied her the opportunity, she longed for it even more; but the pain of her longing was overshadowed by the pain of Bari's rejection. It was as if she was rejected by her very own father.

The attention Bari could have offered might have easily been the cure for the years of pain and anguish that had been inhumanely forced upon the young lady. Had he not been so preoccupied with his own circumstances, he would have noticed her hardship. He often picked up on such a thing instinctively and without delay. More than likely he would have met her relational needs as well as any financial needs that may have existed. He was a great conversationalist and had a gift for helping people sort out personal issues. He would have been more than just a momentary solace for her. He would have taken her out of that situation and granted her a new lease on life. If only he had been himself.

The scent of vengeance, however, was so strong in Bari's nostrils that it distorted his ability to sniff out the needs of others. Again, that often happens when one gets too swallowed up in transgressions committed against them. It seems to always happen to those who travel a vengeful path. They neglect their responsibilities and miss their opportunities to help others who have also been victim to offenses. It is the most critical side effect of un–forgiveness: acute apathy. Bari was feeling full effect of the un–forgiveness he'd allowed to take residence in his heart.

It was a sad occurrence that neither Bari nor the young lady recognized each other's plight. They both were in desperate need of a heart–to–heart conversation. The burdens they both carried were much too heavy to bear alone, and because of that, the emotional faculties of both were in disarray. Bari was perplexed by exploitation and ensuing bitterness. The young lady was confounded by misplaced condemnation and subsequent loneliness. They both could have received a much needed emotional overhaul if either would have been cognizant enough to notice the needs of the other.

The young lady returned to the dining room after she'd collected herself. Bari still continued to pay her no attention as she went about serving tables. He listened and watched intensely for the priests' assistant and the bandleader. He expected them to either enter the dining hall or exit the building soon. He listened intently until he heard the voice of the bandleader just outside the dining hall door. His blood seemed to boil within him, again. Once more, the only thing that stopped him from taking the life of the bandleader was the idea of it costing him any hope of finding his wife and exacting justice on the unrighteous religious men. He sipped from his cup as a means of steadying his nerves. He could not afford to bring attention to himself by the visible manifestation of anxiety.

Bari could hear the bandleader's voice as he bade farewell to what sounded like the voice of the priests' assistant. He rapidly made his way to the door, leaving the greater portion of his breakfast untouched. As he looked through the door, he realized the man was not the assistant, but rather one of the bandits. The bandleader was sending the bandit on his way. The assistant had not yet come out of his quarters. Apparently, he was still sleeping off the effects of the previous night's intake of alcohol and female companionship. Bari watched from the door until the band leader went back upstairs to his room. Only then did he feel it was safe to return to the dining room.

He proceeded back to his table. As he approached it, the young lady was about to remove his dish. She looked around and saw him coming and placed it back on the table. She asked if everything was okay. He did not respond. She sighed and continued on with her duties.

Bari didn't even notice she was there. He sat back down and continued to eat his meal. His eyes shifted in rhythmic pattern between the hallway door and the window to the outside. He processed every voice coming from the other side of the door and every figure that walked past the window. He dared not let anyone pass by unnoticed and miss the opportunity of furthering his investigation of the evil ones and exacting his revenge upon them.

Bari caught a glimpse of the young lady as his eyes shifted between the door and the window. For a short moment his eyes paused as they connected with those of the young lady. Although she had resolved that she would make no more attempts of communicating with him, she still could not stop watching him. For some reason she just knew he was different. She had never misinterpreted that instinctive feeling before. She didn't feel she was wrong that time, either. Maybe there was still a minuscule fragment of hope remaining in her shattered soul.

Bari didn't plan on pausing on the young lady while conducting his cadenced surveillance arrangement. It just occurred as his eyes were systematically surveying the room during their recently fashioned pattern. He had no intention of breaking the cycle of movements between the window and the door. The young lady's eyes caught his during the transition. It was as if his eyes were drawn to hers. It seemed like the soul searching senses he possessed were reactivated if only momentarily. Perhaps there was a small amount of sensitivity in him that survived the transmutation process of un–forgiveness. Obviously something remained, because he suddenly noticed the emptiness in her soul through the despair that filled her eyes. He could not shift his attention away from her, now, as he absorbedly gazed upon her.

It was not a romantic or lustful stare, although he did again notice her physical beauty during the exchange. She was absolutely gorgeous – nicely framed and richly toned with just the right tint to her complexion. Her hazel eyes and long, dark, and glossy hair perfectly complimented the rest of her beauty. Bari wasn't fixated on all of that, however, as enticing as it was to him (as it would have been for any man). He saw into her eyes just long enough to see the pain and the longing for a meaningful relationship like that which once existed between the young lady and her father. He could tell the longing was for a relationship she once knew, but could discover no longer. He could sense that it was a relationship which had been unexpectedly taken from her.

Bari could actually identify with the youthful innocence that had been tarnished by the unscheduled change of lifestyle as she was abruptly forced into the regime in which she partook at the present time. He couldn't realize her entire story in the exchange, of course, but he did see beyond what she had become in recent years. He saw much more than a two dollar hooker in a roadside bar. The old Bari was longing to reach out to her and offer consolation of some sort. He wanted to get to know her story and even offer assistance out of her situation if at all possible. He rose to approach her. As he did, his eyes shifted out of freshly formed habit back to the window. He caught glimpse of the assistant leaving on an animal. The bandleader walked alongside him. What awful timing!

How could he have missed them in the hallway? Was he that engaged in the apparent needs of the young lady that he disregarded the significance of the mission at hand? Nothing was more important to him than the task he began when he left his home the day before. All he could contemplate at that point was that he should never have let himself get entangled in someone else's affairs. He had enough problems of his own. If this near encounter cost him his ability to maintain surveillance on the two hoodlums, he would not forgive himself. Bari disengaged himself of any thought of playing the role of Good Samaritan to the young lady and flung his chair aside. He had absolutely no time to waste in catching up with the criminals.

As he rushed to the door, Bari bumped into the same patron who shoved him the night before knocking the gentleman to the floor. The impact was considerable as Bari was moving with sincere purpose. The man was abruptly ejected from his position and bashed his head on a table as he plummeted to the floor. He appeared to be dazed and in obvious pain. Bari dispassionately stepped over the body and ran out the door of the dining hall. He gave the man a sort of a "serves you right" look as he stepped over him. It never dawned on him that he was becoming that which he hated so dearly.

He rushed up to his room to gather his previously prepared belongings and ran to catch the trail of the assistant and bandleader. The young lady watched him leave the building. The hope she had seen reflecting from his eyes a few moments before exited the establishment with him. He didn't think to leave her a tip or bid her goodbye. He left no promise of his return. She was not surprised that he didn't offer any of those. People often left without a tip or gesture of thanks or anything of the sort; so, she was not bothered so much by that. She was disappointed that she still had not found someone with whom she could connect emotionally, even if only temporarily. She wanted nothing more than a genuine listening ear and an illustration of legitimate concern. She wanted so greatly to experience her father's love, again.

The assistant and the bandleader had been traveling for quite some time when Bari drew close enough to be certain he was trailing the correct party. Upon positively identifying them, he slowed his pace in order to follow from an unnoticeable distance. They were now at the outskirts of the city of the temple. They were nearing a grove of olive trees that grew on a hillside just outside the gate. There was a huge gathering of people along the groves. Someone was standing on the hillside speaking to the crowd as individuals murmured softly amongst themselves. More and more people gathered as the person on the hill continued to lecture on various subjects. The person spoke with such wisdom and authority that no one who heard him could pull away. They wanted to capture every statement the young man had to offer them.

There weren't just common people that comprised the crowd as was normally the case with such impromptu gatherings. There were dignitaries standing alongside the fieldworkers. There were housewives, merchants, fishermen, doctors, tax collectors, professors, lawyers, high–level religious leaders, and politicians. There were even a few prostitutes and men of very poor character among the crowd. All walks of life where gathered around listening to what the hillside speaker had to say to them. No one was really sure of the identity of the speaker. He was a complete stranger to that region, but his message captured the attention of all who stood within the sound of his voice.

The priests' assistant and bandleader pressed their way into the crowd to get closer to the stranger and hear what was being offered in communal declaration. They shoved and shooed people aside as if those congregated were goats grazing on the grassy hill. Well, that's how they reacted to the commoners. They were a great deal more courteous to the not–so–common spectators. Bari ran up behind them attempting to slip into the openings they had fashioned, begging pardon along the way. He wanted to stay within close proximity of the two suspects. He placed the lion's share of his focus on those two, but he also gave some attention to the stranger's appealing message.

Bari listened as the stranger spoke about the benefits of being meek and virtuous. He talked about being merciful and having a pure heart. He spoke about making peace and even enduring persecution. He then discussed being a good example to others. As Bari listened, it seemed as if the stranger was speaking directly to him. He wasn't close enough to see the stranger's eyes, but he also felt as if the stranger was looking directly at him. Bari thought to himself, "If you're talking to me, you're wasting your time."

The stranger went on to say something to the effect of having fulfilled the law. Bari didn't understand exactly what he meant by that, so he didn't make an attempt at committing that portion of the speech to memory. Besides that, anything concerning religious laws did not appeal to him anymore. He had developed serious issues with their laws as of late. It seemed those who wrote and distributed the laws saw themselves as above it. Bari's recent encounter with the polluted religious leaders (which were also their lawmakers and enforcers) left him believing the law was very much unfulfilling. After all he had just been through; it seemed to Bari that the law was incapable of fulfillment. In his mind, it needed to be done away with in its entirety.

The stranger demonstrated how murder was against their law, but he also added that if someone was even angry with another then they were equally iniquitous. That statement sparked Bari's interest and compelled him to listen closer. The stranger spoke against adultery, divorce, and swearing. He said it was wrong to seek vengeance and that one should love their enemies. Bari shuttered and thought again, "Is this guy talking to me? Does he know my thoughts?"

The stranger pointed out some things that not only Bari needed to address, but the religious leaders as well. Bari could not believe he spoke so boldly from the hillside. No one ever confronted the leaders' issues publicly the way the stranger had begun to. The stranger's message began to get extremely interesting at that point. Bari was preparing to move closer to the speaker and more closely heed to the stranger's commentary when he realized that the assistant and bandleader were leaving the crowd. He departed behind them. His desire to obtain vengeance overpowered his increasing interest in the stranger's message.

As Bari left, it dawned on him that the person talking was the stranger everyone was deliberating over at the inn. It was also the same person at the temple who overturned the tables of the money exchangers. Bari assumed it was also the person the woman Yrma met at the market referred to in her discussion of the northern and southern temples. He thought to himself, "If I was beaten nearly to death and robbed of my most precious possession for my simple remark to the money exchangers, how is this newcomer going untouched?" He pondered for a moment, but his mind strayed away from thoughts of the stranger as he saw the temple come into view and the chief bandit and priests' assistant disappearing inside.

Bari meandered apprehensively into the temple. He was afraid someone would recognize him and seek to complete the job they had begun on the Way of Blood some days ago. The money exchanger came up and offered him a tribute to take in with him. It was a different person than before. Bari looked over the tributes and his blood began to boil again. He placed his hand underneath his cloak as if he was reaching for his money bag, but he was actually reaching for his dagger. He had every intention of attacking the money exchanger that time around. He was done with the internal restraints. After all he had been through; the temple workers still had the audacity to offer him the same poor quality as before!

He thought back at the ruckus the stranger had caused there a few days ago. They still had not learned their lesson. Bari felt like the stranger obviously had more authority than he did, but he felt he had the same motive as the stranger and thus would be equally justified in correcting the unethical practice. If he was taken by the authorities afterwards, he could plead his case while exposing the religious leaders and hope that justice prevailed and he would be freed in the process. He was just about to strike when something caught his attention. He noticed a woman moving back towards the inner part of the temple. Women were not allowed into that portion of the temple, so he felt like something was amiss with the situation. He ignored the money exchanger and moved to the inner worship portion of the temple.

He arrived just in time to see the priests' assistant guide the young lady into the rear of the temple. The assistant went back towards the front as the door closed behind him. Bari turned away so as to not be noticed. He was fixated on determining why a woman was allowed into the priests' chambers. That was the place assigned for the priests to prepare for leading the worship services. The priests often invited distinguished guests back there, like politicians and high–end educators, but never women–regardless of their status. They were absolutely not allowed back there.

Bari was not influential enough to enter into that portion of the temple; so, he stayed where he could observe things and witness what was taking place there. He surveyed the area for the bandleader, but did not catch sight of him. He kneeled and pretended to pray. As he watched from under his cupped hands, he felt movement on the other side of him. Then he heard the voice of the priests' assistant as he addressed a party that had just entered into the temple. It was the stranger and one of his close followers.

The priests' assistant was asking the man who followed the stranger whether he planned to pay the temple tax required to participate in the temple worship. The stranger had not only visited, but he had also taught in the temple and had not yet paid the tax. There was a tax of three or four days' earnings for taking part in the temple worship. All male temple visitors above the age of twenty were required to pay the tax, without exception. Bari watched silently as the temple worker questioned the follower. The follower replied, "Of course he is," and walked away. Bari could tell by the follower's facial expression that he wasn't really sure if the stranger intended on paying that tax or not. He watched as the follower went back to talk with the stranger and confer on the mater, but before the follower could present the issue; the stranger posed a question to him.

The stranger said to his close follower, "Tell me, who do the kings collect taxes from, their own sons or from others?" The follower answered, "He collects them from others." "Well then," replied the stranger, "I don't have to pay the tax." After a pause, the stranger continued, "…but, so that we don't offend anyone, let's just pay the tax."

The stranger knew that many would not understand his logic because they were so accustomed to just paying the tax. They did so never making an attempt to determine if it was actually required of them or not. It had been so engraved into the cultural aspect of their belief system that they just paid it without question. They simply rendered it upon request and carried on with their normal pattern of activities. So, rather than upset their system so abruptly, the stranger decided to pay the temple tax without opposition. There would be plenty of opportunities to upset and correct their system in the days that lay ahead.

Bari, as he overheard the exchange, thought to himself, "Who is this person? Even the professors and the lawyers must pay that tax if they wish to teach or worship in here. How is he exempt? Whose son is he that he feels as if he doesn't have to pay?" After witnessing the discussion, Bari wanted to learn more about the stranger. He figured he would need him in his corner whenever he decided to go public about the misconduct of the impious priests and their assistants. As Bari watched the follower pay the tax, he thought to himself, "I guess it is just best to go along with things sometimes rather than confuse and offend folks who don't know any better." He wondered how long a person should just go along with things, though.

The stranger went on to teach in the temple. The lawyers and professors who were present were astonished by his commanding knowledge of their laws and religious customs. He not only taught things they didn't know, but he also corrected things they thought they were knowledgeable of. There were even times during his teaching when he left them feeling quite unknowledgeable. They were so embarrassed from their inferior knowledge, that they began to look for ways to hide the shame they felt was obviously showing on their faces.

They tried trapping him with questions about their law or questions involving hypothetical situations surrounding their religious customs. Nothing they challenged him with was effective. He either countered with questions they could not answer or with answers they could not question. Their frustrations began to mount; and after a while they began to feel threatened by the stranger's superior knowledge and the confidence he exerted in providing answers to their deceptive questions. It did not take long for them to realize that they could not undo his wisdom, so they stopped with the barrage of interrogating inquiries.

Once the questions subsided and the religious inquisitors slowly departed, the stranger stood alone with a few of the men who were his close followers. He held a somewhat private conversation with the small group of men. There were still others around, but the stranger spoke at a level where only those closest to him could hear what he was relaying to them. Bari got a little closer so he could hear what the stranger was saying to the close followers. He still needed more information if he was to acquire the man's assistance in bringing charges against the pretentious religious leaders and he had every intention of doing just that. He only needed to figure out the proper way and the ideal time to approach the stranger with his request.

The stranger was still addressing his close followers when a rich young ruler stepped up to him. The young ruler had been listening to the stranger's interchanges with the religious leaders. He very politely interrupted the stranger. The ruler was absolutely mesmerized with the accuracy of the stranger's knowledge and the strength of his logic. He asked the stranger what it would take to be a part of his efforts to rebuild and correct their religious system. The stranger replied with things that were required by their common and religious laws. The young ruler's reply was, "I have done all you speak of, but I still feel like I am missing something." The stranger then replied, "Well, sell everything you have, give the proceeds to the needy, and come with me." The young ruler's countenance fell drastically. He was a man of great wealth and could not fathom giving it all away just to be a part of what the stranger was presenting, regardless of the message's magnetism. He sadly walked away.

The stranger turned back to his close followers and saw the expressions on their faces as the rich young ruler walked away. Before picking up the previous conversation, he told them, "It is easier for a rope to pass through the eye of a needle than it is for a rich person to make this journey with us." They thought out loud, "Then who can make this journey?"

The close followers were not at all comfortable with the stranger's statement. They knew how well the young rich ruler had observed their laws and customs. His reputation was unflawed. The close followers could not understand how one so popular, so accomplished, and so seemingly just could be shunned away. They felt the rich young ruler could have been a valuable asset to them and their cause. They questioned the stranger's rationale on the decision to allow the young man to walk away.

Bari understood the stranger's logic well. The stranger spoke of someone attempting to get a rope through the eye of a needle in reference to the rich man not having the self-effacing capacity to do the things required of the strangers' followers. Bari saw the idea of attempting to get a rope through a needle equal to attempting to get a camel through a small gate while fully burdened with worldly goods and associated it with the rich ruler's position. The reason Bari understood it that way was because the word the stranger used in his regional dialect meant rope to some and meant camel to others.

In either interpretation, one could get the object to pass through, but not without great effort. In the case of a camel, it would require removal of the goods from the camel to get it through a gate, then reloading of the goods once through the gate. In the case of a rope, disassembly of each strand of the rope would be required prior to passing it through the needle, then reassembly upon getting it through the needle. In either case, the level of effort required would be great.

Bari's perspective was driven more by the camel definition of the word than the rope interpretation. He had vivid memories of the numerous journeys he and Yrma had made between the Temple and his home land. He thought back on how they would not bring the animals, loaded down with their belongings, because it was such a burden to the animals and the people they left at the homestead. He remembered how the well–to–do owners made the trek with their animals completely burdened down. He recalled how they could not get the animals through the gate of the city because of the burden of their belongings. Those owners didn't show any regard to the welfare of the animals or their hired help (or anyone else for that matter). Their only interest was to show onlookers how prosperous they had become in life.

Bari realized that those types placed much more emphasis on what they had than anything else. They would sacrifice the welfare of all others to maintain and have access to their belongings. He knew such a person could not truly devote their time and efforts to helping a "cause" regardless of what the cause wished to accomplish. They were very proud of their possessions. He knew they would most likely falter on the requirement of meekness the stranger discussed on the hillside of the olive grove because of their elevated status and prized possessions. Since Bari had firsthand experience with many of the rich leaders and businessmen and had witnessed their arrogance and selfishness often, he understood the stranger's message. If the rich man was unwilling to part with his worldly possessions, then those personal effects would eventually take precedence over the mission upon which the stranger and his followers were about to embark upon.

Well, at least from that perspective Bari understood the stranger's communiqué. However, he was fixated on the one definition of the stranger's keyword, which was interpreted to camel. Its other meaning was, of course rope, as the others understood the word. Since the stranger used it in a single sentence rather than contextually in a group of sentences, Bari's personal experiences governed how he understood it. The camel interpretation of the word he knew and his association with the animal and the practice of their abuse by some owners led him to his internally held understanding of the stranger's covert message.

From the other perspective, the stranger could have easily intended to encourage his followers' patience in sharing his message with seemingly impossible to reach people. It was impossible for them to pass a rope through the eye of a needle, unless they were patient enough to do so strand by strand. Such a thing would require tremendous patience and dedication to the task at hand regardless of the degree of difficulty or the appearance of improbable completion. If that was the message the stranger intended to send, then neither Bari nor the stranger's close followers received it correctly.

The stranger spoke to the close followers a bit longer, and then went on his way. They followed behind him. Many others began to trail along behind them. When the trail of followers grew increasingly larger, the stranger stopped, turned, and began to teach them about articles within their law and perspectives involving their religious beliefs and practices. A few of the professors and law makers (the religious leaders and teachers) found their way back into the crowd. They were curious of what the stranger would present next. Some were inquisitive with the intent of joining the stranger. Others wished to discover a means for re–establishing their dignity. They really detested the fact that they were so easily outwitted by the stranger in their previous discussions.

The corrupt religious leaders felt less and less important as the stranger taught more and more on what appeared to be a message of personal accountability. He began exposing fallacies that the impure influential ones had created in their teachings. There were misconceptions that were strategically taught by the deceptive leaders to afford them more clout and prestige among the people. The stranger's commentary began to uncover those stratagems. The corrupt leaders were really beginning to feel threatened by the stranger's unveiling of a more logical approach to meeting one's spiritual needs. They began to huddle amongst themselves and seek a way to entice the stranger to make a bad judgment call, so the people would dismiss what he was teaching in his ad hoc discourses.

Since the stranger made the comment about not having to pay taxes, they tried to trick him with questions surrounding paying the taxes their emperor required of all citizens except those who were members of the emperor's court. They wanted to see if the stranger would say he was exempt from paying the emperor's tax, which would have been viewed upon as treason, since they knew he was not a member of the emperor's court. The stranger did not fall into their little trap. They tried to trick him with questions on laws surrounding marriage. He responded with an answer that their laws did not account for, so they could not trick him with that question. They even tried to trick him into prioritizing the laws so that they could justify one wrong doing over another and stimulate debate on the subject. He summed all the laws into two that captured the essence of them all, so they still could not trap him there.

After fielding the corrupt religious leaders' questions, the stranger countered with a question of his own. The question left them all dumbfounded. If they answered one way they were condemned by their response. If they answered the opposite way they were still convicted by their reply. They chose not to answer the question. They just walked away thunder stricken. They realized that they would have to come up with a much better plan if they were to find a way to ensnare the stranger. His knowledge of their laws, his intellect, and his reasoning power was immeasurably superior to theirs.

After the teachers and religious leaders walked away, the stranger looked over at his close followers and said in a very audible voice, "Beware of the yeast of those religious teachers and leaders." His close followers wondered aloud what the stranger meant by the statement. They thought the comment was somehow linked to the fact that they had not remembered to bring food along for the day. Bari just shook his head as he overheard them talking amongst themselves while they tried to decipher the message within the message. They went deep into discussion over it. They were trying their best to determine where they would find food quickly and correct their mishap. They totally missed the meaning of the stranger's statement. Bari didn't.

Bari understood the stranger's cleverly camouflaged message well. He knew all about the yeast that was used in fermentation of dough and liquid. He had grown his own yeast and prepared it for such. He had prepared his own wine with it. He knew the process intimately. He knew the fermentation properties of the yeast were meant to change the chemical makeup of whatever substance it was added to. He knew that when the substance became fermented, it became rotten. He had fermented the liquid of fruit (grape juice) and knew when it rotted (cured) just right, it became grape wine.

So, he understood what the stranger was referring to in his statement concerning yeast. The transformation that yeast brought about on the original makeup of whatever it was added to was a drastic change. Bari understood that the variation could be harmful to those who consumed too much of the substance after it had been altered from its original state. He knew in the case of the fermented drinks, the danger could be readily identified. One could see a person's drunkenness after they'd consumed too much fermented drink. They could easily recognize that something was not right with the substance and that it would not be wise to continue consumption of very much of it, if any at all.

Bari also considered the fermentation effect in his wife's yeast bread as opposed to the unleavened bread she oft times prepared with their meals. The unleavened bread was ready in a short time and it was unformed–resulting in a big lumpy blob of baked dough. Yrma would make unleavened bread most of the time, because it was easy to make and it was nutritious. It had an excellent taste to it and it was really satisfying. Bari would eat some with his breakfast (sometimes it's all he would have) and he didn't think about eating again until lunchtime, because it really fulfilled his hunger.

Bari had also seen Yrma ferment the dough of her unleavened bread many times before and when it cured just right, it became yeast bread. Bari really enjoyed the yeast bread. It was lighter and fluffier, nicely textured, perfectly rounded; and it turned out golden brown every time she baked it. It was certainly more appealing than the unleavened bread. Given the choice between the two, most would choose the yeast bread over the unleavened simply because of its inviting appearance.

His wife's yeast bread took a lot longer to prepare than the unleavened bread, so she usually made a large batch when she did make it. The small loaves of bread were really good, but it never failed; when Bari feasted on the yeast bread, he was hungry again at about mid–morning (long before lunchtime). So, he would grab a few leftover pieces to take with him out to the field or wherever he was working on that day. As he worked through the morning, he'd nibble on the leftover bread he'd stored away until Yrma brought lunch out to him. His wife's yeast bread looked and tasted really good, but it just didn't satisfy him like the unleavened bread.

Bari understood how the yeast bread looked better and offered a better presentation, but the plain bread satisfied better; because he understood the effects of the yeast on the dough. It actually filled the dough with empty air pockets and made it lighter so that he didn't get nearly as full or nourished by a roll altered by the yeast as he would a piece of unleavened bread. That's why he could eat Yrma's unleavened bread and not grow hungry until lunch; but, he needed a carry–over snack when he ate her yeast bread. His wife's yeast bread was offered in a much nicer presentation, but it left him wanting for something else. That yeast was very deceptive. Bari knew that was what the stranger was trying to relay in his camouflaged message to his close followers.

With Bari's understanding of bread tainted with yeast and his new knowledge of the misleading teachings, he knew why the stranger warned his followers to be aware of the yeast those religious leaders and teachers used to supplement the lessons from their religious books. Unlike the stranger's close followers, Bari understood he wasn't referencing physical bread. The stranger was referring to how the impure religious leaders and teachers tainted their laws and customs by adding corrupt doctrine and mandates that weren't there originally. Those additives worked to the leaders' advantage, but they changed the makeup of the people's belief system to a point that it was unhealthy for their relationships – both with each other and with their God. Because of his recent experiences with their leadership, Bari was well in tune with the stranger's covert message. The stranger's close followers could not make that connection.

The stranger turned his attention away from his immediate followers and began addressing the massive multitude that had packed itself into the temple courtyard. He began to show them where the professors and lawmakers erred in their understandings of the law and in some of their religious teachings. He also pointed out instances where some of them deliberately misled the people by adding their own portions of impurity (yeast) to their religious teachings. Bari began to pay close attention as the stranger went through the misinterpretations and fallacies. He was painfully relating his recent experiences to the stranger's account of their leaders' behavior. The more the stranger talked, the more Bari thought, "This is it. This is the moment I've been waiting for. The stranger is about to totally expose our nefarious leaders. Once he does I can go public with my report."

Bari listened restlessly as the stranger methodically exposed the shady characteristics of the impure religious and civic leaders. He began by making the listening crowd aware that because the leaders were in authority over them the people were required to obey the laws and rules they put in place, but they did not have to follow the impure leaders' examples of immorality. Bari realized that many people did as the tainted leaders did simply because they felt they were justified to do so. Some, however, felt obligated because the powerful figures of authority made habit of certain acts to where those actions became the norm. Bari was aware of the seductive effect the leaders could have on a listening body as well. He knew many of their listeners did not know the exact verbiage from their religious books or did not understand the principles those recordings sought to teach them. They just followed the lead of those relaying the meaning of the books' recordings. So, if the leaders ever went off course with their teachings, the listeners rarely recognized the error and unconsciously followed along.

The stranger explained how the leaders placed demands on the people that they were not willing to abide by themselves. Bari had seen evidence of such in the dining room at the inn when he witnessed the uncharacteristic behavior of the assistant. He also knew they demanded that laws be adhered to by their followers, but in secret they broke them. He didn't have to manufacture very much imagination to figure out why they were taking the young lady to the back of the temple. Bari was becoming keenly aware that their hypocrisy knew no bounds. His blood began to boil again as he reflected on his most recent encounter of their deception.

The stranger expounded on the way the leaders acted and dressed a certain way when in public, just so they'd get noticed by those around them. Bari reenacted their behavior in his mind as the stranger spoke out against them. He recollected how once they were noticed, they wanted to be greeted with honor (by name and position) and shown to the best seat in their meeting places and public events. He noticed they were quick to complain about the service or the food regardless of how the commoners appeared to enjoy it. They gave the impression that nothing of common quality was good enough for them.

The stranger continued to expose them. Before Bari realized it, he was nodding in agreement as he took it all in. He listened as the stranger again reminded the listeners to not follow the precedent set by the fraudulent leaders. To Bari, it seemed the stranger placed compelling emphasis on that matter. Bari strongly sensed that the stranger was continually constructing a case for self–accountability. He gathered from the stranger's counsel that if the people took personal ownership of their relationships with their God and with their legal system and with each other, then it would be very difficult to be misled by impure leadership of any sort.

Bari surveyed the courtyard for religious leaders to see if any of them objected to anything the stranger was declaring to the masses. There were several leaders in the crowd, but there was not a single muttered word of protest. Bari saw that as strikingly odd. None of the common people would dare question the authorities, let alone expose them like the stranger had done on that day. "Yet, this man doesn't look any different than any of the rest of us," Bari thought to himself. "He doesn't act much different, either. He dresses like us. He eats with common folks. In fact, he eats with less than common folks. He acts nothing like the ritualistic, chauvinistic, arrogant men of stature whom he's addressing in the crowd. He looks and acts nothing like a man of authority, but he must be one, because they sit and listen to him as if he is their superior." Bari was baffled by the religious leaders' lack of responsiveness.

He became extremely perplexed with what the stranger did next. Eventually, the stranger did proclaim himself to be superior to the religious teachers. He placed them beneath himself and still there was no objection from any of them. That was unusual for one who looked and acted so commonplace, but that was not the action that confused Bari the most. He and the people around him could clearly tell that the stranger was well-learned, far beyond the teachers they were accustomed to. None of the listeners, however, could determine if and how the stranger outranked them. He had no proof of his authority. He had no letter with a higher authority's mark. He had no witness to vouch for him. He had no way of demonstrating his proclaimed position of power. He just proclaimed it as if it had always been that way.

So, it mystified Bari when the stranger looked directly into the eyes of the corrupt religious leaders and accused them of their wrongdoings. He talked through one immorality after the other. He took the very same approach that those leaders did when they witnessed someone else's wrong. They would condemn wrong-doers on the spot and in many cases execute them—without trial or jury. The stranger began the same process against them.

Bari was amazed that the stranger could carry out his complete sentence without a fragment of an objection from any of the leaders. He expected at any moment for authorities to rush in and apprehend the stranger. He could not imagine that any amount of perceived authority on the stranger's part would prevent them from doing so. Aside from that, Bari thought the leaders themselves would have already executed the stranger on location as they were authorized to do for anyone who spoke out against them or their teachings. They did not, however. They stood still and listened as the stranger verbally reduced them to criminal status.

The stranger began his sentencing by labeling the impure religious leaders and teachers as hypocrites. In fact, he would use the word over half a dozen times during his blaring assessment of their character. Bari stood in shock (as did many others) as the stranger labeled them as such. The tone and choice of words he used lacked any hint of respect those leaders so greatly demanded people show to the keepers of the law. In their minds, they were not just the keepers of the law. They were the law. "How can he get away with this?" Bari thought. "Where did he get this kind of authority?" No one else dared take the approach to addressing the religious moguls as did the stranger.

Obviously the stranger was well–aware of their clandestine activities. He informed the leaders that not only were they going in the wrong direction with how they taught and handled their laws, but they were causing others to be misdirected as well. He condemned them for taking advantage of helpless citizens. He declared that the long prayers of the impure religious leaders were just for show and that they would be judged harder for their pretense. He badgered them for their immoralities, again, and denounced the misplaced pledges they often took part in. He exposed how they made certain they followed the ritualistic practices of their religious beliefs in front of the masses– particularly in the area of offering tribute–but they had absolutely no heart for their citizens and worshipers where justice, humanity, and faith were the key factors. He pointed out how they would single out a very simple wrong committed by a person, but ignored the pretentious wrongdoings they were associated with. In their cultural axioms it was referred to as "swallowing a camel, but choking on a gnat." He finished up his sentencing reiterating how they gave an appearance of the perfect moral models, but they were far from such.

After listing his findings against the contaminated religious leaders, the stranger did something that Bari felt would definitely invoke a cry of insurrection. He just knew that the leaders would bind the stranger and have him hauled off to prison or just execute him right then and there. Bari would never have expected an unknown person to get away with what the stranger did next. The stranger called them snakes and condemned *them* to the death sentence – even though he did not attempt to carry it out at the moment. He reversed the order of things for them. In previous settings and times they were accustomed to having the liberty of judging and condemning others. Today, they took the position of guilt as they were judged and condemned by the stranger.

Bari was befuddled by the publicly issued blaring accusations and subsequent sentence. He was absolutely astonished by it. He could not believe what was taking place right before his eyes. He had recently witnessed more than a few unbelievable events. First of all, he could not believe how the things he had encountered in the last few days aligned so closely to the teachings of the stranger. Secondly, he couldn't believe the stranger was exposing them so intensely in the eye of the public.

Bari did not know what to say regarding the matter. He did not know what to do, either. All he had ever believed was now being challenged by the young stranger's unquestionably sound doctrine and irrefutable judgment of the impure leaders. If the things he had witnessed personally didn't change all he thought he knew, the reproachful findings of the stranger against the polluted religious leaders certainly modified his thinking.

The stranger's sentencing of the leaders was so severe that all those within the sound of his inflexed voice began to question the authority and righteousness of some of their religious leaders (the religious professors and lawmakers) rather than that of the stranger. They began to make known their distrust of the dishonest principals.

The leaders were overcome with a feeling of uneasiness because of the murmurs that emanated from the crowd of people. They whispered amongst themselves. They really wanted to subdue the stranger and silence him; but now they feared the people. They knew it would have incited a riot if they had seized him at that moment. So, they dispersed and backed away into the crowds and went on their way.

After a while, the excitement dwindled and so did the crowd. Bari stood at a sizeable distance from the stranger's position. He was still flabbergasted by what had taken place. He had absorbed all that the stranger said and had processed it and agreed that it was absolutely correct. He felt confident he could trust the stranger with his plight, now. He walked toward the stranger pondering how he might approach him for his assistance in exposing the deceitful leaders even further. As he reasoned within himself, he realized that the stranger was actually already in the process of deposing the highly influential religious counterfeits. He really didn't need to bring his personal battle into the picture. He came to a standstill and began to ponder his next move a bit more.

Bari was extremely pleased with how the stranger was progressing with his plan. There was only one thing that Bari was having trouble with in processing the stranger's teachings. Bari's witness of the stranger's overturning of the exchangers' tables and the discussion with his close follower about the temple tax left him in a bit of disarray. With those events, the stranger had all but nullified the purpose and the power of the tribute. Not only had the stranger worshipped in the temple without offering tribute, but he had also taught there without being obligated to pay the temple tax. He never paid tribute and the only reason he paid the temple tax was to not cause unnecessary offense towards the innocent.

That troubled Bari somewhat. The tribute was an extremely important element in their religious culture and the stranger had just rendered it insignificant. It was very difficult for Bari to disregard what he had known and done for so long. There was so much that was tied to the tributes they gave on each temple visit. Their gratitude to their God could not be achieved without that tribute. The forgiveness of their occasional wrongdoings could not be obtained without that tribute. The stranger was not only breaking down their tradition, but he was also removing what they saw as their rudimentary means of worshiping their God and obtaining necessary forgiveness. Bari knew the stranger definitely had some type of authority. That was more than obvious; but he wondered how the stranger could just wipe out the need for or the significance of the tribute. He wondered what the stranger would replace it with. The people still needed a means for atoning for their wrongs. They still needed reparation that would allow them a meaningful worship experience. Bari wondered to himself, "What on earth could ever take the place of the tribute?" That perspective of the stranger's message left Bari feeling a bit uneasy.

Bari felt somewhat uncomfortable with how strongly the stranger reprimanded the leaders as well. He did not feel the corrupt kingpins had just walked away from the tongue lashing without a planned counterattack in store. Bari had experienced the consequence of being found in open disagreement with them. He knew they did not like to be challenged overtly by anyone, let alone a stranger. He had the scars and the broken life to prove just how far they would go towards achieving retaliation for someone contesting their authority and judgment. He felt certain they would take some form of reactive countermeasure on the stranger. Bari was worried for the stranger's safety. He had a very uncomfortable feeling about the situation the stranger was creating for himself.

Bari saw that there were several people who agreed with the stranger's corrective approach in dealing with the corruption, but the stranger didn't appear to be forming any type of resistance party to fend off an attack from the leaders. Bari felt absolutely certain that an attack was forthcoming. He just knew the leaders would have the Rhomine troops come and take the stranger away. It was only a matter of time. Because of the certainty in his theory, Bari wondered why the stranger wasn't mustering troops of his own. He could have assembled a militia much easier than Mathes had back in his day. The stranger had accumulated a tremendous following. Bari was one who had determined that he would join the stranger and go to battle when the time came – as he was certain that time would arrive soon. He was willing to fight on the front line at that. He thought to himself, "When is he going to begin forming his posse?" He went away, pondering on and following the actions of the stranger to see what would be his next move.

Bari secured a room for the night, but he did not get very much sleep. Too many thoughts were flowing through his mind. He was still mulling over the degree at which the stranger had outwitted the professors and lawyers. He still marveled at how authoritatively the newcomer had reprimanded the impure religious leaders. He was especially astounded by the fact that the stranger had the audacity to condemn them in front of such a vast multitude without a single word of objection from anyone of them. Bari truly had experienced a personal satisfaction in witnessing the stranger's proceedings on that day. He suspected at some point the stranger would take over at the temple and restore things to order. Everything the stranger had done in the presence of the crowd pointed towards a changing of the guards at the holy place. Surely something phenomenal was about to take place.

Every action the stranger took that day was an act of defiance against the profane status quo. Every word he spoke against impurity was harsh, yet indisputable. The people could not reprimand the stranger. The religious leaders could not rebuke him. Through it all, Bari had developed a great deal of respect for the young man and adoration for his teachings. He still wondered, however, why the stranger hadn't begun to put together a band of fighters for when the time came to complete the cleansing process.

Bari recognized the fact that the stranger had a few men that stayed with him at all times, but that was only a dozen or so. They were mainly common people. He knew that four of them were mere fishermen. He was aware of a tax collector among them. He knew about the doctor in their midst. There was also a political activist that he knew about. The others he wasn't sure of, but he was certain they carried no martial clout. They did not appear to have any military experience, either. They wouldn't stand a chance against a company of the sort that the religious leaders could muster with the assistance of the Rhomines.

Bari was now thinking more like Mathes without realizing it. He had gone from a feeling of disappointment in the situation the tainted religious leaders had placed him in to a burning desire to clear the temple of the entire clan. He wanted to waste no time in reasoning with them. He didn't want to offer them an opportunity to correct their wrongs. He wasn't considering rehabilitative measures, temporary exile or anything of the sort. He had no forgiveness to offer them whatsoever. He wanted nothing more than to drive them completely out – even if driving them out entailed loss of life, including his own.

Bari was so consumed by the debauchery of bad leadership that he'd forgotten the second and most important half of his mission: finding his lost wife. It was really ironic. The malevolent leaders had gotten so engrossed in the system they had created for their self–sustenance, that they had forgotten their responsibility towards the people. Bari had gotten so enthralled by the situation they had created for him that he forgot his responsibility towards his wife. He was experiencing a transformation that was causing him to act totally out of character.

Bari began to realize that although there were many avenues of un–forgiveness, they all led to the same terminal point. He knew that place was marked by mental and physical signs of anguish, which he began to clearly recognize. They were overcoming him, making him something he did not desire to become and he knew it. The sad part of it all was although he recognized it and noticed its advances; he still could not halt its progress.

Bari began to feel the mental effects of the un–forgiveness. He was educated enough (both from a religious and academic viewpoint) to recognize exactly what was going on, but he still was helpless against it. The un–forgiveness had matured into anger and was rapidly approaching malice. His anger was driving him towards self–centeredness. He acted solely on his own interests and cared nothing for anyone else's. He acted out his anger in ways he normally would not have. He regretted his acting out less and less as it began to occur more and more.

On certain occasions, Bari's unforgiving anger escalated to mouth–foaming madness that drove him towards a hatred of anything that smelled like corrupt religion. He wanted nothing more than to destroy everything that the impure religious leaders had constructed through their elusive antics. There were also episodes of heart–wrenching sadness that caused him to question "Why?" to everything he had ever known about his religion. He felt as if he was being torn apart inside. He was learning firsthand the overpowering effect of un–forgiveness. He had often marveled from seeing it manifest itself in others, wondering how it could harden them so. Now he understood why. It was a very tough lesson to learn from such a personal perspective.

Bari went back to the temple the next morning to see if the stranger had returned to teach again. He felt as if the stranger would be there early the next day. Sure enough, he was there. The stranger progressed as if he had no time to waste in propagating his ideologies. He appeared to be on a tight schedule. He started the day with teaching. He ended the day with teaching. All during the day he was helping the temple worshippers to understand the need for changes in their thought process regarding their religious laws and customs. He carried his message into the communities as well.

He was intent on making sure those who did not worship at the temple also understood the importance of spiritual awareness and a meaningful relationship with their God. It was obvious that the stranger wasn't bound by their religious traditions and he did not seek to bind others with those practices.

Bari began to understand that the stranger's teachings were designed to move people to a sense of oneness, rather than generate classes among them as was evident in their current system. He paid close attention as the stranger addressed equality among his close followers. On one occasion, the followers were bickering over who would have the authoritative right to sit on the stranger's left side and right side when he would one day rule. The stranger gently explained to them that the true character of a leader was to place everyone else's needs before their own rather than seek how they might rule over them. He warned them not to follow the example of civic leaders who wanted nothing more than to govern others. Some of the religious leaders were already following that model and the stranger wanted to ensure that his close followers were not influenced to do the same.

Bari began to see that the stranger's intent was to make their religious experience a personal one with their God, rather than a blind adherence to what the impure leaders required of them. The stranger stressed self–accountability to one's own knowledge of truth verses pure devotion to another's interpretation of it. Bari gathered from the messages that if a person knew right, then it would be extremely difficult for anyone to deceive them into doing wrong. Of course, they may still choose to act immorally, but that would make it autonomous misconduct versus influenced improper behavior.

Bari truly understood that leaving the responsibility of one's knowledge of truth in the hands of others was a drastic mistake. Mostly everything he thought he knew about righteousness had been undone by his recent experiences. Although he could see the pure logic in the stranger's instruction (which was enough to prove its legitimacy), he also had personal experience as evidence of the accuracy in the stranger's teachings. He could definitely relate to the stranger's final statement to the crowd after having exposed the impure leaders: "If you will learn the truth, the truth will set you free."

Bari also began to notice how the stranger lived out his belief system among the people instead of confining it to the secret corridors of the back of the temple as did the impure religious leaders. He watched as the stranger freely provided comfort, assistance, healing, and relationship to people where they were, rather than requiring they come to him at specific times and on specific terms and with specific tributes. As Bari watched the stranger's interaction with the people in their environment, he thought again how the priest on the Way of Blood couldn't even come close to him in his most dire time of need – even if the priest had desired to do so. "What a horrendous contrast to what truly should have been," Bari thought.

Even in sharing of information, the stranger showed variance to the religious leaders' methods. He brought his messages out to the people. On some days, the stranger taught in the courtyard. On many other occasions he taught in any place he found a need to do so. He generally positioned himself in a place where all within earshot were welcomed to hear him. Had he done only the traditional temple teaching, his audience would have been very limited which was the case with the other teachers. Although the stranger did teach there, he also taught where the areas were open to anyone who desired to hear his message.

Bari found himself devoting all of his attention to the stranger's teaching. He was overjoyed with the refreshing change from the traditional condemning rigor of the impure religious leaders. It seemed those impure leaders spent the bulk of their time informing the people of what they had to and could not do according to laws and customs. It almost seemed the impure religious leaders' training was geared towards keeping their listeners in bondage – subjected to them and their rules. Those messages always left the listener feeling as if they would never be quite as good as those presenting the message. They would never be accepted as they were, but must continually keep coming and doing as they were requested in order to keep growing toward acceptance.

The stranger's approach was one of forgiveness and acceptance. His teachings seemed geared to freeing them from bondage of earlier inadequacies. His instructions made the listeners believe they could be accepted just as they were and grow from there. Bari grew extremely fond of the stranger's teachings. More and more he anticipated the day when the stranger would claim his place in the ruler's seat.

On one particular day, Bari listened as the stranger instructed listeners in the courtyard. He noticed a great deal of disgust in the face of the stranger when he addressed the hypocrisy of the religious leaders. The stranger detested dishonesty more so than Bari and he spared no effort in letting the infected leaders know that. As he verbally thrashed them, Bari's mind went back to his current dilemma each time the stranger addressed one of the unscrupulous events he'd recently encountered at the hands of the leaders. He was stunned at the accuracy of the stranger's description of the impure religious leaders' dealings. If he had not experienced the trickery firsthand, he might have not believed it. In fact, he would have probably indicted the stranger on being too harsh against the perceived righteous ones.

Bari watched the stranger's eyes as they followed the actions of people who came around the offering tables and placed monies into the baskets near the wall of the courtyard. The purpose of giving those monies was different from the reason of the tributes given inside the temple. The tributes were always given by the male head of household. They were a pre–determined item representing a certain degree of sacrifice. The offerings he witnessed now were given by free will. As stated before, the purpose of the tribute was to supply the needs of the temple workers as well as act as atonement for the wrong doings of the people. The additional monies given in the courtyard were to be dispersed among the poor as a means of sustenance. It was for those who could not support themselves.

Not all those monies made it to the disadvantaged. The impure religious leaders would redirect some of the monies for their own personal use. The stranger knew that. He used harsh words against the religious leaders concerning their greed and misappropriation of those offerings. Bari recalled a similar action was taking place at the exchange tables. The amounts they were asking for the tributes were inflated substantially. When he saw the temple worker spending money so loosely at the inn, he deduced that the exaggerated amounts for the tributes were redirected for their personal benefit. He felt certain the same occurred with the tribute. Bari knew that if they were scheming with those freely offered tokens in the courtyard, then they surely must have been conniving with the required tokens at the changers' tables.

Bari could clearly see that much of the benevolent offering didn't reach the people whom it was intended for. Anyone could tell that most of the people in the courtyard congregation were extremely poor. The majority were homeless widows and children.

The remaining folk were men with severe handicaps. There were some who lived within close proximity of the temple. Some lived right around the temple–camping out along the temple walls. The blind and the lame that could not get about so freely were assisted to the temple grounds each day. They would often call out to the people on their way through the courtyard gate requesting financial assistance or a morsel of bread. Other poor folks would come in to hear the messages, but they also waited for the temple workers to put out the excess foods that were not consumed in the temple.

Bari closely examined the number of people who passed by the offering baskets. There were large numbers of people gathered in the courtyard and the majority offered something for the baskets. Some announced what they were giving as they placed it into the basket. He listened to the amount of monies announced by those who offered large sums. There was more than enough in those baskets to care for all the individuals in the local congregation who simply could not care for themselves. There would have been enough to care for the ones in the surrounding community as well. It would not have afforded them a lavish lifestyle, but it would have certainly met their needs. That's all that their law required of it anyway. That's all most of the people desired from it. Since those people's needs were not being met, Bari could safely assume that those benevolent offerings were not reaching them as they were designed to.

Bari watched as they filed around to the baskets. Most of the professors and lawyers announced how much they were placing into the basket as they passed by. As he listened, Bari noticed those who were impressed by it would acknowledge them with clapping of hands or verbal expression. An old woman came and placed an amount without making an announcement and to no acknowledgement. She had placed a very small token into the basket. Those who were in close proximity of the basket could see that it was a minuscule amount. They all but ignored her, because her offering was insignificant in their opinion. They could not understand how any good could come from such a small amount.

It was insignificant to them, but it was very significant to her. It was the total sum of her fiscal assets. Even though she was obviously not very well off, she wanted to aid someone who was even less fortunate than she. Bari listened as the stranger pointed out to those who were paying attention to the amounts being given that the old woman's offering was more meaningful than any of the others. Bari understood the stranger's sentiment. He could tell the others were giving for acknowledgment or simply out of their abundance, but the old woman was truly concerned about the needs of others. She was so concerned, in fact, that she gave her all. "What an awesome gesture of genuine concern…" Bari thought to himself, "to give your all for someone else' welfare."

Bari's attention was drawn away from the offering basket as he noticed a bit of commotion from the corner of his eye. He turned and saw that a small mob was heading to the center of the temple court. It was the assembly of adulterated religious leaders coming back towards the stranger. They were moving at a rapid pace and in deliberate fashion. It was obvious to Bari that they had now decided to take the stranger into custody. That was the thing he feared the most. He knew the moment would eventually come. That was the reason he was puzzled by the stranger's slothfulness in forming his company of resistance.

Bari was sorely afraid for the stranger and a bit perturbed that he afforded this opportunity to the leaders. Bari's fears and frustrations almost propelled him into jumping in front of the mob and attempting to hold them back until the stranger could get away. He felt sure some of the bystanders would move in and assist him. He was just about to lunge at them until he noticed something odd about the mob of polluted leaders.

Two of them were dragging a woman along. Bari could not see the woman's face or features. Those surrounding her obstructed his view. They pulled her along so fast she could hardly keep up. Her feet literally dragged the ground at some points. There were three leaders in front of the two with the woman and all the others followed along carrying stones in their hands. They had all surrounded the woman. Bari moved closer to better witness what was taking place. He watched as they pulled her along and tossed her at the feet of the stranger. They were gathered around such that Bari could not view the activity. He moved in closer in order to at least hear the conversation between the religious leaders and the stranger.

The leaders addressed the stranger as a great and wise teacher. He dismissed their spurious reverence and asked their purpose for summoning him. They told him they had just caught the woman in bed with someone other than her husband. They explained the consequences for a married person sleeping with someone other than their spouse based on how their laws governed marriage. They took their time and explained the law carefully and at a very audible level. They made it known that the penalty for such an offense was immediate death.

They weren't explaining the penalty for the stranger's sake. They knew he was aware of how their laws addressed the matter. He had proven that he knew their laws better than any of them. They took care in explaining it so all those in audible range could hear and see what the stranger's reaction would be to one of their strictest laws.

Bari was relieved that they did not come to apprehend the stranger, but he still did not feel comfortable with how the situation was taking form. He could tell they were attempting to lure the stranger into another of their tricks. He recognized the trap. He knew that if the stranger told them to follow the law and stone her to death, then the sentimental types in the crowd would see the stranger as no different than the unrighteous leaders he had been exposing the last few days. It would show that he was just as impassionate as they, given the right situation.

Bari also knew that if the stranger just freed the woman against the will of the accusers, then he was ignoring their sacred laws. Those in the crowed who revered the law (which represented the majority) would see it as an act of treason against everything they believed in. If that were to happen, the stranger would not be allowed to walk away freely from the confrontation with the religious leaders as he had in the past. Those who stood by would demand the leaders take him into custody for such an act. Bari felt bad for the stranger. He didn't see any way out for him.

Bari also felt bad for the woman. Although she was obviously guilty, he still knew she was just a pawn in their plot to ensnare the stranger. He was a bit curious how they could have caught her in the act, though. These men were of the same class as the one who bypassed him as he lay in the ditch on the side of the road at the brink of death. The only rationale he could unveil for having been passed by was that the leader could not legally come near him, because of his unclean condition. "How then," Bari thought, "could they have caught her in the act? Has she been somewhere she shouldn't have been or were they somewhere they shouldn't have been?" The speculation occupied Bari's mind as he watched to see how the discussion would progress from that point.

According to their law, the woman's offense was gravely serious. It was punishable by death without a trial. She was to be executed on the spot. Most in the crowd of spectators had witnessed it in the past and they expected to witness it that time as well. The people were unsympathetic and the Weshuan law was uncompromising in cases of infidelity. It stood firm for anyone caught in that situation regardless of their gender or their social status.

The religious leaders asked the stranger, audibly so all could hear, "What should we do with this woman?" The stranger did not respond. The leaders stood around looking down their noses at him. They glanced occasionally at each other with somewhat of a smirk on their faces. They discreetly celebrated their impending victory over the stranger's logic, which had proven untainted up until that present moment. They waited patiently for the stranger to respond to their inquiry.

While the religious leaders awaited the judgment from the stranger, some in the crowd around them grew restless. They began to goad the leaders to make a decision. They knew the law. They didn't need a response from the stranger. They screamed insults at the lady. Some even spat in her direction. Some picked up dirt and tossed it in her direction. They were too far away for the results of their ill mannerism to reach the lady, but they knew that. They just did it as a sign of detestation. They probably got more dirt and saliva on themselves than anyone, but that was of no consequence to them. They just performed the act to show their objection to the woman's unlawful activities. To those who protested, most of their religion consisted purely of visible, yet ineffective acts anyway. Few of them could conceptualize the principles behind those acts.

The lady was absolutely terrified with her predicament even though she had heard of the stranger's commanding knowledge of their laws and how well he defended himself against the crafty questions of the leaders and lawyers. The stories of his victorious debates with the leaders had circulated the city more than once. Discussion of such had even bounced around the hallowed halls of their temple. The leaders and their assistants had sat in debate as to whether the stranger meant to establish good or evil by engaging in debate with them. It was apparent to many that he meant well. No flaws existed in the ideologies he introduced during those debates.

Still, the lady felt there was absolutely no hope for her in the current situation – not even with the greatest lawyer their society had ever known standing in her defense. She knew when the law was against a person, it did not matter who they had standing in their favor. She didn't feel anything the stranger could say or do could help her at that point. She almost went unconscious from the fear induced by the impending judgment of the religious leaders.

She was petrified; because she knew that regardless of how she pleaded for or demanded compassion; no one would hear her case. No one there would question the sentence of the religious leaders. None of the ones in authority over those leaders would and no one beneath them. They were considered elite untouchables by all other classes. Their judgment was final and there would be no deliberation to accompany their pronouncement of guilt.

The lady was well aware of that. She remembered days when she was positioned as a condemner versus being the condemned one. She would never have screamed or taunted or spat or thrown things at the accused; but she would never have pleaded for their pardon, either. She would have silently sat aside and watched as the law took its course. She knew everyone standing around her felt the same about the law as did she. Those who did not verbally demand justice would silently stand and watch it unfold regardless of whether the "it" was justice or injustice. She knew there was nothing that could alter the course of the written law and the leaders' interpretation and enforcement of the same. The law condemned by design, so she felt her life was utterly doomed.

Thoughts raced through Bari's mind as he sat along the sideline with the crowds. He almost had compassion for the lady, but he didn't think the stranger could do anything to alter the religious leaders' judgment, either. He didn't really know if he wanted the stranger to do anything. The law was clear in the case of infidelity. After witnessing the leaders distort and misuse the law in other cases, Bari wanted to see it work the way it was designed on this occasion. He was fed up with them allowing it to work only when it was convenient. "Let it be what it was meant to be!" He thought to himself. Bari would not join in with the ranting, but he had resolved within himself that it had to be that way.

Each of the leaders held the stones they intended to kill the woman with as they waited for the stranger's reply. The stranger seemed to be in no hurry to respond to them. He stooped down before them as he deliberated within himself. He picked up a stick and began writing something on the ground. Bari was too far back and too many people stood between them for him to make out what it was, but it must have been profound. As each leader looked down at the ground to read what was written, they froze in place. Those who were tossing up their stones and catching them again suddenly stopped tossing them. Those who were patting their feet all of sudden stopped patting them. Those who were whispering amongst themselves suddenly became quiet. They no longer looked around at each other. The victorious look in their faces had dissipated completely. Their expressions of assurance were replaced by the familiar look of defeat conveyed after each challenge of the stranger's intellect. Their eyes were fixated on what the stranger scribbled on the ground.

Without looking up, the stranger offered his response (just as audibly as they had). He stated that any of them who had never committed a wrongful act had every right to stone the woman for her infraction of the law. Apparently the right to execute such judgment as they desired to carry out required blamelessness of the executioner. The stranger asked those who fit that description to be the first one to cast their stone. He waited patiently for a counter response or a motion to move forward with the execution. Everything was quiet. There was no discussion amongst the leaders. There was none among those standing in the crowd. It appeared that no one in the vicinity could lay claim to being blameless, hence none could be the first to cast their stone. It may have been the first time that those religious leaders had admitted to being less than perfect before such an enormous crowd of witnesses.

Nearly a minute passed after the stranger made his proclamation. It seemed like an eternity to the accused woman. After the pause in action, she was startled by movement among the leaders. One by one those closest to the stranger dropped their heads. Subsequently they dropped their stones. They moved away and the other leaders moved forward to view the inscription on the ground. As they did, each of them dropped their heads, dropped their stones, and turned to walk away as well. After a few more seconds, the stranger looked up and they were all gone. He stood and asked the woman where her prosecutors had gone, again in a very audible tone. She sighed in utter relief, "I guess they choose not to prosecute me." He replied, "Neither do I. Enjoy your freedom, but discontinue your wrongdoing."

The woman was overcome with joy after having been excused from certainty of the death penalty. She felt as if she was floating on air. She knew she had absolutely no defense for her wrongdoing; but somehow the stranger had obtained for her a full pardon. He completely forgave her crime even though the law stated that there was no forgiveness for such. By law, even if someone would have offered tribute on her behalf, as the law allowed in many cases, there were no such restitutions for the wrong of which she'd been convicted. None of the tributes they had to offer could pay for that wrong. Yet, the stranger made provision for her – somehow. She didn't understand it, but she certainly didn't question it. She just stood in place enjoying her new found freedom. She fell to her knees crying tears of joy as the stranger walked away. His small band of devoted followers joined in behind him.

The crowd stood silent as they witnessed the entire episode. Once it ended, they burst into conversation over the matter. Eventually they dispersed amongst a great deal of deliberation. Most were wondering how the stranger had convinced the prosecutors to not execute the law against the woman. They wondered on what grounds she had been freed from her proven wrongdoings and ensuing death penalty. They wondered how he had the authority to question the judgment that had been rightly placed on the woman by the religious leaders. They also wondered why the leaders even brought the matter before the stranger in the first place. As they walked away, none of them thought to stop and read what the stranger had written or drawn upon the ground. They just marveled at the grace and authority with which he rerouted the woman's fate.

Bari was absolutely flabbergasted. He wondered to himself,

How can this stranger just pardon that lady for a crime that's punishable by immediate death? Our law requires that she dies. She is clearly guilty. Why did the leaders just walk away from their duty to punish her for this hideous crime? How could they have been persuaded to offer forgiveness when, by law, forgiveness is unattainable? Who is this stranger that he can convince them to overturn our sacred law?

The questions in Bari's mind seemed to go on and on.

Even though he pitied the woman, Bari still took the side of the religious leaders. He knew the law. The lady's act was unforgivable. The law was easily interpretable on the offense and he was prepared to assist in the execution of the law, if requested to do so. Although it appeared that the religious leaders were prepared to perform the execution themselves, normally they would have others do it while they watched in the background. They took that approach to keep their hands clean of the blood of the guilty party. So, Bari was prepared to do his civic duty, if called upon. He had even picked up a stone should they have called upon him.

He was not called upon that time. It seemed the religious chiefs wanted to perform this execution themselves. It appeared they had a personal interest in that particular trial. Bari could not understand it all. He questioned why the lawyers went through so much trouble to bring the lady before the stranger to exact punishment according to law, but then did not continue in their pursuit of justice. He knew they had the law on their side. He knew they were granted the authority to execute that law. He still wanted to know what happened to alter the course of her trial. He thought to himself, "It must have had something to do with what the stranger wrote on the ground." So, Bari rushed up to see what had been scribed into the sand. The inscription was obliterated by the time he got to the spot where the trial had taken place. Either the stranger had deliberately erased it or the crowd had trampled over it. Whichever the case, Bari would never know if what was on that ground was evidence in favor of the woman or against the prosecutors.

Bari just could not get over his amazement of the stranger's authoritative move in the temple courtyard that day. He stood still as everyone cleared away. He thought, "Now, I know this stranger is about to establish a new protocol." He began to think like Mathes, now. He was ready to prepare his troops. He was ready to arm himself and fight alongside the stranger. If the stranger did not begin mustering troops soon, Bari decided that he would muster the troops for him. He got up to go back to his home and make ready, but he thought he would go over and console the woman and bid her well before he departed the scene.

The woman was still in a state of shock. She had not moved from the place where she had recently received her new lease on life. The array of emotions she'd just undergone had drained her of so much energy that she could not budge from her present location. In a matter of minutes she had gone from experiencing the worst fear she'd ever encountered to the greatest freedom imagine–able. She had just stood face–to–face with inescapable death and all of a sudden was offered a way out with absolutely no probation, without any time served, without an ounce of criticism, and without a penny of required retribution. It was an amazing feeling and the woman was overjoyed by it. She just kneeled there, still crying, and basking in her newly attained liberation. She couldn't move. She stayed there on her knees sobbing through a silent prayer of thanks.

Bari was dying to know what argument the stranger offered in the woman's defense. He looked at the woman as she continued to whimper with gratitude and non–belief. He wanted to go closer and ask what the stranger had written or said or done to save her from her deserved death sentence. He was a little reluctant, however; because he had already condemned her and was willing to execute her despite not having heard her side of the story. He had sided with the law, believing it was the correct approach to the situation.

Now that he faced the victim recently acquitted of overzealous regulatory activists, he felt a great bit of guilt from the reactive part he played in the ad hoc court procedure. He began to think perhaps he should have thought things through a little more before approval of such a horrible and permanent sentence. The guilt almost persuaded him to walk away and try to forget the entire ordeal. His desire to know the stranger's formula for freeing the woman from judgment, however, was far greater than his guilt. He began to move toward the woman and seek answers.

Bari walked very slowly in her direction. He did not want to startle her. Besides that, he didn't want to raise suspicion from anyone who might still be observing the two of them. He knew he could easily be associated with the events that landed her there if he went too close too soon. He did not want the label of "guilty by association." He needed a clean reputation if he was to go after the impure leaders and he still had every intention of doing just that. Bari called out to her from a distance as he walked toward her, "Woman, I mean you no harm!"

The woman's entire body shuddered as she heard a voice of acquaintance calling out to her. She turned away and hid her face as if she did not want to have any conversation at all with a–a man. Bari hesitated for a moment, but continued on his quest to harvest the information necessary to understand the stranger's argumentative approach to setting a proven guilty offender free. The burning desire to learn the stranger's method of defense was still much stronger than the embarrassment he might have to endure, either from the woman's retaliation or from the murmurings of passersby. He called out again; this time with a friendly greeting, but still to no response. Bari felt a little déjà vu, only in reversed order. It was an obvious indication that she did not wish to converse with him. Still, he was determined to know the stranger's antidote for completely removing the guilt of so blatant a crime. Bari loss interest in protecting his image or his feelings and walked closer.

The woman bent down even further and turned to prevent him from communicating directly with her. Bari did not look at her–partly out of respect and partly out of shame. In fact, the shame had increased to the point where he no longer felt the desire to obtain more information. His approach had transformed from one of inquisitiveness to an advancement completely centered on offering empathy. He moved a little closer to her and softened his voice as much as he possibly could; and said,

> Look. I know you want nothing to do with me and probably anyone else, right now. I didn't come to condemn you all over again. I had before; just as everyone else. I don't, anymore. I see now that I have no right to. You should go and start over, like the stranger said. Those who had evidence against you have dropped their charges and forgiven you. The stranger has also forgiven you. You should take that forgiveness and go rebuild whatever life you had before this.

The woman responded to Bari's genuine concern. She communicated brokenly between the uncontrollable sobs:

Yes, Bari. Those religious men have forgiven me. Even though it was they who created this situation for me, they can no longer hold the wrong against me. The stranger has also forgiven me. He knew my innocence from the start. He knew my guilt as well. Although I began in innocence, I found myself engrained in guilt. I was guilty of un– forgiveness. I wanted nothing more than to take the life of everyone that placed me into this predicament – even you. The people who came to watch me die knew my guilt. They wanted only to see that justice was served and rightfully so. They, too, have dropped their stones and ended their cries of invectiveness and have left me to my forgiveness. Despite the magnitude of my guilt, the stranger ushered me back to my innocence. Everyone else has forgiven me, Bari; but, have you forgiven me?

Now, Bari shuddered at the familiarity in the sound of *her* voice. All the compassion he brought to console her with had dissolved into detachment. He came to cheer her up; but now he was the one distressed. He came to explain to her the power of the forgiveness that she had just received; but now he needed to understand the force of forgiveness for himself. He was completely taken aback by the crisp, cutting words of the woman.

He stood there speechless and motionless for a long time. He could hear her words echoing through his head over and over again, though she only said them once. "Everyone has forgiven me, but can you forgive me?" He tried desperately to answer, but he couldn't. Bari was at a loss for words. He could not find words sufficient for responding to his wife's question. Her inquiry tugged mightily at his heart's string. He felt an even greater aching once he realized he was still holding tightly to the stone with which he was to execute the justice he and the others had deemed appropriate. He turned as he could not bear to present himself before her any further. As he walked away, he flung the stone as far away as he possibly could. He could not, however, so easily toss aside the guilt.

4 RESTORED

B ari wandered almost aimlessly back to the inn where he was staying while in town. He sluggishly made his way up the stairs to his room and proceeded inside. Absolutely no vigor remained in him whatsoever. He appeared to be moving about without a purpose. He had no more objectives, no more motives, and no more plans. He didn't have a clue as to what to pursue as his next step. There was no heroism left in him. There was no more desire to right all the wrongs. There was absolutely nothing.

He walked over to the bed and plummeted face first as his almost lifeless carcass discharged a huge sigh of relief. The repose came from the occasion to lie and rest his wearied body, but his mind could not take pleasure in the same. It was still charting its way on a very tempest laden journey. He laid there and went over the events that had transpired so recently. Several of the words he'd overheard from the stranger echoed through his head as he tried to make sense of it all and determine a viable next step.

He still wanted badly to enforce the eye for an eye rule on those charlatan leaders, but he remembered overhearing the stranger say that instead of retaliating, one should turn away. He didn't see how he could still have peace within himself if he just left them to their fraudulent activities without any attempt of bringing their racket to light. He felt like he would be less than a man to ignore the deceptive, degrading acts against him and against his wife. Still, he knew that everything the stranger said made sense, so turning the other cheek must also make sense. He just didn't know how to draw the inherent logic from it.

Bari dwelt for a moment on the religious writings to see if he could remember something from them that could shed light onto his current situation. He often found solace in the religious writings during his most difficult time. He desperately needed that type of consolation at the moment. His life was in absolute disarray and he could think of no way to bring it back to order.

Bari's mind took him to one of the sacred books written by one of their prophets by the name of Lamak. That particular book had a message to the Weshuan people from their God. It was not a good message. The first portion of the message was to all of Weshua and that message was basically that they had profaned the religious practices they were required to perform in order to have a good relationship with their God. It discussed how they had polluted both the temple and the tribute they brought to it. The bottom line is that they weren't offering their God their best. They were just performing the activities required by their laws without any heartfelt emotion.

The second part of the prophet's message was directed to the temple leaders. It was not a good message, either. The message stated they had stopped glorifying their God and were glorifying themselves. It said they had also stopped teaching from the books the way their God instructed them. It notified them the relationship had gotten to a point where their God was not happy with it. In fact, He was very unhappy about it according to the message. That was the whole reason he sent his prophet Lamak with the message of warning.

The final part of the message was that their God promised to purge and purify the temple because of the way they had not kept the agreement he had with them. They had not done the things he required for having a good relationship with him. He told them he was sending someone to clean up the temple. As Bari deliberated in his mind, he wondered if the time had come for the fulfillment of the prophecy. His mind shifted for a moment and recalled the old woman at the temple that he gave the provisions to.

After several hours of contemplation, Bari suddenly realized that nightfall had arrived un–expectantly. He went down to the dining room for his evening meal. He didn't want anything to eat. He just went to get away from the plethora of discussions going on in his mind. He felt if he could get among other conversations they might drown out some of those taking place in his head. He had grown extremely weary of asking and responding to his own questions.

When he got to the dining room he found it was just as crowded as the other, which made him feel his idea of using the other distracting noises to drown out those in his mind just might work. It seemed every visitor in town came to eat at the same time. He looked around at the crowd. It was the same class of people he'd seen at the other inn. They were just as boisterous and were debating over the same topics. He didn't try to filter the noise that time. He embraced it. He needed it. Perhaps he could escape his troubles in there–if only for a little while. He lazily scouted the room then went to a back corner as had become his custom.

The waitress came to deliver his dinner. She greeted him rather dryly. He never looked up. She said nothing further to him. She placed a plate of food and a cup of wine before him and walked away. He didn't touch the food, but he drank the wine in a few large gulps. He sat there after finishing it and gaze around at the crowd again. The woman came by a few moments later and refilled his empty cup. She refilled the cup a number of times. Each time she came and went without a word.

Bari was not a reveler. He was not one to sustain drinking long enough to purposely intoxicate himself. Sure, there were occasions for wine with his meals, but that was normal for their culture. Everyone had a little wine with their meals on occasion. Many did so on most occasions and such activity was not considered unscrupulous. The wine was nothing more than juice that sat at room temperature for some time. As a result, it had a tendency to become slightly fermented. Bari, as did many others, drank it as a dinner beverage, nothing more. He had real wine on occasion as well, but again, never with the intent of losing sobriety. He never drank the beverages that contained high levels of alcohol. He neither drank hard liquors to be social, nor to celebrate, nor to drown his sorrows. He simply refused the offer whenever it presented itself.

Tonight, however, without even giving it a second thought, he gulped down cup after cup of the lightly fermented drink until it began to have the effect of high proof whiskey. After he'd gotten to a point of observable inebriation, the woman stopped refilling his cup. Perhaps she could see that for this one patron drinking was not customary. Perhaps there was a limit that the law or the establishment mandated for serving customers drinks. For whatever reason, she no longer supplied Bari the means for further intoxicating himself.

The depressant influence of the wine began to settle in. After a few drinks, the loud voices of the other patrons were no longer effective in drowning out those in Bari's head. He sat and reasoned with himself on what could have possibly made his life go from as well as it was before the recent array of events to as rotten as it had become since then – all in such a short span of time. He wondered (almost aloud) what he could have possibly done differently as he began to blame himself for the abrupt downturn.

He started to reason with himself as to how he might have avoided it all. He thought if only he had just gone with the order of services, regardless of how unfulfilling they were, he would not have wound up in the situation in which he currently found himself. He figured if he would have just given the tribute as the religious law required, not being concerned with the lack of personal fulfillment he desired from the worship experience, then everything would have remained normal. He felt he could have continued in the ritual of his religion and his life would have gone unnoticed and unchanged forever. He would not have been (as a result) so viciously targeted by the offended infected religious clan.

As he continued to reason within himself, Bari knew that would never have sufficed, regardless of how he ignored their undesirable undertakings. He knew deep down that his longing for something other than just a liturgical pattern of activities made him seek more from the worship experience. Even a perfect tribute at the right rate of exchange would have eventually become less and less fulfilling to him. There had to be more to worship than what he was accustomed to. He wanted the experience to be a more personal one. He wanted much more in his relationship with his God. He wanted to feel something from the encounter. He didn't want to just bring something to the gathering. He wanted to take something away. That is, something from a spiritual perspective.

On that particular trip, however, he had taken away much less than with which he came. He was crushed by his last experience with the temple and its residential wrongdoers. He wanted nothing more than to be absent of the debauchery of the impure religious leaders and the cunningness of their collaborators. They had created more than a lifetime's worth of suffering for him. He felt now that if he never saw them again, it would be too soon. Well, his *never* would come sooner than anticipated – much sooner.

Bari attempted to stand up and make his way back to his room. He decided he should go upstairs and sleep off the toxins. He would wait until the next morning to decide what to do with his life. At the moment he didn't have a clue. The intoxicating properties of the drink caused him to stumble over the table and stagger onto a party of diners next to him. One of the party members shoved him back to his seat and openly rebuked him for his drunken state. He blurted out religious reprimands to Bari referencing words from their religious books concerning a man's responsibility with taking strong drink. Their religious custom and beliefs prohibited such. The man who yelled at him was with a religious faction. They were a group of temple workers who had recently retired of their duties for the day. They were money exchangers and priests' assistants. Bari recognized a few of them from his temple visits.

Each of them began to chime in as they rambled off quotes from their religious books, reprimanding Bari for allowing himself to fall into such a pitiful state. They felt justified in pointing out Bari's condition despite the fact they were in the same environment for the same reasons. They just hadn't consumed as much fermented drink as Bari – yet.

Under normal conditions, Bari would have respectfully agreed that he was out of order, but Bari was at break point, now. His condition was no longer normal. He was everything but respectful to the religious types. He lashed out at them with a "How dare you look down at me…" speech. He audibly recounted all the things the stranger had spoken to the impure religious leaders in the temple courtyard concerning them and their impure activities. Others in the crowded room who had heard the stranger's speeches began to support Bari on the indictments.

Bari then took his dispute with the religious clan to a personal level. He made the people in the inn fully aware of his identity. Although they had not recognized him before then, they quickly associated with the voice once he identified himself. Everyone who didn't personally know him at least knew *of* him. They'd all heard great things about the grandson of Mathes. Even with the scarred face, they could still see the resemblance once he identified himself. There was a strong similarity in the facial features of the male members of Mathes' bloodline.

So, they recognized him, but they gasped at the appearance of his disfigured face. They wondered aloud what could have happened to him. Bari ignored the gasps and remarks and continued announcing all he had been through in the last few days – even down to the details of his wife's exploitation. The crowd went into total silence as he rifled down the actions of the religious clan. The temple workers began to show concern as soon as he began explaining his ordeal. They began to look around at each other. The crowd glared at them. The workers began to feel an aura of uneasiness overtaking the room.

The moment Bari ended his outburst of anger, the place grew extremely rowdy. Most of the patrons had already migrated to the side where Bari sat to signify their support for him. Bari, with the crowd behind him, began to move toward the crew. The religious party (along with their few remaining supporters) where backed into a corner and vehemently defending their innocence in the matter. They begin screaming out alibis. "I've never seen this man!" "I wasn't on duty that week!" "I didn't know anything about that!" "I never knew it would go that far!" They went on and on, further incriminating themselves in the process.

The more they cowered and tried to excuse themselves, the more irate Bari became with them. The crowd behind him also became more and more roused as he increasingly harassed the small party. The inn keeper sent for the authorities. He felt as if the crowd might break into a full – fledged riot at any moment. He was not in opposition to Bari's quest for justice, but he did not wish to wear the label of the birthplace of the largest insurrection his generation had known.

The authorities came in just as the crowd began to move toward executing judgment on the religious party. They pressed themselves between the two groups. Along with the authorities were a few religious leaders. Bari recognized some of them as well. He had seen them about town and in the temple. Apparently he had gotten the attention of the high authorities, because those leaders would never trouble themselves with such a small matter in a street–side bar. They saw a need, in this case, to come in and resolve the matter quickly. It seemed it presented much greater implications than a meager dispute among drunks.

One of the leaders tried to calm the crowd to the point where they could talk things through. They knew they would be better served if the incident did not go beyond a heated debate. They knew if it grew into a bar brawl or anything worse, it heightened the opportunity for their exposure. They weren't so naive that they didn't believe people were already aware that certain things about the temple operations were improper. They knew people had known about and ignored those actions for some time and would continue to do so. The information Bari was delving out, however, would not be overlooked so easily. They realized the importance of extinguishing the altercation as quickly and as quietly as possible.

While one of the religious leaders attempted to pacify the crowd, some of the others were endeavoring to get the temple workers out of harm's way. The riotous crowd recognized that the authorities were trying to rescue the party and began to push back. They attempted to force the authorities out of the door. There was scuffling between the groups and Bari was right in the thick of it. The authorities pulled out their weapons and began maneuvers to subdue the crowd. They formed ranks and raised their weapons while screaming threats to anyone who attempted to interfere with their efforts.

The crowd behind Bari backed down somewhat, but he would not allow the event to end without incident. He felt too many people had gotten away with too much for too long. He would not allow them to get away with it any longer. It was time for restitution. The wine, the anger, the disappointment and the un–forgiveness had made for a powerful toxin and had entirely exterminated Bari's previously present better judgment. His reasoning ability wasn't just crippled. At that point it was virtually dead.

Not only was Bari's group far outnumbered by the authorities, but few of them had weapons to attempt a worthwhile defense. Bari didn't know how many of his supporters had weapons, but he knew he had one. So, he didn't recede one bit. One of the religious leaders stepped up to Bari to try and calm him down. Bari would have no part of rationalization with what had become the bane of his existence. Bari pulled his dagger from beneath his cloak and in one motion ripped through the man's flesh from the lower right portion of his middle section to the upper left part of his chest. The leader let out a terrifying scream.

That incited the crowd behind Bari even more. It provoked their thirst for defiance in a way that only comes with the drawing of first blood. Quite a few of them had daggers and swords tucked away. The others began looking for makeshift weapons. They broke legs from chairs and made clubs. They used the eating utensils from their tables. They picked up anything they could find and drove the authorities and the other religious clergy members out onto the streets.

Once the commotion moved to the streets, others joined in. It grew into an all–out riot. The temple workers were beaten and thrown aside. The authorities retreated or were trampled upon. The rioting crowd made its way down the street and overthrew anything in their path and thrashed anyone who offered resistance. Bari screamed at the top of his lungs alerting all who wanted to join that they should take a stand with them. They were determined to get to the temple to reclaim it and cast out all that resided there. No longer would they tolerate the mockery of their religious beliefs brought about by the debauchery of a portion of their religious leaders. Many of the people followed Bari with pronounced enthusiasm. The Mathes of old had been resurrected and they were just thrilled about it.

Bari led the way with venomous chants, provoking that justice be served and righteousness restored to its fullest. The crowd that followed regurgitated his intonations. There were many in the crowd who had heard the stranger's judging blows against the religious leaders and law makers. They were feeling the same disgust that Bari felt, only to a much lesser degree. Most of them were not yet privy to Bari's knowledge of just how immoral the actions of those leaders were. That didn't matter, though. When it comes to opposing oppression, it doesn't take much effort to motivate indigent, indignant followers to take up the cause.

Bari had a formidable mob by the time he got to the street upon which the temple stood. There were thousands of armed and angry citizens following behind him. He turned the corner, leading the pack, desperate to see the temple in his view. He was eager to lead his posse in for an overthrow of the corrupt clergymen. He felt the impurity had to cease that instance and he was about to bring it to its end. He wasn't alone in his sentiment; because by now it seemed half the town was walking behind him. He couldn't wait to make that last turn and walk onto the temple grounds.

He made the turn, but instead of fixing his view on a clear path to the place of worship he was met face–to–face with a full regiment of Rhomine soldiers. There was a sea of swords and shields and spears in the hands of very well–trained and very well–conditioned professional soldiers. The religious leaders had summoned the ruling government's military to subdue the fast–growing insurrection. They knew their religious authorities and temple guards would not suffice in stopping the mob's forward progress. It had advanced into a full–blown insurgence at that point. Hence, they were able to enlist the help of the military. Although the government would not get involved in their domestic religious issues such as the altercation back at the inn, a rebellion of the magnitude it had grown to was viewed upon much differently.

The presence of the soldiers was an alarming sight to the riotous group. The crowd saw the solders and immediately began to disperse. They all knew they didn't stand a chance against the massive formation of armored soldiers. They knew how rigorously the soldiers prepared for battle and how mercilessly they went about carrying out their missions. When those soldiers went to disperse of an enemy, they did not seek to leave any standing; they did not allow any to flee; and they did not attempt to take any prisoners back with them. The crowd hurriedly reasoned among themselves and dispersed before the soldiers began to move toward them.

The soldiers did not pursue the rebels. They stood in formation and awaited the command to attack. When the military leaders saw the crowd dispersing, they determined the threat had ended and did not give the assault signal. Bari was so driven by his vengeance, his un–forgiveness, and his drunkenness that he did not realize his collaborating cast had abandoned him. He continued towards the soldiers issuing blaring insults at the religious leaders along the way. The religious leaders dispatched their personal security force to overtake him. He was easily subdued and carted off to prison.

Bari was later charged with inciting an insurrection. That in itself was a serious offense, but it was announced afterwards that the leader he attacked at the onset of the riot died from the injuries Bari's blade inflicted upon him. Bari was then tried for murder and sentenced to be put to death before the public on the next scheduled day of execution. The religious leaders handed down his sentence then went back to business as usual. The people fell back into the status quo of meaningless exchange and worship at the temple. It was a sad day for those who knew the truth behind the matter.

Bari cringed at the sound of screeching rusty hinges and the clanging of metal doors as the guards shoved him into the dungeon–like prison. He stood slouched over at the door of the cell. He was slumped over partly because of the weight of the chains on his wrists and ankles and partly from the uneasiness of facing what lie ahead. He was sober of the wine by then, but was still drunk with un–forgiveness. His raging fury and thirst for revenge had not subsided one bit despite his most recent setback. There was a small degree of disappointment with having gotten so close to making a difference and being halted abruptly. Nonetheless, he was satisfied that he had opened up awareness of the corrupt activity he'd witnessed firsthand with the detestable religious leaders. He did not feel his encounter and even his current predicament had come about in vain. He felt their purpose would serve the people well. He felt he was now mentally prepared for his day at the gallows when he would take his last opportunity at provoking the people to make the shift towards a permanent change. Still, there was a noticeable amount of uneasiness.

Bari sat down on the cold hard floor. He'd been tossed stale bread and there was water nearby, but he did not touch either. A fellow inmate picked up the bread and motioned to him a gesture that suggested that if Bari didn't want it he would eat it. The inmate wasn't as interested in the bread as much as he was in striking up a conversation. Bari motioned back that he would not be eating it. As he gnawed at the bread, the inmate queried Bari as to why he was there. Bari explained the previous evening's events to the inmate. The inmate shook his head. He said, "My friend, you have the right motive, but obviously the wrong method."

There was no immediate response. After a long period of silence, Bari asked the inmate why he was there. The inmate offered his reply:

> Just as you, I went too far with my criticism of faulty leadership. I suggested; no, I was insistent with the emperor that his marriage was unlawful and I did so in the company of some very influential people. I proved to him that either by our religious laws or by his governmental laws or by most people's moral standards it was illegitimate. I could have easily waited for a more appropriate time or used a more sensible approach in exposing his fault, but my distaste for dishonesty drove me to loss of reasoning.

The inmate continued talking as Bari took in what he said. Bari was only half listening at that point. He was busy pondering the inmate's opening statement that his motive was right but his method wrong. He was thinking within himself how he might have done things differently and to a greater degree of success. He wondered what the steps were that his grandfather took years ago to usher in his success. Bari wondered what failed steps on last evening caused his recent campaign to be unsuccessful. He pondered as long as the inmate continued to give his account of why he was there.

Once the inmate stopped talking, Bari asked him what the punishment was for his ill–advised actions against the emperor. He didn't want to give away that he wasn't really paying attention to the inmate's conversation. The inmate was not certain. He stated that the ruler almost fully ignored the incident and discounted him as a mad man. His wife, on the other hand, was absolutely livid over the entire episode. It was because of the wife that he received prison time. Otherwise, he might have just been verbally reprimanded and sent on his way.

The inmate changed the subject on Bari. He told Bari to not be overly concerned with his failed attempt at correcting the corruption at the temple. He told him that he was certain that things were about to change regarding their religious laws and customs. The inmate then recited quotes of their religious books that spoke of a person who would come along and challenge all misappropriated authority of leadership in both the religious and the governmental realms. He said that the person would restore order to their religious practices and clear up all the misunderstandings that had been generated from the misinterpretation (both deliberate and unintentional) of their laws and traditions.

Bari was familiar with the quotes. He had even pondered on them earlier. It wasn't until the inmate recited them did he finally become convinced that the stranger was the one whom the books spoke of. Everything was beginning to make sense to Bari, now. He almost leaped out of his chains with excitement. "He's already here! He's already here!" he exclaimed in excitement.

Bari's sudden and enthusiastic response startled the inmate. He thought Bari's recent ordeal was having an adverse effect on his mental stability. It took him a moment to realize what Bari was saying to him. "You've seen him?!" he asked Bari once he grasped the proclamation. "Yes!" Bari said as he began recounting to the inmate the teachings and the deeds of the stranger. "Certainly, he must be the one!" Bari replied after he described the activities of the stranger.

The inmate became just as excited as Bari. His ties to the religious leaders were deep and he longed for change just as much as Bari. He was a religious teacher himself, although nothing like the arrogant, self-righteous educators the stranger had addressed during his discourses. The inmate had a very thorough understanding of the books of their religion – much more so than Bari. He had his own close followers just as the stranger. His followers would come and visit occasionally and keep him abreast of the current events as well as make sure his needs were being met (as much as the guards would allow. The inmate's followers would bring food, fresh clothing and toiletry items for him.

The inmate's followers had not mentioned the activities of the stranger to him. Either they did not see the events as significant or they had not yet witnessed any of his deeds personally. Perhaps they were operating in areas other than those of the stranger. Whichever was the case, they had not mentioned the stranger to the inmate as of yet. The inmate decided on their next visit he would send them to ask the stranger if he was the one who would restore order to their religious system.

The next day the inmate's followers came to visit. The inmate presented the directive to them and they sought out the stranger at once. They found him performing great deeds for the people of their communities. The feats were much greater than anyone in the area had ever witnessed before. Not only was he doing great deeds, but he was also teaching out in the poor communities. He was communing with people most considered the lowest form of life. The other teachers would never have gone into those places. He was breaking their tradition into pieces. He was meeting the people at the point of their needs. He went right into the middle of their place of despair. He went to offer hope in places where they never knew hope. He went to renew hope in those who had lost it. It was a very refreshing change from what they were accustomed to.

The high class religious leaders and educators would never go into those areas or gather with those types. It was extremely taboo for someone of their caliber. And since those people would never have gone to the temple, if the stranger hadn't met them where they were, their needs would have never been met – not if they were waiting for the religious leaders to meet those needs. The inmate's followers found that the stranger was much different than the other teachers and religious leaders. The stranger made sure everyone had an equal opportunity to his giving, his teachings, and his unconditional compassion.

The inmate's followers went up to the stranger and told him the inmate had sent them. They asked if he was the one whom they had heard of. The stranger told them to return to the inmate and tell him what they had witnessed in his actions. He told them to tell the inmate what they heard in his teachings. The stranger knew once the inmate saw the impact the stranger was having on the people and the improvement in their lives and lifestyles; the inmate would know that the stranger was the one he had been informed of.

The inmate's followers went back to the prison and made their report. The inmate was elated over the information. He was confident now that things were to soon be set in order. He let out a huge sigh of relief. Before now, he was concerned that he may not get out of prison to teach and meet the people's spiritual needs. He felt they were doomed if left in the hands of the impure religious leaders with whom Bari was so closely acquainted after the last few days. Now, he felt that if his life was taken at that moment it was okay, because he had fulfilled his purpose. He felt the stranger would take it from there.

Bari asked the inmate,

Why doesn't the stranger just gather together enough people to relieve the immoral religious leaders of their duties and do away with these corrupt rules and practices? Does it not seem obvious that their rules were a burden that our forefathers could not bear and are equally unbearable for us? They create classes among people that should not be. They make demands of people that are not fair and just. They place more weight on ritualistic acts than meaningful interaction and relationships. They don't provide solutions to real issues, they simply postpone the inevitable. Just look at the un–forgiveness element of their methods and messages. If we continue in this "eye for an eye" mode for too long we will ultimately destroy ourselves. We're like a house divided against itself. How can we stand?

The inmate could sense the disgust in Bari's voice and observed the pain in his eyes. He calmly countered,

It's not the stranger's intent to do away with our laws or traditions. They are not as inadequate as you might think. They simply have been misinterpreted or misused to the extent that no one seems to fully understand them anymore. The way with which they have been distorted by the fraudulent leaders has caused gaping holes in some folks' ability to employ them effectively. The capacity to forgive certainly has suffered through the misconceptions fashioned by so many years of misleading messages as well as practices that accompany those messages. However, the stranger doesn't want to do away with the law because of the evil intentions of keepers of the law. He just wants to fill in the gaps where the wrongful leaders' interpretation and enactment of our laws and traditions lack that complete forgiveness that you allude to.

There's a huge element of un–forgiveness in our current laws and traditions; that much we as law–abiding citizens can see. However, laws are not written for law–abiding citizens. They are written for those who have no regards to law. They are basically for the lawless. Their purpose is to condemn unlawfulness. Since they are designed to condemn, they can't possibly offer any provision for forgiveness. Now, can they? One cannot extract fresh water and salt water from the same stream.

Don't seek for the stranger to destroy our law, Bari. That is not his intent. He seeks to fulfill the missing elements of the law. And he will do so by offering the forgiveness aspect it lacks so greatly. Once he fulfills it in that manner, its condemning properties will no longer be in effect.

Bari intensely pondered the inmate's response. He recognized the fact that there really was no room for forgiveness in some of their laws or in some of their customs. Based on the wrong committed, one might not ever obtain forgiveness. Sure, some wrongdoings could be "paid for" by the tribute, but of course recurrence would require repayment. And then, there were some wrongs that simply could not be eliminated, even with the tribute. Bari looked at the situation with his wife. Even if he had wanted to seek forgiveness for her during the trial (had he known it was her), no matter the tribute he offered, he could have not obtained pardon. So, if he could not conjure a way to obtain forgiveness for her through the religious laws and traditions that governed his life, how could *he* personally forgive her? According to their laws, the wrong she had committed was unforgivable (despite the unpleasant persuasive factors of her situation).

Bari knew that was the dilemma the stranger faced when asked what he would do by the religious leaders who wanted to stone her. The stranger knew there were no provisions in their laws and customs to forgive her. So he made provisions for her forgiveness. Somehow he made it such that the law could not condemn her and the people who executed the law could not condemn her, either. Bari still did not know what those provisions entailed, but he knew they were sufficient, because the leaders would not oppose the stranger concerning those provisions. Somehow the stranger fulfilled that missing element of their law. Bari thought to himself again, "What *did* he write on that ground?!"

Bari was lost in thought until he was startled by an unexpected array of clamor. The Rhomine guards had entered into the prison. They came in, took hold of the inmate, and dragged him into an empty cell. They forced him to kneel against a stone bench and placed his head on the bench. The executioner beheaded him without muttering a single word. It happened so fast Bari did not have time to ask what was going on. He didn't have time to offer objections. He didn't have time to even react except to turn his head in time to not have to view the horrible act. He was paused in shock. The punishment for the inmate's crime was now obvious.

The emperor had not planned to end the inmate's life so viciously. In fact, the emperor did not intend on harming the inmate. He had no more ill feelings against him. He was well over the inmate's unflattering comments. He really could not argue against them. The inmate's rather personal message was error free as were the other public speeches he'd made on other occasions.

The fact of the matter was: the emperor had grown fond of the inmate's discourses in their entirety. He had stopped and listened to the inmate's dissertations more than once. He felt as if the inmate's teachings were far superior to what he had heard from the impure religious leaders. He truly admired the inmate's messages. He saw the hope that the inmate's teachings offered to the listeners. He failed to see the same in the other teachers' messages. He noticed a liberating element in the inmate's teachings as well. That element was not evident in speeches from the others.

The inmates' teachings appealed to the people's intellect as much as it petitioned their emotions. The messages contained the personal accountability factor often depicted in the stranger's messages. The emperor saw how the people were drawn to the teaching, yet he didn't feel threatened by that. It did not show dishonor to him or the other religious leaders. He even knew of some of the impure religious leaders who had listened to and began to follow the teachings of the inmate. He was confident that the teachings could bring about nothing but good to his empire. So, the emperor could not bring himself to harm the inmate. He merely imprisoned him as a means of letting the people know the consequences of addressing authority in what might be viewed as an act of disrespect.

The emperor's wife, however, was absolutely infuriated by the inmate's comments regarding their marriage. If she had her way, she would have forgone the imprisonment and would have put him to death instantly. Unfortunately for the inmate, she eventually found a means for getting her way, even though it was in an indirect manner. She would not have dared to make the request directly to the emperor to do away with the inmate. She knew his mindset concerning the inmate. She knew that to request that he alter his decision would have constituted insubordination. Such an act may have cost her drastically – perhaps her head. Still, she found a way to get the emperor to know and grant her request.

The emperor was providing a dinner feast in honor of some very distinguished guests. As entertainment, the emperor's stepdaughter (his illegitimate wife's daughter) performed a dance before the company. The emperor was so pleased with her performance he granted her a wish of anything she desired. Not knowing what to ask, she quietly queried her mother for ideas of what to wish for. The mother responded that she should ask for the head of the inmate on a silver platter, delivered immediately. The daughter internally questioned such a morbid request, but honored her mother's plea (as was their custom) and audibly requested the same of the emperor.

The emperor's countenance changed from its jovial disposition to a puzzled and disappointed expression. For a moment, he was shocked that the young lady would make such a gruesome request. It didn't take him long, however, to figure out the true origin of the appeal. Still, because he had offered to do anything she wished (and had done so in the company of such an esteemed crowd); he was compelled to grant her desire. He never looked over to his wife. He didn't check the faces of the on looking guests. He dispassionately motioned to his guards to go and carry out the request and then motioned again for everyone to continue with their festivities.

Bari just stood there as the event swiftly unfolded. He watched them snatch the inmate up from the floor and forcibly restrain him against the wall. He observed as they nonchalantly unlocked his chains without any indication of what was about to happen. He followed their movement as they dragged him over to the adjacent cell. He watched them strike him at the back of the knees coercing him to fold over forward onto the floor. He observed as they forced the inmate's face onto the bench.

Once he realized what they were about to do, Bari turned his head as he could not bear to watch the act. His heart raced with fearful anxiety. His body was overcome with numbness. Destabilized by the idea of what was taking place, he fell to his hands and knees. He heard the whiffing sound of the blade as it moved swiftly through the air. He heard the clanging of the blade as it landed against the bench having effortlessly severed the inmate's head from his body. He heard the thump of the inmate's head as it landed on the concrete floor. He kneeled there for quite some time in disbelief. He could not cry a single tear. He could not scream a single yelp. He could not feel a thing. He kneeled there oblivious to the world.

Upon hearing new movement in the other cell, Bari was startled back to consciousness. He remained on his knees, but turned slowly to see what was happening now. He fought off the frightful idea that they were returning to repeat the task as it may have been his turn to face the executioners. He was somewhat relieved to see that it was not the soldiers making their return. His eyes adjusted to the sight of a small group of men and women assembled around the inmate's body. Apparently, the inmate's followers had been alerted of the catastrophic occurrence. They came in to claim the body. They took it away for proper burial after obtaining permission from the lead prison guard.

Some of the females stayed behind after others had wrapped the body and carried it away. They cleaned up the area then quietly departed the cell. Bari could not even address them while they carried out their duties. He did not know what to say to them. They were apparently too sorrowful to say anything to him, either. They never even looked over to acknowledge his presence. He watched silently as they finished up and left the scene of the most horrible act he'd witnessed in his entire life.

Bari tried desperately to get the image of what had just taken place out of his head. Although he turned away before the incident occurred, the sounds were vivid enough to complete the image of the act in his mind. He grew faint from the idea of it all and almost lost consciousness again. It took him a while to regain his equanimity. Once he did, he had to remind himself that the inmate completely fulfilled his purpose before the horrible sentence was enacted upon him. Bari comforted himself with the fact that he did not hear a single word of protest or a single plea for mercy from the inmate.

Bari knew the inmate was at absolute peace with the fact that the stranger would correct things. He wanted so badly to have the type of peace the inmate displayed, but he was still much too engrossed in the un–forgiveness that had overtaken him. He knew that even if he found a loophole in their religious law which would allow him to forgive his wife, there still was the problem of forgiving the religious leaders who were behind the immorality that had brought this havoc upon his and Yrma's lives. Discarding their culpability would require a huge degree of personal forgiveness. Bari did not feel as if he was capable of such forgiveness anymore.

"Why should I forgive the temple workers either for swindling the worshippers?" he thought. "How different is that from the Kreges who disregarded the sanctity of our place of worship? It is the same principle." The thoughts against the religious clan pulsated in his mind. They overtook the uneasiness he felt from witnessing the brutal death of the inmate. He could not, for the life of him, differentiate between the repulsive acts of the religious leaders against the temple during his time and those of the non–believers who ridiculed their religion in Mathes' day.

Of course, he also thought about the band of thieves who inflicted the initial pain that proceeded what he was currently going through. Even though their motive may have had no association with lack of religious discipline, it was still criminal in every aspect. Those bandits knew the cost of their crimes. They knew the consequences should they ever have to face the Rhomine courts for their crimes. Bari wanted badly to make them face those courts and if that were not possible, he wanted his opportunity to invoke punishment on them. He was even willing to face the Rhomines for his renegade justice if given the opportunity to enact it. He wondered how the religious leaders could have been hypocritical enough to join with such forces and commit such acts. He could not find a reason why any of them should go unpunished.

Word returned to the stranger that the inmate had been beheaded in his cell. He was deeply sorrowful. The inmate was not only a friend of his, but also a member of his family. They were nearly the same age (just six months apart). The stranger knew of the inmate's love for and dedication to their religion. He knew of his concern for the people. He knew how the inmate despised the immoralities of the impure leaders. He had heard how the inmate had stood in opposition to their practices and had spoken out against them on occasion. He lamented the sudden and violent death of his slain cousin and comrade.

The stranger left the crowds and went away to a private place. He wanted to be alone as he mourned the inmate's death. He would not be in solitude for long, however, because the crowds would soon seek him out. They had begun now to trust the stranger's teachings and seek his guidance more than that of their religious leaders. In fact, many who did not take part in the religion of the Weshuans were attracted to the teachings and company of the stranger. Even some of the religious leaders left their misunderstandings behind and began to live by the teachings of the stranger. News of his commanding wisdom and his unbelievable acts were spreading fast. He was having a huge impact on the lives of the people in the surrounding areas and even in places abroad.

Quite naturally, the contaminated religious leaders and educators began to feel the pressure of the stranger's growing popularity. They felt as if the stranger had taken away their purpose for being there. It was as if their rule was no longer necessary. In fact, by the stranger's judgment of them, they were more a hindrance to their parishioners than a help. Their once faithful followers began to realize that fact. The religious leaders were no longer revered by as many of the common people as before the stranger's arrival onto the scene. The fouled influential faction felt a pressing intimidation from the stranger's rising status.

The stranger basically ignored the impure religious leaders after the incident in the temple courtyard. From that point on, he moved forward with building the correct understanding of the people's religious beliefs and practices. It was a hard blow to the egos of the impure leaders. It did not afford them further opportunities of winning back from the people any degree of popularity. Those who had heard and agreed with the stranger's teachings wanted nothing to do with them.

The leaders were so distraught by it they decided the stranger must be removed from public presence. They resolved to wait for opportunities to discredit him and if that didn't work, then eventually they would just dispose of him. They made several attempts at discrediting his character. There were occasions when they questioned either his authority or his method of teaching or the services he made available to the people. In every case, he either did or said something to silence them, but they continued to plot against him.

The stranger spent the bulk of his time teaching the people and giving clear example of how they could better obtain their religious fulfillment and improve their worship experience. He would often go into private places and teach his immediate followers (the dozen or so) on a more personal basis. He warned them again to not follow the pattern the impure religious leaders had currently set for them. He showed them how those leaders could take the teachings and change them just a little, but the impact of that change would be great. He warned them how the religious leaders would attempt to cease the advancement of his message because of its nullifying effect on their impure approach to leading the people. His followers listened intently and received all he had to say.

The stranger also introduced the principle of grace to them. He made sure his band of close followers understood the power of forgiveness. It seemed he placed more emphasis on that principle than any of his other teachings. He let them know that they were absolutely required to forgive without exception – regardless of what their religious laws and customs had demanded of them in the past. He also made them understand that once they were forgiven, that pardon was permanent. There was no need to go back again and again to compensate for the same wrongdoing as was with the tribute principle. Once forgiven, the process was complete. The stranger made it clear to them in his teaching and he illustrated it in his full and free offering of forgiveness to Yrma in the courtyard when he required no payment or further action on her part. Her forgiveness was complete.

Grace (being freely forgiven) was a concept that the stranger's followers had a hard time grasping at first. The continuous payment of tribute to atone for their wrongdoings was deeply engrained into their religious psyche. They couldn't fathom any other approach to obtaining forgiveness. They felt they had to make some form of payment or perform some kind of action to be truly forgiven of their wrongdoings. After having lived by that creed for so long, they just felt there could be no other way.

Complimentary forgiveness was also a concept that the religious leaders grumbled against strongly. The stranger was forgiving wrongdoings without requiring a tribute and he did it on an immediate and permanent basis. The religious leaders felt the stranger was not only pushing their authority aside, but also weakening the effectiveness of their religious laws. The bulk of their powerful influence came from their ability to use those laws and customs to exact judgment or request payment for the people's infractions. The stranger was becoming more and more of an inhibitor of their way of life. They began to plot harder to find a way to derail his campaign.

The stranger was offering instruction near a cornfield and told his followers to go out to the field and pick corn to serve as their midday meal. It was on the seventh day of the week. Again, that was the day deemed a time of rest by their laws and customs. Absolutely no physical labor was supposed to take place on that day of the week. The religious leaders sought the opportunity to show the people that the stranger had no respect for their laws and customs. They shouted aloud so that the crowds might hear, "Your followers are doing something that is illegal!" Their intent was to get the crowd's attention so they might witness how the stranger would respond to their condemnation of the wrongdoing.

The stranger responded at a level the crowds could hear as well. He reminded the religious leaders of how their religious books recorded an event involving one of their most decorated military leaders who eventually became king. He was a very devout and religious man and a key figure in Weshuan history. The stranger reminded them of how the leader was forgiven for taking food from the temple that was pre–ordained to be used by priests only. The military leader did it to feed his soldiers during a time of battle when no other food was available. The stranger explained that the leader was not penalized for his actions, so neither should his followers since that was their only means of obtaining food for that day.

The stranger also reminded the leaders that their priests had done things in the temple on that day of rest which were much more offensive to their laws than his followers' actions on that day. Those activities were also recorded in their books. That quickly ended the conversation. The impure religious leaders were well aware of events that took place in those secret corridors of the temple. They were not about to get caught up in other indictments the stranger could have presented concerning their current priests.

When the leaders did not respond, the stranger walked over to one of the classrooms where the elite religious teachers taught classes. The religious leaders followed along. They were not satisfied that he had so effortlessly escaped the accusation of his follower's wrongdoing. Still, they could not argue that point anymore. There was too much risk involved in continuing that conversation. Now, they sought a way to make *him* break the law that prohibited them to do work on the seventh day; since it was apparent that he did not oppose to what his followers were doing on that day.

The religious leaders had previously witnessed how the stranger took his meals without first performing their ceremonial washing of hands. That washing was not for the sake of hygiene as they only dipped their hands into a bowl of water and dried them with a towel. Certainly such an act could not have removed the dirt and germs from their hands. It was merely a traditional feat performed when eating in public or social environments. It signified their position of purity more so than accomplished actual cleanliness. They asked the stranger why he ignored their tradition as if it was not important to him. The stranger knew their intent was to demonstrate that his teachings and actions had no regard for their established laws and traditions (which was not the case). He knew the question had nothing to do with their concern for health or hygiene.

The stranger explained to them how certain of their laws and traditions only illustrated that certain positive actions should take place. They did not prove that the illustrator was actually performing those positive actions. He explained how they gave an appearance of purity, but did not prove that the person's intentions were pure. He used the example of their law to honor their mother and father. This law required that an adult must do all they could to make sure their parents' needs were taken care of. That was especially true in the case of aging parents who were no longer self–sufficient. The religious leaders taught the law often. They gave the appearance that they were very concerned about the well–being of their parishioners' elderly parents. However, what they practiced regarding that law was contradictory. The stranger made them aware of it by responding with a question of his own:

Why do you break the command of our law for the sake of your tradition? For our law states, "Honor your father and mother," but you say that if anyone declares that what might have been used to help their father or mother is devoted to the temple, then they are not to honor their father or mother with it. They should rather give it for temple use. Thus you nullify the command of our law for the sake of your tradition.

The religious leaders were aware of what the stranger referred to. They made a habit of teaching their parishioners to give tribute to them, even if it meant the worshippers' elderly must do without basic essentials. They were taught to give tribute to the religious leaders even if it meant they had to tell their aging parents (or anyone in need for that matter) that after giving to the temple, no money was left to help them. That was totally contradictory to the requirements of the law to honor their father and mother. It was also against another law that stipulated the head of the household was to take care of home before anything or anyone else.

The religious leaders would instruct the parishioners to be sure to pay tribute even before taking care of their financial responsibilities at home. The stranger pointed it out to them that by doing so they were adhering to double standards. He then told them, "You honor the law with your lips, but not with your hearts." They taught one thing, but practiced another. He ended the conversation by calling them hypocrites. Again, they expressed no emotions towards his condemnatory comments.

The religious leaders still continued to seek flaws in the stranger's new model for having a pure and meaningful relationship with their God. They paid close attention to his teachings and practices to see how they might go about doing so. They ignored the logic of his teachings and the goodwill and positive outcome of his actions. They had witnessed on occasion how the stranger healed individuals with ailments. So, they brought one of the bandits who had attacked Bari before the stranger. It was the bandit whom Bari had ripped the risk ligaments apart. The incident left his hand wilted and useless. He could not even move the fingers on that hand.

The bandit had been listening to the teachings of the stranger and following his actions. He felt confident that the stranger's way was better than what he had experienced with the impure religious leaders. He followed the stranger from venue to venue hoping to eventually ask forgiveness for what he had done previous to having heard the stranger's teachings.

The religious leaders had noticed the presence of the bandit at each setting and could sense the bandit was about to convert to being a follower of the stranger. Hence, they saw no more use for him. They brought the bandit to the stranger to use in their next attempt at enticing the stranger to err before a crowd of witnesses. They asked the stranger if he would tend to the bandit's wound on the seventh day. Once again, that was the day on which they were to perform no physical activity, regardless of the action or the intent.

The stranger knew the religious leaders were not concerned with the ex–bandit's health. As Bari sat in his cell and listened to the recount of the events, he also knew they weren't really concerned. He knew based on his own experiences. It was, of course, another trap. The stranger countered the ploy by asking them if they had a farm animal stuck in a pit on that seventh day, which of them would not have rescued it immediately rather than waiting until the next work day. None of them answered him. He then asked them if they were willing to help the animal (their silence was evidence against them), then why would they not help a fellow human that needed help on that same day. There was still no response. He then asked them if their law would permit him to perform a good deed on the day they were supposed to do no work. Again, he did not receive an answer.

The stranger then illustrated how that particular aspect of their law (not working on the seventh day) could not be fully met due to its contradicting nature. He showed them how they themselves violated it at times. He reminded them that they had another law that required they perform a certain act on their male infants eight days after birth. The act involved physical labor. The act had to be performed on the eighth day regardless of which day of the week that eighth day after birth fell upon – even if it fell on the day when they were to do no physical labor.

The religious leaders were involved in the rituals to which the stranger referred; so they were very familiar with the law and with the activity. They knew they were violating one aspect of their laws in order to fulfill the requirements of another. They could not hold the stranger to a standard that they themselves could not possibly meet; at least, they couldn't do it openly with all those witnesses standing by. So again, they dropped their heads as they knew their trap had failed miserably. As they stood seeking a way out of the conversation without showing admission of defeat, the stranger tended to the ex–bandit's wound. He restored it back to health.

The religious leaders grew really sore with the latest encounter. It clearly proved that they could not rightfully object to the stranger's logic. They were mad enough to take him and execute him based on the fact that even though what he did was logical, it was still an infraction of the recently cited law. Even though the stranger had shown them there were contradictions in the law and therefore should be exceptions to the law, the law itself did not make allowances for exceptions. The law did not allow for thinking outside of the written box.

The impure religious leaders did not wish to think outside of that box, either. They ignored the fact that the stranger presented reasoning that the law did not accommodate for, showing that the law was unfulfilling in that case. He chose to fulfill it. He chose to make it accommodate the people and not encumber them. The leaders talked among themselves and agreed that despite his well–presented argument and perfect intent, there was still an infringement of the law and that was enough to take him in.

They broke their huddle and motioned for the temple guards. The temple guards were not associates of their religious community. They did not report to either Weshuan religious leadership or its civil authoritative body. They were rather Rhomine soldiers posted within their community by the emperor. They provided for the safety of the Rhomine government–appointed officials, such as the governor and his cabinet. They stood to make sure Rhomine imposed laws and mandates were followed by all. They were posted throughout the city–even there at the temple. They would intervene in any situation where the infraction or threat was against their government. They would not intervene in domestic or religious matters.

The religious leaders instructed the guards to go and arrest the stranger. The guards went over towards him. He continued to teach as if they weren't even present. After listening for a while, the guards went back to their posts. The leaders went over to the guards and asked them why they hadn't arrested him as instructed by the religious principals. The guards replied "No one has ever spoken as well as this man speaks." Not only did they see no threat to or violation of their law in what the stranger taught, but they were also impressed by his teachings. One of the leaders replied, "Don't tell me he has persuaded you, too?" The guards ended the conversation and assumed their post position.

The ex–bandit went back to some of his friends and told them what had taken place. He explained the entire exchange between the stranger and the religious leaders. Some of the bandits wanted to see and hear the stranger. They decided that he definitely had something better than what they had lived with and for. The remainder of the thieving band ignored him and continued in their chosen profession. Those who decided to follow the stranger's doctrine decided they would take the paralyzed bandit when they went to meet the teacher and seek medical attention for their friend.

The ex–bandits sought out where the stranger would be next. They learned he was currently on a ship crossing the sea heading towards their location. They met him coming in from aboard the ship greeted by an anticipative crowd. There were a few of the impure religious leaders in the crowd. The ex–bandits were somewhat apprehensive in letting the leaders know that they had chosen to follow the leadership of the stranger, but still they pressed forward carrying their friend on a mat.

They knew it was a clear sign of disrespect to the leaders if they passed them by to seek immediate and direct assistance from the stranger; but they did not let that stop them. They were willing to be labeled as conspirators by the impure leaders if it meant they could get closer to the stranger. They marched boldly towards him. The stranger watched them as they walked past the fraudulent religious leaders and sought him out. Before they could begin to make a request of him, he told the bed–ridden ex–bandit that he was forgiven of his wrongdoings.

The bandits were amazed that the stranger knew what had taken place. They had not even made their request, yet. They were overjoyed as a result of his pronouncement. The leaders were appalled with it. They made it clear that they felt the stranger had no right to forgive wrongdoings. According to their laws, there were several religious requirements that must be met before forgiveness could come about. The stranger knew, again, they were not concerned about the ex–bandit's pardon. They were concerned that the forgiveness of the ex-bandit was offered without consideration of the tribute required by their laws and customs. They were also upset that forgiveness was granted without their counsel and without anything that involved their opinion, their authority or their judgment. They just simply could not grasp the concept of grace.

They grumbled amongst themselves. With all the other noise in the area, the stranger could still hear and understand their murmuring. He asked them why was it so easy for them to watch him heal the man's ailment, but not to forgive him for his wrongdoings. The stranger knew it was important to the man that he walked again; but he also knew that the ex–bandit had a more pressing need to be forgiven of his wrong. He knew the spiritual healing was more important if the ex–bandit was to leave there restored completely. Apparently the religious leaders failed to recognize that. The stranger told the religious leaders that just as he had the ability to heal the man's physical wounds, he had the ability to heal his spiritual wounds by offering forgiveness.

With that, the stranger healed the ex–bandit's wounds. The religious leaders were again beside themselves. They wanted so much to arrest and punish the stranger for taking authority over what they felt only they were entitled to by law. The crowd was so amazed at the stranger's logic and his abilities that they cheered and celebrated for an extended period of time. With that response from the crowd, the leaders knew that they had better not try and seize the stranger just yet. They would never have made it out of there alive. So, they went about their business. The stranger went about his.

Each time such an event occurred, Bari received information on it from the guards or other prison workers. He was given the intricate details of each lesson and each activity. Bari was extremely pleased to hear how the stranger was asserting himself in dealing with the impure religious leaders and their tactful attempts to stop him. Bari was also pleased at how the stranger was taking all of the ritual secretiveness out of their religious activities. He was especially pleased with how the stranger brought the messages and meaning of their religion to the populace rather than necessitating the people come to him. Bari could tell, based on the news alerts he received, that the stranger was just as satisfied teaching from a hillside, a house, or a boat in the harbor as he was with teaching in the grandeur of their mesmerizing temple.

Each day Bari sequestered information from anyone who came to the prison concerning the whereabouts and actions of the stranger. He kept careful mental record of the deeds and the debates and the number of people who decided to follow the stranger's leadership. More and more people were beginning to realize the stranger had a more appealing and logical approach to religion than did the impure leaders they were accustomed to. Bari had surmised that there were more than enough followers now to topple the polluted political stronghold of the tainted leaders. He knew the time was drawing nearer for the stranger to move into position to take over. It became more and more exciting as he watched it all unfold. Bari reveled in the news each time a report of a new deed the stranger had done or a new misunderstanding he had corrected, which resulted in more followers joining with him.

There was only one of the stranger's activities that Bari just could not come to terms with. It was the fact that the stranger forgave the ones who Bari thought he came to overthrow: the ones who'd cause the most havoc in the communities. Bari heard of how some of the impure religious leaders denounced their practices and faulty teachings and began following the stranger. The stranger gladly welcomed them into his fold. He did not hold any of their past wrongdoings against them. He offered them the same forgiveness he offered to the others. Bari learned that he even spent the night at one of their houses. The stranger treated the impure leader as if the leader had never done wrong his entire life.

Bari also disagreed with the stranger's forgiveness of those bandits who had attacked him and how he healed their wounds. That was beyond Bari's comprehension. His idea of an overthrow did not include pardons for the opposition. It certainly did not entail offering assistance to them. He wanted the eye for an eye vengeance he was lawfully entitled to. He wanted to inflict pain for pain and injury for injury. Obviously, Bari did not quite yet fully understand the stranger's principle of grace.

Bari's thought process was still following the pattern of his grandfather's. He wanted more than ever to force the impure leaders out. He did not wish to see any of them prosper anymore from the fraudulence he had witnessed of them. He was willing to take life and limb to see that they did not. He did not want to run the risk of offering them forgiveness just to see them later revert to their old ways. He wanted to see them overthrown completely. He spent day and night wondering how he could launch a revolt before they brought about the death sentence they had placed upon him.

As the stranger preformed great work after great work, his popularity grew stouter and stouter. The counterfeit religious leaders felt more and more at risk. They called a meeting to discuss the situation. They spoke among themselves:

Why are we sitting around like this? This stranger is doing a lot of great things. If we don't stop him, not only will the people continue to flock to him, but the Rhomines will sympathize with him, too. Once they see the majority of the people flocking to him, they will remove us from authority both in the temple and in our internal government.

They discussed back and forth amongst themselves. There was disagreement of whether they should proceed with a plan to rid themselves of the stranger or just leave him be. Some of them had already concluded that the stranger was absolutely correct in his teachings and actions. They walked away from the conversation.

They would eventually join the ranks of the stranger. There were those who wished to follow the stranger's teachings, but they remained because they did not want to lose their status in the community and among the remaining leaders. The discussions continued amongst those that were left. Finally, they agreed they had to do away with the man they considered a menace to their society. They began to plot even harder how they might get rid of him.

They made several attempts at seizing and killing the stranger. Each time something happened to prohibit them from laying hands on him. On some occasions the crowd of people who agreed with him was too immense, such that they were afraid to make an attempt to detain him. On other occasions, he sensed their intentions and maneuvered away from them. After countless failed attempts at taking him into custody, they decided it was easier if they just fabricated charges against the stranger and had him arrested by the Rhomine authorities. They found a few people to bare false witness against him. They would take the charges to the authorities and demand his apprehension. The authorities would then be obligated to at least bring him in for trial.

The leaders made sure everything was in place to take the stranger into custody. They even bribed one of the stranger's close followers to lead them to a place where he would be at a time when there were no crowds around him. They gave the bribed follower payment equivalent to four months of common laborer's salary for agreeing to complete the deed. It was the most money he had ever owned at one time. He could not resist the temptation. He agreed to lead them to one of the stranger's most secret getaways.

There was a huge garden where the stranger often went to pray in the late hours of the night and sometimes on into the early hours of the next day. He went there on several occasions and his close followers would trail him there. They would usually wait in the distance while he prayed alone in a secluded corner of the garden. The bribed follower knew he'd be in that garden and in a specific location at a predetermined time. He led the Rhomine guards (along with a few priest assistants) to the garden and straight to the stranger. He told them to stay back and let him go greet the stranger first. He let them know that he would go up to the stranger and greet him with a kiss on the cheek, as was their custom. The kiss would be their signal to rush in and apprehend their suspect.

It happened just as they planned it. There was very little struggle. The only incident was when one of the stranger's followers drew his sword and attacked one of the priest's assistants. The stranger restrained him. The stranger let him know that he did not want any bloodshed during the encounter. The stranger looked at the soldiers and said, "All this time you have seen me teaching and have not confronted me. Now, you come at me with weapons as if I'm a criminal." The soldiers' countenance wilted and they provided no response.

The soldiers put away their weapons and were reluctant to take the stranger in. Some of them were privy to the great deeds the stranger had accomplished in such a short time. Some had heard him speak and could find no fault in his teachings. They actually were afraid of confronting the stranger. However, he convinced them that it was their duty and they must do so. They agreed and led him away peacefully. As they did he asked his bribed friend, "Do you mean to tell me you betrayed me with a kiss?" The bribed friend dropped his head. He, too, had no response.

The rest of the stranger's followers fled the scene fearing their lives were in danger. They did not want to face the ruthlessness of the Rhomine soldiers carrying out the warrant of arrest. They would often murder or viciously beat anyone who stood in their way or appeared associated with their target. Rather than risk guilt by association, the close followers all dispersed into the trees and bushes planted in the garden. All except the bribed follower fled the scene. There was no need for him to fear the guards. After all, he had led them there. He had acquired their trust. He just stood and watched as the stranger was escorted away.

Once they were out of sight, guilt began to settle in the mind of the betrayer. He could not believe what he had done to the stranger. He gathered himself and went back to the religious leaders and denounced his association with the plot. The bribed follower told them he wanted no more to do with it. He told them they were convicting an innocent man. He offered the money back to them.

They refused it and told him they had no more use for him. His part in the matter was complete. They had already determined how they would obtain the death penalty for the stranger. They did not need a statement from the stranger's once-trusted companion.

The bribed follower threw the money at their feet and departed the room. Depression set in rather quickly. He knew the stranger would forgive him. The stranger had forgiven much worse crimes than his. The bribed follower, however, could not find a way to forgive himself. He just did not know forgiveness at that level. He could not forgive himself and he could not move himself to seek forgiveness from the stranger. Despite all he had heard the stranger say and had seen him do, everything in his religious and mental repository still made him believe that such an act was unforgivable. Apparently he had not come to understand the stranger's full philosophy on grace. The bribed follower battled ferociously with the guilt. The remorse would ultimately win. He was found dead later that day. He'd hung himself.

From that day on, the religious leaders worked at carrying out their plot against the stranger. They expended a great deal of effort in finding all who chose to continue spreading the stranger's teachings. They commissioned their most decorated religious leader and judge to go out and punish anyone found spreading the information once taught by the stranger. The appointed leader carried a blanket arrest warrant permitting him to use any means he saw fit in silencing the stranger's band of followers. He would have them beat, thrown in jail and there were occasions when he had them executed on location. Those who chose to continue teaching the stranger's ways trembled at the very mention of the lawman's name. Nonetheless, they still chose to spread the stranger's message. The threat of facing the leaders' punishment was greatly outweighed by the hope they discovered in the stranger's message.

The other religious leaders who maintained that they were innocent (or at least justified) applauded the efforts of the commissioned assassin. He and others would experience very little resistance in executing their orders. The Rhomine government did not interfere as this was, again, a domestic religious matter. They just refused to involve themselves in the religious matters of the Weshuan citizens. The people would have to settle those matters themselves. For some reason, however, those who followed the stranger's doctrine did not band together to resist the persecution. They simply scattered themselves abroad and hoped not to cross paths with the gruesome dispatcher.

No one among the ranks of religious leadership spoke against the dreadful decree, save their most senior teacher of the law. Through all the turmoil, he still stood in good standing with all the people – both those who agreed with the stranger and those who did not. He seemed to not have adapted to the tarnished ways of the impure religious leaders; yet he did not commit fully to the stranger's teachings.

On one occasion when a few of the stranger's close followers had been imprisoned and were about to be executed, the senior teacher ordered a halt to the execution. He reasoned with the religious leaders to reconsider the penalty for the stranger's close followers. He stated that if what they taught was indeed nonsense, then nothing would come of it. He also told them that if it was of truth, then killing them would not stop it. It would continue to spread anyway.

The senior teacher's words were convincing enough that the leaders could not argue against him. They called the stranger's close followers back to the room where they delved out their sentences. They revoked the death penalty and reduced it to a non–public flogging. They still commanded them to discontinue spreading the stranger's message and threatened harsh punishment if they continued doing so. The stranger's close followers did not cease in their efforts. They returned to disseminating the doctrine as soon as the authorities released them.

Bari sat in prison as the process ran its course. After a short while, he lost track of the acute details of what was taking place. No one had visited the prison to provide news since the decree of the religious leaders. He received no word on the whereabouts and activities of the stranger. He didn't know anything about the arrest. He was unaware of the scattering of the group of followers. He did not know about the fate of the bribed follower. So, he sat and waited for his day to come.

That day finally arrived when Bari had to pay his debt to society. The guards came in and taunted him as they unlocked the cold steel door to his cell. "I guess you're only half the man your grandfather was, eh hero?" they teased. "You could only take your revolution half way to the temple." Bari did not respond to the mockery. He saw no value in it. Perhaps he still felt there was a chance he'd have his opportunity to get back at all of them. Maybe an all-out revolt would begin once the people saw him in person. Maybe the stranger had been told of his plight and was already preparing a way to set him free. Bari still did not know of the most recent development regarding the stranger's fate. He still had faith that change was imminent and the stranger was on the brink of establishing his place as leader of their people. Bari held on to his hope as they led him away.

He squinted as the guards dragged him from the dark dungeon–like prison into the bright sunlight. It was the middle of the day. The sun was at its brightest point. There was not a cloud in the sky and nothing else to block the intense rays of sunlight. The chains prohibited him from raising his hands high enough to block it. He had to be led by the guards as he could not see anything. They brought him before the emperor and other very prominent religious and governmental officials. He was placed on a raised platform alongside another alleged criminal. His eyes still were not fully adjusted, so he could not determine who the person was standing next to him.

Bari was still restricted by his chains. The guards had not removed them before leading him out. The person next to him bore no chains at all. Bari made the assumption that there was no reason to bind that person. He felt perhaps that person's crime wasn't as great as his own. He looked around and saw the silhouettes of a huge multitude of people. Based on the format, he was certain that he was about to be placed into the hands of the executioners. He began to feel anxiety settling in. He asked himself the same question he'd asked the innkeeper at the beginning of all the madness: "Where am I and how did I get here?"

He continued to look around as his eyes adjusted to the light. Finally, his eyes made their way back to the person who was on the platform with him. He was able to focus in on him that time around. He could not believe his eyes. It was the stranger! "What is he doing here?!" Bari thought. He never would have guessed that the impure religious leaders would find a way to bring charges against the stranger – not with the way the stranger defended himself against their tactics. From Bari's assessment, there was absolutely no fault in him. He wondered, "What could the stranger have said or done to make him guilty enough to stand opposite of me?" He could not make sense of it all.

Bari listened in disbelief as the emperor and the religious leaders exchanged dialogue. The emperor asked what the charges were against the stranger. The leaders brought forth a false witness. The testimony did not prove true; so, the charge was dismissed without deliberation. Time after time the religious leaders brought forth their charges, but none of the accusations survived evaluation.

At the end of the exchange, the emperor stated that he found the stranger innocent and began the motion to release him. Before he released the stranger, however, he proposed to them a choice. Since it was the time of their annual festival, the people would get to choose a "criminal" to be freed. It was a custom they had practiced for some time. As a part of the festivities, a clean slate was offered to someone who had been recently sentenced for a crime regardless of its severity. Since the religious leaders presented the stranger as a criminal the emperor offered to free either Bari or the stranger at their request. This is where the leaders felt their plan would come to fruition.

The emperor made the official announcement to the crowd. That was the opening the corrupt religious leaders had been waiting for. They seized the opportunity by initializing a chant, "Free Bari! Free Bari! Free Bari!" A small portion of the crowd joined in. The chant began to spread like wildfire. It seemed Bari was still just as popular as ever. Perhaps everyone still felt the connection with Bari and his lineage. Perhaps they did not feel the same with the stranger whom they barely knew of. Although there were many in the crowd who felt the stranger had a very strong case for changing things – an impeccable case in fact – it seems they had quickly forgotten his good.

The cadence grew louder and louder. If anyone there was shouting on the stranger's behalf, they could not be heard among those chanting for Bari. It was amazing how quickly they abandoned the stranger. It wasn't as if the work he had done could have been dismissed so easily. He'd uncovered major fallacies and mistakes in their religious leadership. He had restored many broken lives and created hope where none existed before. He had healed the ailments of some of the very people in that crowd. Could they have forgotten the stranger's love and kindness so quickly or were they just afraid to defy the religious leaders and demand his freedom? Then again, maybe they just got caught up in the moment, which is always prone to happen. Even the most well-grounded people get caught up in the emotions of an event. Whichever the case, Bari's name was all that could be heard at the massive gathering.

The emperor was amazed beyond measure. He had heard of all the good the stranger had accomplished in such a short time. Even he was *almost* convinced that the stranger should have been their religious leader instead of those currently in place. He had listened to all the accusations as each one failed to hold true. He understood that even if any of the accusations against the stranger were valid, Bari's charges were much more serious. He even considered the appearance of the two and determined Bari much more criminal in appearance than the stranger. He had no idea what had recently transpired to alter Bari's appearance that way, but by his eyes' judgment, Bari was the greater of the malefactors. The

Emperor could not comprehend it all, but he chose not to wrestle them out of their decision. Again, those were their religious affairs and he would not be entangled in such matters. The religious leaders knew he would not intervene on that occasion. That was one more aspect of their fail-proof plan.

The emperor did the ceremonial "washing of the hands" to signify his purity in the matter and that he played no part in their decision. Then he motioned to the guards to set Bari free. The leaders looked around at each other with victorious expressions on their faces. They had finally managed to mitigate the threat of being completely relieved of their religious supremacy. They knew the risk of the choice they had made in freeing Bari. Bari could still be very influential among the locals. If he chose to follow the path of his grandfather he could be an issue. However, he was not nearly the risk the stranger had become for them. They simply had no defense against the stranger. They could not provoke him to misinterpret their religious laws. They could not invoke their civil laws against him. They could not claim religious indemnity from his critique of their mishandling of the laws and traditions. They had no defense against his non–refutable dissolution of their stronghold.

On the other hand, should Bari decide to begin a campaign against them, they had each of those options at their disposal. They knew Bari did not have the commanding knowledge of their laws as did the stranger. They could easily trap Bari should they see the need to do so. They also knew that Bari did not possess a peaceful demeanor like that of the stranger–at least not any more. They felt Bari would begin an uprising at the first opportunity. However, they would have no problem in obtaining a military force from the Rhomines to dispel such activity. The impure religious leaders were pleased with their accomplishment. They had retained control of their pious dynasty.

The guards loosened the chains from Bari and motioned for re-issuance of his personal belongings. He felt the pressure recede as the shackles fell away from his feet. He felt the burden lifted as they fell away from his hands. He felt instant gratification from the people's choice to pardon him for his wrongs; however, the satisfaction did not last for very long. Bari considered the looming fate of the stranger as a result of being the chosen one. He wondered what would become of his people's belief system if the stranger was no longer there to lead them. The stranger had proven to be such a powerful and upright leader.

All of a sudden, Bari wasn't as thrilled about his status as the people's choice. He didn't feel he deserved to be the one to go free. He really wasn't certain that he wanted to be anymore. Bari felt that his own crimes (though provoked and presumably justifiable) were punishable. He felt that nothing the stranger had done was worthy of punishment. He felt that the stranger was paying the cost of *his* freedom. Now, he felt an obligation to finish what the stranger had started in freeing the people of their religious bondage. The burden that was lifted with the release of Bari's chains had just been replaced with the burden of liberating his people.

He rubbed his wrists slowly and gently. He reached down and did the same for his ankles. Then he looked out at the crowd and threw both fists into the air. The religious leaders snickered amongst themselves. The crowd, however, went into turmoil. They celebrated uncontrollably. They felt as if they had done the ultimate good. They had pardoned the wrongdoings of their favored son. They had come to his rescue. For a brief moment, they were the law. Just for an instant they possessed the power of condemnation or redemption that was normally only granted to their religious leaders. The feeling was truly gratifying.

Bari soaked it all in for a few seconds. After a while, he realized that he really was free to depart the judgment stage. So, he gathered himself and his belongings and began to move slowly toward the exiting steps of the raised platform. As he walked, he haphazardly looked over to the stranger, who was now to take his place in the hands of the executioners. He was deeply moved for the moment. He knew that it was he who should be staying there and the stranger who should have been set free. He didn't know what to feel after that. On the one hand, he was glad to be free. On the other hand, he felt somewhat guilty for what he had brought upon the stranger. He surmised that the stranger's unwarranted conviction was a direct result of his transgression. He began again to feel a rushing influx of un-forgiveness. He knew he would not be able to forgive himself for this.

As the guilt swiftly invaded his psyche, he glanced into the eyes of the stranger. In them, Bari witnessed the same satisfactory sentiment as with the inmate when he met with his material demise at the hands of the guards in the cell adjacent to him in the dungeon. The stranger had a fulfilled look about him. Just as with the inmate, there was not a single word of protest or a single plea for mercy.

For some strange reason, Bari felt himself offering a congenial smile to the stranger just as he had done on their first encounter. It was his only means of offering gratitude to the one who had saved him from certain death. The stranger offered a doubly amiable smile back. The atmosphere was eerily comparable to the encounter at the temple. Bari sensed instantaneous relief from the rushing flood of un-forgiveness that had taken over him. Again the stranger had made the emotional aftermath of a terrible experience dissipate into nothing. Bari felt revived all over again. He was truly grateful to the stranger from that moment forward.

Bari had witnessed (from a distance) the latter part of the stranger's life story. He recollected how the stranger had sprung up like a tender plant out of dry ground. He appeared on the scene quickly and out of nowhere. Bari witnessed how the other religious teachers and leaders around him had been thorny, dry, and brittle towards him, but their actions had absolutely no effect on the stranger. Bari realized they despised and rejected the stranger. He realized that the stranger's current sorrows and grieves were not his own but those of the people's. He realized that his immediate liberty was a direct result of the stranger's unwillingness to protest the unfairness of his situation. Bari walked off a free man (in every aspect of the word). Behind him, the oppressors flogged the stranger and led him away to the site of the execution.

Bari had gone a great deal further than the stranger in exhibiting his frustrations for the inadequacies in their laws and customs and the impure leaders' misuse of them. Even though he had no authority to take the actions he had taken, he still thought to himself, "I was justified in what I did." In a sense he was right. No one, as Bari felt, should be condemned by the very laws that were designed to protect them. So, he had every right to use those laws in defending himself, even in defense against those who were charged with upholding the law. In another sense, though, he could not have been further from the truth. He knew he was not justified in using un–forgiveness to combat the same. That was the greatest shortcoming of the law which he disagreed with. Un–forgiveness was not the weapon for defeating un–forgiveness. It would take a pure forgiveness (an amazing grace) to win that battle. The stranger understood that perfectly. Apparently, Bari had not quite grasped that concept.

Bari walked away from the scene and made his way across town to the temple courtyard. People began to gather rather quickly. In almost no time there was a huge crowd surrounding him. They began to chant his name again, "Bari! Bari! Bari!" Again, he began to feel a strong sense of responsibility towards the people. He had become the Mathes they so badly needed right then. As he gazed among them, he began to ponder as to which approach he should take in fulfilling their needs as best he could satisfy them.

He knew if he took the path of his grandfather, there would be lots of bloodshed. He wasn't at all opposed to the shedding of blood for the sake of religious equilibrium. That was his intent on that trip to the temple anyway. He intended on starting an all–out revolution with a single act of vengeance against his adversaries there. He knew the choice he'd made presented a very uncertain end. Still, that was his choice. It was time to fight. He would muster enough troops to take over the temple and advance from there.

This time he had the support of many more people than just those who occupied and lived around the inn. He had enough to overthrow the temple, now. He knew, however, that if he overthrew the religious body, he still had to contend with the governmental body. It could be done, though. It had been done before and it could be done again. He knew he could be the one to do it. He wasn't "half the man whom Mathes was" anymore.

On the other hand, Bari also knew that it would not end there. Although he still felt a driving urge to take an eye for an eye, his deeply rooted-understanding of the principle still remained strong. His philosophy that retaliation could never bring about good was still intact – especially now since he'd heard the stranger's teaching on the matter and witnessed the stranger's non-violent approach to dismantling the effects of evil.

Bari knew that if he were to be successful in overthrowing the temple, animosity would mount and at first chance the episode would play out again in reverse order. The religious clan would retreat to the Rhomines' homeland. The Rhomines would reinforce their local army. Then they would all come back for another round. The personal battles and communal wars would just continue time and time again. Someone would just be waiting for an opportune moment to change the system back to its original state or to something worse.

Bari knew if he went the way of the stranger, he could almost guarantee the outcome. The leaders would take little time in expelling him just as they had the stranger. In fact, he knew he could not gain popularity as fast as the stranger. No one could do that. He knew he would do well locally, because he was already a hero in their eyes; but beyond that he was nobody. So, beyond the local communities, he was facing peril. Not only did he face the problem of being an unknown outside of his extended community, but he also had to deal with the new, stricter enforcement of the religious laws. He had just learned of the leaders' decree that their most capable legal representative had permission to comb the area and mitigate any instance of the stranger's followers' attempts to continue propagating his message.

Bari pondered the two choices before him; but he felt he had a third option, as well. He could just ignore it all and go back to a fairly normal life. He could regroup, re-marry, and rebuild his life. He hadn't lost anything from a fiscal standpoint. He still had his home, his land, and his business. His health was almost back to normal. He had a few scars of remembrance (both physical and mental), but he could learn to ignore those. Perhaps others would learn to ignore them as well. He determined that it really wasn't such a bad option.

Still, Bari wondered if he would ever be satisfied with going back to status quo. He thought back one more time to the look on the face of the stranger as he walked away from the judgment stage. He recalled the peaceful satisfied look the stranger displayed despite his ensuing dreadful situation. He again remembered the same serene demeanor exhibited by the inmate at his material termination. Bari remembered how he had longed for such peace as displayed by the inmate when he sat there in that cell in a hopeless state of mind. He then began to understand his heart–to–heart discussion with the inmate on the stranger's intent: "It's not the stranger's intent to do away with our laws or traditions. He just wants to fill in the gaps where our laws and traditions lack that complete forgiveness you allude to. There's a huge element of un–forgiveness in our laws and traditions…"

At that point, Bari realized that the stranger had provided the fulfillment that the law so desperately needed. He had established a way to fill in the gaps without destroying what was already in place. He had provided a way to complete their religion such that the core of their belief system rested in their hearts and their everyday actions versus in the temple and its liturgical practices. The stranger had created a path that led them from provisional impurities to irrevocable innocence in their religious experience. It cost him his life, but he he'd done it.

He had offered unconditional forgiveness at the personal level. The veil of un–forgiveness between their God and His People had been ripped down the middle by the stranger's personal offering. If everyone would receive that level of forgiveness for themselves and offer the same to others, then the law between them was no longer necessary. The condemning aspects of the law would be rendered ineffective. Bari found delight in his little personal epiphany. He had finally achieved that satisfied feeling he had so desperately longed for.

Bari leisurely surveyed the crowd now gathered in the courtyard. It had grown to a sizeable amount. There were common people just as there were elites. There were businessmen alongside laborers. The only thing missing was any sign of the impure religious leaders. He assumed they had all gone to witness the execution of the stranger.

The crowd continued to chant Bari's name. He raised his hands as a motion for silence. Once everything was quiet, he began on his quest to lead them to liberation. He began delivering his first speech as their new and improved Mathes. He started his speech by exclaiming to them, "There is an element of logic missing from our laws and customs that leaves us with the inability to forgive or to be forgiven. It leaves huge gaps in our religious fulfillment. There is a way to fill those gaps. The stranger has shown us the way…"

After his discourse, he watched the crowds slowly disperse one small group after another. He listened closely to the departing conversations so as to gauge the effect his words had on them. He wasn't concerned about their approval of him, but rather of the message. They were discussing the powerful logic in his teaching. They compared it to that of the stranger. It was an easy comparison, because it was just a continuation of what the stranger had begun teaching them. It was the same message relayed through Bari's own experiences. He watched for signals that they agreed – even if they did not say a word. He saw the sign. It was the satisfaction expressed on many of their faces. It was similar to that of the stranger and the inmate. It was a duplicate of *his* new found contentment.

He observed the crowd as they moved on. Some acknowledged him with a pat on the back. Others offered a huge smile and a nod of appreciation. As he watched them leave his level of fulfillment increased astronomically. He was not basking in his own glory as if he had achieved or sustained a personal agenda. He simply felt a spiritual oneness that had been lacking in previous religious gatherings in that same temple courtyard. The contentment he felt overcame the fear of being punished for teaching the message of the stranger. It drove him to continue in spreading what he considered good news.

He knew of the penalty for speaking out the way he had just done in the temple yard. He knew he ran the risk of being rebuked by the religious leaders. He knew he could face public flogging or prison time or even worse – death.

None of the probable consequences frightened him. He did not bite his tongue nor did he rush out once he completed his speech. He gave the opportunity for those present to ask questions and clear up any misunderstandings they still had concerning the stranger's message as relayed by Bari. He stood there until every single one of his listeners filed out – all but one.

A young woman walked towards him slowly. He watched as she came in his direction. As she got close, he opened his arms and offered an embrace. She fell into his arms with tear–drenched eyes. Bari began to fight back tears of his own, but he woefully lost that battle. They just held each other. No words were shared among them. No faults were assigned by them. No excuses were made of them. There was just a mutual understanding of forgiveness shared between the two of them. After an extended period of time, he gently pulled himself away from her. She watched as he made his way into the temple.

Bari's eyes adjusted to the dim lighting inside. Once they were focused, he gazed into the eyes of the money exchanger. It was not the same worker as before. He was younger and still had the appearance of innocence. Bari shifted his focus over to the eyes of the assistant. The assistant was new as well. They carried out their duties as if none of the events of the past few days ever even took place.

Bari wondered to himself if either of them knew who he was:

> Do they know my recent history? Did they hear my discourse in the courtyard? Are they totally ignorant of the fact that I was the second greatest factor in what has transpired the last few days? Do they realize the things I have done and might still be capable of?

He concluded by the unassuming looks on their faces that neither of them had a clue.

Bari reached for his moneybag. As he did his hand brushed against his dagger. Every bit of the hurt, anger, and disgust he'd felt those last few days made their way back into his psyche. They filled his veins with every quickening pulse of his palpitating heart. He recalled the bandits who had almost killed him. He remembered the abduction of his beloved wife. He recalled the priest who showed absolutely no concern for his life. He remembered the priest assistant's "Serves you right" expression as he passed him lying in the roadside ditch hovering at the brink of death. He recalled the impure religious leaders who pulled his wife into a hopeless situation. He recalled the guilt he'd felt for placing himself in a position to allow all of those events to come to pass.

All the emotions associated with his recent experiences welled up inside of him, rekindling a heated hatred for the entire entourage of religious counterfeits. At that moment, he knew he could definitely kill again. In fact, he felt as if he was about to. He was on the verge of exploding when the money exchanger interrupted his trance with a heartless, nonchalantly offered second request, "Well, have you decided? Which choice have you made?"

The question brought Bari's mind back to words he'd heard the stranger say to his close followers, "If your righteousness is no better than that of the impure religious leaders that mislead you, then you cannot continue with me." Bari revisited his views on the "eye for an eye" rule. He knew by their laws and customs he had every right to begin his quest for vengeance right there at the exchanger's table. He could prove his story now that he had Yrma as an eyewitness. The worse punishment he would have to face is payment of tribute to compensate for the anguish with which he exacted retaliation.

He had two options: vengeance or forgiveness. If he chose vengeance, then he was choosing the way of the impure religious leaders he despised so greatly. In doing so, he would remain entrenched in a belief system that was incapable of full forgiveness. If he chose to pardon, then he was choosing the way of the stranger he had developed absolute admiration for. With that choice he would finally have a means of offering complete forgiveness and receiving the same.

Bari moved his hand away from his dagger and felt for his moneybag. He untied the bag and pulled it away from his waist. He made certain the dagger remained hidden from view. He gave the exchanger the requested amount for the overpriced, under kept tribute. He took it from the exchanger and moved along towards the place where he would offer the tribute to the assistant and began to prepare himself for worship. He started to pray softly as he moved along: "Father, bless this tribute so that it will be what I desire rather than what they have reduced it to."

Bari's prayer came to an abrupt halt. Although he'd prayed countless times before, he just could not think of anything else to pray for that time around. There was much, much more that he knew he needed to express to his God, but he simply couldn't do it. He felt the same hopelessness he felt while lying in that roadside ditch at the brink of death, having been passed up by those he trusted most to help him. He began to feel faint and shortness of breath. Finally, words the stranger had spoken to his close followers while teaching them to pray gently echoed through Bari's head. The words revived him. He continued his silent prayer,

"Father, forgive my wrongs as I forgive those who have wronged me…"

Bari took a final look around as he exited the temple. He wasn't quite sure if he would visit their again. He didn't feel as if he really needed to. After pondering it a while, he determined that he would come back. If for nothing else, it would be for the sake of fellowship with those who had decided to go with the way of the stranger and to encourage and teach his principles to others. He knew, however, that the grandeur of that facility and the emphasis placed on the liturgies performed there would no longer be as significant (as they once seemed to be) to his religious experience.

Although he had no intention of disrespecting the impure religious leaders, he no longer felt obligated to live under the convictions they imposed through their impure intentions. He no longer feared their judgments, either. They were no longer responsible for managing the relationship between him and his God. He realized that *he* was responsible for making sure the relationship remained in good standing. He had learned that discipline of self was one of the key elements in achieving such a relationship. He knew that dispensation of grace was the other. He would no longer be misled and he would be extremely careful to make certain he was not intentionally misleading others.

Bari left the temple and rejoined with his wife in the courtyard. There were no more cheers from the crowd. There were no more pats on the back. It was still rather early in the afternoon, but the courtyard was empty, save Bari and Yrma. The event that radically changed their lives was over. It was as if the entire episode never occurred or that it happened so long ago that everyone had forgotten it. He and his wife prepared themselves for the journey home. They decided not to take the Way of Blood – for obvious reasons.

Bari was glad to see the inn in sight. He and Yrma agreed to stop for the evening, and then continue their trek home on the next day. He couldn't wait to introduce his wife to the innkeeper and also perhaps the do–gooder. He still longed desperately to meet the one who saved him. There was so much he wanted to thank him for. He felt like he owed not only his life, but his future to the do–gooder. Everything he would do or become was made possible by a stranger's unconditional affection for his life. It would have been nice to meet him and say thanks. Bari's mind paused for another incoming epiphany, "Perhaps I've already met him."

They walked into the inn. The innkeeper recognized him immediately and ran over to greet him with a hug and a kiss on the cheek, as was their custom. Bari introduced his wife. By the end of his introduction the innkeeper was in tears. He was so happy for Bari and Yrma. He ordered up the best room, his finest wine, and a special meal for them as he and Bari continued their conversation. At the end of the long discussion, Bari reached for his money bag to pay the innkeeper for the meals and his night's stay. The innkeeper brushed his hand away from his belt and insisted that the stay was free of charge. Bari and his wife thanked him over and over then went to their room to prepare for dinner.

Bari and Yrma entered into the dining hall and pressed their way through the crowded dining room. Bari instinctively went to the corner, pulling Yrma along behind him. He prepared his wife's position. After Yrma sat down, he went around and sat opposite of her. They engaged in casual conversation as they awaited the specially prepared meal to arrive at their table.

The room was packed as always. Bari filtered through the noise as he did once before. He sorted out the conversations and found the people were still on the same subject. It seemed the stranger was even more popular than before. Bari filtered it all out as he began to describe to Yrma his last encounter at the inn. He went through every detail including the kindness of the waitress and his uncharacteristic unkindness to her. He paused in his discussion as he was overcome with emotions. He was woefully ashamed of how he had mistreated her. Yrma placed a hand on his shoulder and reminded him that there was something else driving him at that time.

They sat a moment in silence as he recomposed himself. During the silence, Bari caught a whiff of a conversation that was going on around them. While overhearing a debate concerning the stranger's intentions, he heard arguments in favor of the stranger. He realized that it was the bandit that the stranger had forgiven and healed and sent on his way. As the man went on with his plea, another jumped into the conversation in support of the bandit. As he explained the incident where the stranger had healed his hand, Bari realized that these were two of the men that attacked him. He watched intently as the two of them tried to convince some in the crowd that the stranger's new approach to their relationship with their God was unflawed. It was a tough crowd. They were mostly Rhomine citizens intermingled with temple workers.

After a while they became a bit unruly. The two debaters were outnumbered fiercely. The religious clan got to a point where they were disgusted with the debaters. Eventually, they took hold of them, beat them badly, and tossed them out of the inn. They then returned to their conversation as if nothing out of the ordinary had taken place. Bari watched almost emotionless from his table as the incident unfolded before him. Yrma watched in shock. After it all ended, Bari asked Yrma's pardon as he excused himself from the table. He stood up and moved toward the door. His dagger scrubbed across the table as he left.

He went outside to see what had become of the debaters. The innkeeper was helping them from the ground and apologizing for the actions of the religious clan. Bari made his way over to the debaters. They looked at him. They knew who he was. Neither spoke – not the debaters; not Bari; not the innkeeper. There was an extremely eeric aura shared among them.

Finally, Bari broke the silence. "What will you do now?" Bari asked them. "You've turned against your own. So, not only have you destroyed your means of employment, but you have also obliterated your means of protection." His expression was stern as he delivered the inquiry. They replied without the slightest delay, "We will continue to teach the stranger's way. That's what he instructed us to do."

Bari continually looked intently at them. The expression on his face did not change one bit. They knew he was contemplating something, but they had no idea what. After a long and awkward silence, he gave them directions to his home and invited them to come and work for him. He told them he would give them all the time they needed to prepare for and to teach the stranger's way. He told them they could come and go as they needed – earning wages in between their campaigns by assisting his hired help. They accepted the offer with gratitude as they all shook hands and embraced as a means of confirming the agreement. The two ex–bandits went on their way.

Bari and the innkeeper made their way back into the dining hall. As Bari sat back down at his table, he saw the same young lady who waited on him before. He practically yelled across the room to beckon her to come near. Bari began greeting her before she could even get to the table. Once she arrived, he introduced her to his wife and explained again to his wife how the young lady had been so kind to him on his previous stay. Of course, he had to ask for her name as he never attempted to learn it before.

The young lady was confused by his inviting behavior. It was so different from the last cold encounter that lacked any congeniality whatsoever. Certainly, something had changed within the man standing before her. She didn't ponder on it, though. She gladly accepted the warm, nonjudgmental salutations offered of Bari and of his beautiful wife.

She placed their drinks on the table and almost in a skipping fashion went away to bring their specially prepared meals. As she went away, Bari leaned over to his wife. He whispered something into her ear. She had a somewhat startled look on her face at first; but it immediately adjusted to a smile. Bari had just explained to her the young lady's means of extra revenue at the inn. He then presented an idea that offered grace to the young lady. He asked Yrma if she had interest in providing the young lady the opportunity to come and help out around the home place. She would not come as a servant or as property, but as a family member with full rights to their possessions and their loving kindness. Bari knew they might have to purchase her freedom from the innkeeper, but he was more than willing to do so. Yrma was equally willing.

MORAL OF THE STORY

Every now and again an appalling, anguish–inducing incident takes place in the Christian community that forces us to really take inventory of who and what we believe in. More often than not, the pain of the incident is inflicted upon us by impure leadership. It's easy to see the signs of impurities long before they make national news headlines, because they always reveal themselves in one way or another. The series of events leading up to the revelation of the infection often involve several participants and factors including misappropriation of monies, abuse of authority, and/or sexual immorality. Those factors are not all inclusive, of course; but history reveals that one or more of them are central in nearly every occurrence of exposed impurity. Although it's almost always a single fall guy publically associated with the exposed impurities, there is almost never just one contributor. That means defilement exists and many are fully aware of the wrong for some time before its revelation. It is ignored or overlooked by all who are either beneficiaries to the corruption or not personally affected by it.

There are some outside of the Christian community who will place maximum effort in ridiculing our faith or attempting to draw us away from our faith or condemning us wholly as just another cluster of cult–based conspirators each time an impure leader is exposed to the world. Those critical of our faith will squander their energies attempting to discredit the entire body of proclaimed Christian believers because of the impurities of one (or a select few). Meanwhile, we within the community are exhausting our efforts in trying to determine how and why such an event could occur, yet again. Most often we will attribute such an act to the work of the devil. Since many deem the events as "evil," (both those inside and outside of our circle) it's so easy for us to tack a *d* onto the evil and be done with the discussion: "The *d*evil made them do it."

Might I pose another more probable cause, though? Certainly evil (immoral character) has its place in all of this, but could it be that every now and then God desires to get the attention of His believers who are being misled by those impure religious leaders? Might He be protecting them from being enticed into straying too far away from the relationship He desires with them? Could it be that he is reminding the believers of their personal responsibility of making sure they have the right relationship with Him rather than leaving that relational responsibility solely in the hands of others? Could this be the crux of why He exposes those who are misleading His followers by the application of impure intentions?

In the way of a disclaimer, I advocate that I do not wish to suggest that God goes on an all out attack to completely annihilate the impure leader's character when such exposure takes place. No, the Bible gives clear exhortation in why God brings about their chastisement. He does it for the simple reason that he wishes to restore the right relationship between He and the mischievous party. It is the parental principle with which we all are so thoroughly familiar. The purpose of God's punishment (same as any parent) is to correct their improper behavioral patterns.

The idea that God exposes impure leadership just shows that the human error factor is ever–present in individuals, regardless of how well they lead others; regardless of how high they climb in the sphere of leadership. They will err at times. The errors can be corrected if the leader in question is willing to take the necessary steps in rectifying those mistakes. Even when impure leaders intentionally mislead, forgiveness and restoration are still available for them according to the teachings and practices of Jesus Christ. This was parabolized in the story you just read.

I must offer the following disclaimer as well; so as to minimize the risk of being quoted or evaluated out of context concerning this proposal that God exposes impure leadership with a purpose. To suggest that God deliberately exposes impure leadership does not imply that God wills the misleading events into existence. No, if we do a complete root cause analysis, we will see that the exposed events are the direct byproduct of someone's freewill wrongdoing. Their behavior involves the aforementioned element of immoral character. The leader is responsible for his or her actions as much as the followers. If the leaders direct wrongfully, they do so under their own freewill efforts. Freewill is a wonderful thing until it becomes soiled with impure intent.

So, the events are certainly not God's doing. The Bible teaches clearly that He neither performs evil actions against us nor does He provoke us to such (rf. James 1:13). It does seem, however, once the action takes place, God eventually exposes it. It seems if He doesn't bring this exposure about, then the leaders with impure intentions will continue on their course of misleading others. If the body of believers is not made aware of the impurities, it seems they will continue to follow those leaders. Of course, there are known cases when even after such impurities are exposed, supporters still feel obligated or inclined to continue following that impure leader. In such cases, it's obvious that their relationship with their impure leader is stronger than their relationship with God, but that's an entirely different discussion – perhaps another book's worth.

So, why does God bring about such exposure? Could it be that sometimes Christians get so intimate (not necessarily sexually involved, but rather passionately close in trust) in their relationship with their religious leaders that they forget their personal accountability in seeking progressive knowledge of God as a means of improving their personal relationship with Him? Could it be that in such cases fewer and fewer individuals go back to God's Word and use it to verify the words of those leaders to make certain that the leaders' intentions stay pure? Could it be that at some point they begin to seek God's Word less for their Spiritual growth and rely more on those whom God appoints to impart His Word? Could it be that those who are appointed to impart God's Word, at some point, discontinue holding individuals accountable for their own personal progressive relationship with God? If that's ever the case, then isn't that equivalent to those leaders placing themselves in position to be the sole source for those individuals' growth? Isn't that the model Christ came to tear down? Doesn't he want to be that sole source?

We who are of the Christian faith might ask ourselves, "Why does God have to expose those events to the *entire* world? Couldn't He just deal with the impure individual(s) and save face for the remainder of the Christian community?" Then perhaps Christians wouldn't have to cope with the ridicule that so often extends from non–Christians. We wouldn't have to question ourselves as to what's going awry in our Christian faith–based organizations if the exposure was contained somewhat. It seems like it would be a much better fix if God would just surgically remove the cancerous cell(s) rather than submit the entire body to chemocriticism; doesn't it? (Put the dictionary down. I just procreated a word to fit here. You won't find it in your dictionary. The purpose of chemotherapy is to prevent cancerous cells from dividing and growing into other parts of the human body. Although its purpose is to destroy only bad cells, it does adversely affect some of the good cells. However, overall, the body is made stronger in the process. A thing such as *chemocriticism* might have the same effect on the Christian body.)

Those outside of our faith community are not oblivious to the events that occur within our community. It seems to me that they are sometimes more aware of our inadequacies than us. Perhaps they observe our actions more than they listen to our jargon as they try to determine what constitutes Christian behavior. Our lives and lifestyles might be their only measuring stick for determining if Christianity encourages a wholesome standard of living and introduces a path in life they might deem worth following. Of course there is more to the Christian pathway than lifestyle, but one must start somewhere in determining a practical, practicable belief system.

If there is no public chastisement for the impurities of those who are leaders within our belief system, then those outside who are watching their actions (and we know they're watching) might think the impure leaders' dealings are common and even acceptable among their followers. Unless the impurity gets punished and those within the body of believers openly show variance to the contamination that's created (and consequent agreement to the punishment), the viewing world might just take those impurities as normal practice for the Christian body as a whole. That would be a terrible discredit to true Christianity; now, wouldn't it?

History reveals that events often occur that involve impure religious leadership's desire to modify God's formula for maintaining a great relationship with Him. The things that took place in the preceding parable have taken place since the inception of Christianity and continue to do so. Some leaders will probably always have their followers performing certain tasks or maintaining certain views or values that hold no significance in sustainability of a good relationship with God in Jesus Christ. They'll do it (among other reasons) for personal material gain (wealth), to esteem themselves above others (power), or to place someone in a compromise–able situation (sexual misconduct). These are all visible signs of impure religion and we should pay close heed to them, lest we fall victim to the same. We will find ourselves either contributing to their impurities or ignoring them. In either case, we are damaging our personal relationship with God in the process.

An open exposure of the signs of impurity and a resulting schism within the believing community is sometimes the only thing that will cause those who ignore or overlook those signs to begin to pay attention to and take action on them. Schisms and shakeups often won't occur until such events reach a point of vulgarity that causes the non–Christian world to take notice. The public exposure forces believers to take a moment to internally assess what is really taking place. With honest assessment, true followers of Christ will publicly object to the impurity of their leader's intentions rather than defend that leader's actions against the rest of the world's judgment. It is obvious that our beliefs are not subject to world's judgment, but our actions (especially those that pertain to immoral character) are certainly subject to such.

The manner in which God exposes the impurity to the world seems to vary, but the end result is unchanging. Those of us within the Christian faith who wish to maintain a wholesome relationship with God and credibility of our belief system with others will honestly evaluate what has taken place by comparing it to God's Word. We will then reevaluate where the impure leader is attempting to lead us. In most cases, the re–evaluation creates a major change in perspective.

There have been a few noteworthy exposures of impure leadership in Christian history (for those who are familiar with our history) that have really shaken up our community of believers. There have been some recent exposures as well. I could name and discuss a few of the more prominent schisms and exposures, but I don't wish to cause offense – just awareness. I *can* say that they closely resemble those parabolized in the story you have just read through.

The schisms that resulted from exposures of those impurities of the past are recorded in books that have lined the shelves of libraries and desks of classrooms (both secular and Christian) since their occurrence and consequent exposure. The most recent ones are still littering the headlines of newspapers, magazines and television news stations. In some cases guilt is assumed (which is an awful thing), but in other cases it is obvious. At any rate, schisms are developed with every occurrence. In each account, believers in God are forced to reevaluate their relationship with Him, regardless of which side of the division they draw towards after the comprehensive dissection of viewpoints.

There have been recent shakeups of lesser caliber than the ones that make their way into history books. Not all incidents warrant discussion in Bible institutes or debate by biblical scholars; yet, they are still equal in principle. In each case (high profile or low), impure leadership is proven to have altered the formula God has in place for what it takes to have a meaningful relationship with Him. Those leaders mislead followers into abiding by their altered formulas. Sometimes the formulas stay in place for years and years without exposure. When they are finally uncovered or addressed, many will honestly evaluate the impurities and choose to no longer follow the modified formulas. They will choose, rather, to go back to the purity of God's original formula for Christianity. It almost seems as if it's all a purification process that God occasionally takes the believing body through in order to keep us aware of our personal responsibility in our relationship with Him.

Now, you may consider this just another arguing point for theological dialogue in a seminary classroom and as such deem it irrelevant to the everyday Christian. You may be thinking that there is absolutely no correlation between what is currently happening in the Christian body and what has happened in the historical shakeups captured in books of various genres – including the Bible. You may be thinking God would never risk causing a major schism or ridicule from non–believers just to expose impure leadership within the body of believers. Well, we have just traced Christianity back to its origin and can see (even without the parabolically injected inferences) that not only does God use such exposure as a purification process for our belief system, but He also used it in birthing our belief system.

Christianity was founded on the exposure of impure religious leadership. It should not devastate us, then, when God sees it necessary to use exposure of those same impurities in the modern body of believers to bring us back to the foundation of our belief system: a relationship with Him that is based solely upon grace offered through our Lord and Savior, Jesus Christ. He does it quite often. Leaders exerting excessive authority over others, sexual scandals, and embezzlement or misappropriation of funds are the key signs of that impure leadership. When there is proof of such (not just accusation by individuals or insinuations by media but actual proof), those who follow the impure leaders should thoroughly reevaluate that leader's intentions and determine if they wish to continue allegiance. If they do, then they are being irresponsible in their personal relationship with God. If they failed to see the impurities before us, then they were not paying close enough attention to their personal relationship with God. Perhaps if they were, God wouldn't have to continue to use so much exposure to take them back through the purification process.

You still might be thinking to yourself, "Okay, maybe you're right. Maybe this is how God gets our attention; but I still don't understand why? Why would God do such a thing to introduce us to Christianity and why would He continue to do this to bring us back to our foundation? Isn't there a less harsh way?" Well, as I see it, the only way to cause us to fully depend on His grace for maintaining our relationship with Him is to completely wipe out our trust in anything that we consider necessary above and beyond grace.

Before we were ushered into this period of Grace we're currently in, those who had a good relationship with God completely relied on the policies and processes of the Law (as you saw in the parable) to maintain that relationship. They had to do it that way. It was all they had at that time. Now, we must rely on grace to maintain the relationship. Now, every time we find ourselves struggling in our relationship with God, we discover it's because we've come to rely on someone or something other than God's grace for maintaining the relationship. So, it seems God has to do the same thing He did at the onset of Christianity to usher us into this period of Grace. He has to expose things again to let us know that grace is still the single most important element in our relationship with Him.

ABOUT THE AUTHOR

James is married to Lucinda (1986) and they have two 'kids': James, II and Marcinda. He currently serves as Youth Pastor at Big Miller Grove Missionary Baptist Church in Lithonia (Atlanta), GA. He enjoys writing, family, fishing, gardening, and working with youth. His philosophy on life is to *never let a teaching moment slip by you and recognize every opportunity to learn something new*. He holds a Ph.D. in Psychology with a concentration in Christian Counseling from Louisiana Baptist University in Shreveport, Louisiana. He is a member of the American Association of Christian Counselors. He has also authored *The Other SAT* and *Up from Poverty*.

www.ingramcontent.com/pod-product-compliance
Lightning Source LLC
Chambersburg PA
CBHW031437240626
47154CB00001B/308